The Natalie McMasters Mysteries by Thomas A. Burns, Jr.

Stripper! (2018)

Revenge! (2018)

Trafficked! (2019)

Venom! (2020)

Sniper! (2020)

Killers! (2021)

Sister! (2022)

Shooters! (2024)

Shooters!

A Natalie McMasters Mystery

Thomas A. Burns, Jr.

Published by Tekrighter LLC 2024

Thomas A. Burns, Jr.

Printed in the United States of America

Kindle Edition: January 2024

ISBN-13 979-8-9872099-5-0

Paperback Edition: January 2024

ISBN-13 979-8-9872099-6-7

Dedication

To my late Aunt Helen Burns, a troubled soul.

I am the master of my fate
I am the captain of my soul.

From Timothy Mc Veigh's final statement

Prologue

"So, when was it exactly when you knew you were a ho in a dude's bod, Rex?" Adam Tymko asks his guest on his podcast, *Tymko's Times.*

It's a few days before Christmas. In his own inimitable style, A.T. is interviewing a 6'6", 350-lb transgender woman who used to be the goalie for the St. Stephen's Icemen, a college hockey team from the northeast. Today she wears a fetching crimson gown that doesn't quite conceal the bulge of her beer belly.

"A.T., those of us assigned male at birth who now identify as women don't like to be called hos, bitches, cunts, or by any other similarly derogatory term. You may refer to me as a transgender woman, an MTF, or simply as a woman. My pronouns are she and her. And Rex is my deadname. I now call myself Roxanne."

At the end of the table, Taras Tymko, a smaller, more compact version of his brother, gives a derisive snort. Adam smiles in his direction.

"I really wish you wouldn't use that kind of divisive language, A.T.," Roxanne stresses.

Taras snorts again as his brother answers.

"So have you still got your dick, Rexy? I mean…, Roxy."

Taras is now red-faced, holding a hand over his mouth so he doesn't guffaw into the open mic.

Roxanne, also crimson for a different reason, is obviously controlling herself. Her voice cracks slightly as she responds. "Your question is extremely rude, Adam. It's my choice to share the physical progress of my transition or not."

"I'm only asking because I'm sure the *Tymkoverse* would like to know."

"Why would my bodily status be so important to anyone?"

"Because the truth is important to everyone, Rex, or at least it should be. If you've got a dick, by definition you're a man. If you've had it cut off, you're still a man anyway, just a man with no dick."

Taras bursts into spontaneous applause.

"The truth is that my physical configuration has nothing to do with my gender identity."

"Bullshit! It has everything to do with it."

1

"It's my psyche, my attitudes and my actions that make me a woman. Not my bodily constitution."

"More bullshit! Simper all you want. You'll never have an actual pussy. You'll never get preggers. You'll never fully function as a woman. No tranny can."

"Then tell me how a trans woman just won the *Miss Cosmos USA* pageant." Roxanne challenges.

A.T.'s face suddenly becomes a stone mask. "What did you say?"

Realizing she's just gained the upper hand, Roxanne bores in for the kill. "Oh, you hadn't heard?" she says smugly. "The news came out just before I came in today. Rickie, formerly Ricardo, Ortega, was announced the *Miss CUSA* winner last night. She'll go on to compete for the title of *Miss Cosmos*."

"That just ain't right!" says Taras.

"No, it isn't," agrees A.T. "This fucking country is going to shit."

"Or finally starting to get woke," says Roxanne smugly.

A.T. looks at his guest with unabashed hatred. "Get the fuck out of my studio, you fucking pervert."

Roxanne, mindful that A.T. was formerly half of the pro-wrestling world tag-team champions along with his brother, decides not to argue.

After his guest is gone and A.T. has regained some self-control, he addresses his audience through his headset mic. "Guys, we've got to stop just sitting back and taking this shit. If we want to keep our country, we need to fight back."

"How we gonna do that, A.T.?" asks Taras. "Chase down that fucking tranny and kick its ass?"

"While that would give me a great deal of satisfaction, little brother, it won't get to the root of the problem." A.T. assumes a reflective expression. Finally he says, "I've got it! Tune into our next show, gang, and I'll have the answer for you. And I promise you, it's gonna be epic."

***

A soaking rain drenches the streets of Manhattan, but it does not, nor could it ever, cleanse them of two centuries worth of accumulated filth. The sweet sewerstench that rises from the pavement as a shimmering haze seems nearly tangible, or is it just the multicolored lights of the businesses that line the streets, reflecting through billions of raindrops swirling in the air?

At two o'clock in the morning on a warm May evening, the man called Irwin Irwin, staggering along the mostly empty sidewalk on 1st Avenue, has other things besides the weather on his mind. His hands are clutched between his legs, as if he's trying to drag his body along by the sheer strength of his arms, and he's bent nearly double as he stumbles uptown.

"God damn her!" he grates to no one in particular. "God damn that motherfucking whore bitch of a motherfucking Stacy!" His voice nearly breaks because of the pain emanating from his crushed testicles lancing through his belly.

After passing a bodega on the corner of 16th Street, his destination, the cylindrical glass tower of Mount Sinai Beth Israel Hospital, finally looms out of the mist. A ragged sob breaks from his lips, as he hauls his broken body beneath the steel latticework of the construction shelter surrounding the building, frantically looking for the emergency room entrance. He spots the bright crimson sign and lurches forward just as an ambulance with red lights strobing pulls up to the curb. Two EMTs leap out and dash around to the rear, where the doors burst open as the medics inside push out a gurney with a patient strapped on. The crew outside grabs and lowers it till the wheels touch the pavement, then roll it through the double doors of the emergency room, nearly running over poor Irwin in the rush. He screams in anger and frustration, but the EMTs never even look back. Such is the story of Irwin's life.

Of course, when he finally makes it inside, the staff is fully occupied with the patient just delivered, and Irwin is totally ignored. It isn't until his legs give way and he crumples to the floor with another pitiful cry that a white-clad nurse notices and comes to his aid. Maddened with anger and pain, he strikes out with his fists as she bends to help him, knocking her to the floor and breaking her nose. In the ensuing chaos, he finds himself hauled to his feet by several burly nurses' aides and strapped onto a gurney, then he's promptly wheeled to an alcove and left alone with his agony.

He screams raggedly until his throat is raw—it becomes obvious that no one is going to come near him. He closes his eyes and tries to sleep, but the incessant throbbing between his legs that thrusts knives into his vitals effectively prevents that.

Eventually, a hefty black nurse approaches the gurney, dragging an IV stand. "You gonna be good, now?" she asks him, checking him out with a wary eye.

Black people are generally on Irwin's shitlist for a variety of reasons, but he figures he'd best be nice to this one. "Yes ma'am. I'm sorry I did what I did. I hurt."

"Where does it hurt?" she asks, and he tells her, rating his pain at a 10 out of 10. He's grateful she doesn't ask how the injury happened.

"OK. Hang on and I'll fix you up."

She slides a needle into a vein on the back of his hand, connects it to a bag of fluid that she hangs on the stand, then plucks a syringe from her pocket and sticks the needle into the port on the tubing leading from the bag. Irwin's pain vanishes instantly as the opiate rushes into his veins.

Sinking into a cloud of warm whiteness, his last conscious thought is "Goddamn you to hell, Natalie McMasters!"

***

In a beautiful A-frame mansion nestled in a wooded suburban lot on a gorgeous mid-June day, Maria de Guadalupe Ibáñez sits in her wheelchair facing a computer monitor. Her husband, Danny Merkel, leans over her shoulder. He'd much rather be outside enjoying the late spring weather, but he'd promised to help her complete the form now displayed on the screen. He's close enough so he can smell the earthy, spicy aroma arising from her skin. He loves the smell of her, but he knows there's a reason it's so apparent right now. Fear.

"What do I put down for my birthplace?" asks Lupe. Her voice sounds strained. "If I say Culiacán, they will know I am illegal."

Danny sighs audibly. "First of all, you are not illegal. You have a green card."

"But I was illegal when I came here. If they know that, they will not want me to be around the children."

"They won't care, sweetheart. The new program that the legislature just instituted is designed to get more minorities into important positions in the public schools. You're a bisexual Hispanic woman. You've never been arrested, or even charged with a crime. You more than qualify."

"I had to go before the judge that time, then I ran away when she said I had to prove I belonged here."

Danny sighs again. *When will this lady get some self-confidence? She's been through things that would break a Marine, but she's still going strong, working and going to community college.* "They expunged your record when they gave you your green card. It won't even come up if the school checks."

"I am an addict. I am going to meetings and still taking suboxone."

"That just means that you're committed to staying clean."

"And there is this way that we live. Nattie is my wife. I call you my husband, but we could not even get married under the law…"

"Read my lips. It… won't… matter…"

Lupe's expression becomes puzzled. "Why should I read your lips? I can hear you just fine."

Despite himself, Danny breaks out into laughter. While Lupe's English is nearly perfect, there are still some Americanisms she's ignorant of. Noting that her expression has become pouty because he laughed at her, Danny leans in further, turns her face toward him, and softly kisses her lips. "Read my lips means I want you to really pay attention to what I'm saying. You love kids. You will make a great teaching assistant, and they're actively trying to hire people like you. Fill out the application and send it in. After what he's experienced lately, Eddie needs you close by."

Eduardo is Lupe's eleven year-old son.

"If you say so…"

"I do say so. And by the way, you need to get out of that wheelchair and start walking. The doctor told you, you don't need it anymore. It's actively hindering your recovery."

"All right, all right!" She turns back to the computer. "Now help me with the rest of this damned form."

***

In another part of the mansion, a second couple is huddled in front of a computer. Amos Murdoch, seventy-two, is also in a wheelchair, but unlike Lupe, he won't ever be leaving it. Next to him is Supervisory Special Agent Maribeth Murdoch, *nee* Woodrow—they were married a couple of weeks ago. She looks about ten years younger than Amos.

Shaking his head as he surveys a spreadsheet on the screen, Amos says, "I'm tellin' you, sweetness, I think the 3M Detective Agency is about as dead as a coon in the middle of a pack of Plott hounds."

M.B. winces at the visual that pops into her head. "It does seem like your business has definitely declined since the Ellis affair," she says, "but now y'all have your licenses back and can work again."

She's referring to the family's recent altercation with billionaire Jerome Ellis, who kidnapped Natalie and Eduardo, then used his money and influence to get the agency's licenses suspended when they fought back.

"Problem is they ain't nobody to work for," says Amos. "Most of our insurance clients moved their bidness to our competitors and are keepin' it there."

"It will pick back up again. You just have to give it time."

"Time won't pay the bills."

"What bills? Nattie, Lupe and Danny don't charge you for rent or utilities even though you insist on paying them. And there are plenty of insurance companies out there that can use your services. You just have to make some calls."

"I got to pay my people."

"Bosh! Kidd gets along fine on his pensions from the Marines and the CCPD. And Danny and the family are doing fine. I'll be retiring from the Bureau again at the end of summer..."

"Damnit, woman, I ain't no charity case!" Amos squawks.

"Nobody's saying you are. This is just family helping family. Isn't that the way you've always said it should be?"

Amos glares at his new bride, well-knowing she's right. After a minute he looks down at the floor and says, "I jest don't want to feel useless."

"And there it is," M.B. replies. "Nobody thinks you're useless, hon. They know you're just getting over a hump, and they're willing to help you. Why won't you let them?" She tries not to smile at his woebegone expression. "Jobs will come along. You just wait and see."

***

A warm breeze blows in from the lake, carrying a grassy aroma with a muddy hint of fish. Worming its way into my loose clothing, it evaporates the sweat on my skin and brings my nipples erect.

My name is Natalie McMasters. I'm twenty-four, blonde (OK, it's bleached) and way cute. Only I totally don't feel that way right now.

Shooters!

I'm at Tai Chi practice. Lupe and Danny didn't make it today—they stayed behind to work on her teacher's aide application. So it's just me, my *sifu* Ye-ye and his caretaker Vivian.

Ye-ye, eighty if he's a day, is wearing baggy white pants and a matching tunic that drops below his waist, held closed with braided buttons. He's got typical round Chinese features, a little pointy beard and a long mustache. His silver hair cascades halfway down his back and it's kept out of his face with a white headband. His eyes are totally covered with a white cloth tied behind his head.

Vivian, a little taller than me and slender as a reed, is as dark as I am blonde. She's got on an outfit similar to Ye-ye's. *Moi*, I'm in cut-offs and a t-shirt—that Chinese lewk is way cheugy for me.

Us girls stand side-by-side, facing *Sifu,* mirroring his movements as he goes through the form. I shake my head and try to concentrate on the complicated progression..

Pivot on the left foot, make a quarter turn to the right. Rotate arms clockwise, bringing right hand, palm in, to shoulder height and the left hand, palm out, to my waist with fingers down, grasping my invisible adversary by the shoulder and hip…

…holding my wrists behind my back, that bastard Irwin forces me down into the couch as he relentlessly shoves his dick up my ass. I try to relax to lessen the pain, but I just can't. Waves of agony ripple through my thighs and my belly as the assault goes on while I scream "No!" over and over…

Step empty to the east with the right foot, rolling the right hand, palm down, to chest height. Shift weight to 50/50, letting the right hand keep descending to waist height while stepping into *hu gongbu.*

…in another place at a different time, my biological father, Jay Ellis, grasps my ankles, spreads my legs, and slides himself into me. His face is in a rictus as he closes eyes and grunts like a pig—hot liquid spurts inside me, burning like molten lead…

Pivot on the left foot, turn left side to center, left hand pushing forward… or is it the right hand? Shit!

Ye-ye stops, apparently noticing my mistake. How can a blind man do that?

"Oich!" he says. "Wassamatta you? You been doing this form t'ree years now." He takes a step toward me and places two fingers of his right hand against my cheek. His mouth puckers, suggesting confusion, then a broad grin replaces his bewildered expression. "Now I unnerstand. Congratulations!" He says.

I'm thinking he's still throwing me shade. "You don't need to get sarcastic," I tell him. "I've just got a lot on my mind, is all."

"No sarcasm," he says. "New mother always deserve congratulations!"

WTF?

***

Later, I'm back at the house, in the bathroom, peeing into a Dixie cup. I grab the testing device off the sink and dip the end into the yellow fluid, stirring it around so violently that it splashes on my hand. Yuck!

I don't want to stare at the fucking thing for the five minutes that it takes for the results to develop, so I turn it upside down on the sink and stare at my phone instead.

It can't be! I shoved him off so only a little got inside me!

It seems to take an hour for 1:07 to turn to 1:12. My hand actually trembles as I reach for the device to flip it over and read the results.

Two lines.

Two. Motherfucking. Lines.

No!

Chapter 1

It takes me almost three months to get up the nerve to tell the fam I'm preggers. I spent all that time doing my best not to think about it, hoping that it would just go away. Finally, the growing bump in my belly forced me to say something.

"Holy shit!" says Danny. "Nattie, that's outstanding!"

Obviously, there's something else I didn't tell them.

"It's wonderful," echoes Lupe. "Now Eduardo and Shannie will have another brother or a sister."

I should have expected this reaction. They think it's Danny's baby!

"We should tell the kids right now," Lupe goes on.

"And have a celebration," says Danny. "Why don't we call Mom, Amos and M.B., round up the kids, then all go out to dinner tonight? We can tell everybody at once."

"We can go to that new seafood restaurant that just opened," adds Lupe. "You know, Nattie, the one you said you really wanted to try."

Come to think of it, it could be Danny's. I've never been religious about taking my pill every day. It didn't seem to matter much when he was the only guy I was with. Danny looks at me and suddenly looks alarmed. "Nattie, you're crying!"

Of course, I'm crying, you idiot. How can I tell you this baby might be my biological father's?

"Of course, she's crying," says Lupe. "Hormones! It's what new mothers do."

***

Dinner seems to last forever.

I'm at the head of the table, with my husband on one side and my wife on the other. Good old Danny made a detour on the way and got flowers, which the waiter put in a vase in front of me, and multicolored helium balloons that spell out B-A-B-Y are tied to my chair. The strong fishy odor in the restaurant fills my nose and makes me want to heave. How the fuck will I ever make it through this dinner?

Thomas A. Burns, Jr.

Eduardo is sitting next to Lupe, and Shannie, the eleven-year-old homeless girl we recently adopted, is beside Danny. Next to Shannie is my mom, and M.B. is by Eduardo. Finally, Uncle Amos in his wheelchair is at the foot of the table.

It's cray hard to put on a chill face. I order a salad for dinner, drawing a puzzled look from Danny, and I push the lettuce around on the plate, pretending to enjoy it. Sitting at a table full of people who read other people for a living and who know me maybe better than I do, how can I even think I can get away with hiding that I'm scared shitless? The only thing I've got going for me is that nobody will know why I'm so pressed—they'll just think it's just hormones.

Everyone is so fucking happy! If one more person congratulates me, I swear to Christ I'm gonna knife 'em!

Later, back at the house, I slink off to my room. When Lupe, Danny and I established our throuple, we decided that each person should have their own space to avoid being smothered. Now I'm totally grateful that we did that. That is, until there's a knock on the door.

I don't answer. Maybe they'll think I'm asleep.

"Nattie? It's me. Can I come in?" Mom lives in the guest house on the property. She usually tries *trés* hard to give the three of us our space. Apparently not tonight, though.

Shit. "Yeah, come on in."

She opens the door and comes in. She's still wearing the frilly blouse and white pants she had on at the restaurant. She sits on the bed next to me and ruffles my hair.

"Sweetiekins, what's wrong?"

I hate it when she calls me that!

"Nothin'. I'm just way blown away that I'm gonna be a mom."

Her dark brown eyes bore into mine. "I think there's something more to it than that."

I never could get away with capping her. I open my mouth to speak, but the words won't come. I burst into gales of tears. She wraps her arms around me, pulling my face into her bosom just like she did when I was a little girl and lets me cry it out. When I'm done, she pushes me away and gives me the eyes again. "Now tell Mommy what's the matter."

"You remember last month when you told me about how I was born?"

She nods. She told me that her and Daddy couldn't get preggers, so they finally went to a fertility clinic in New York City. *In vitro* did the

10

trick, but what Mom and Daddy didn't know was that the clinic didn't use her eggs and his sperm—instead, they used some from Jay Ellis, the nutcase billionaire who owned the clinic, and his crazy-ass GF Geraldine, my biological mother. I tell Mom some of what happened while me and Eduardo were prisoners at his estate. That I met my twin sister who was in an incestuous relationship with her parents, and who set me up to get raped by them. Later, the three of them were killed when their helicopter exploded while they were escaping from the cops.

"There's a pretty good chance this baby is his," I finish.

WTF do you say to something like that? She just sits there slack-jawed, shaking her head. Finally she leans over and takes me in her arms, pressing my face into her neck. The warm smell of her hair is just as I remember. "Oh Honey, I'm so sorry that that happened to you," she says. She sits back up and looks me in the eyes. "You have to tell Danny and Lupe."

"I just can't, Mom. They're so fucking happy. I won't fuck that up for them."

"Then what are you going to do? If you want to get rid of it, I'll understand."

Yeet! As a devout Catholic, that's a huge thing for her to say.

"Problem is, I don't know Lupe and Danny will get it," I reply. "Lupe's totally Catholic—she's got enough shit on her plate with being bi and married to both me and Danny to put that on her too. And Danny's totally trad. There's a chance this baby is his, you know. He'd never forgive me if I got rid of it. Shit, I'd never forgive myself!"

"But you were raped…"

"I don't want to tell them that!" I holler, then I lower my voice, hoping that nobody heard me. "I know this is on Ellis, not on me, but I still don't want Danny and Lupe to know!"

We sit there for a minute just looking at each other. At last, she says, "Then maybe you'd better see somebody and find out for sure who the father is. You don't have to say anything to Lupe or Danny in the meantime. Once we know what we're dealing with, we can take it from there."

I don't miss the switch from you to we. "I love you, Mommy."

"I love you too, Sweetiekins." She suddenly becomes all business. "Call a doctor next week and get an appointment as soon as you can."

"I'll do it first thing, Mom."

I lean over and put my arms around her again, hugging her for all I'm worth. Maybe this mess will work out OK after all.

Chapter 2

Irwin is sitting up in his bed at Mount Sinai Beth Israel, chowing down on a Dixie cup of chocolate ice cream. The sharp tang of iodine in the air makes the ice cream taste like shit. He's basically dead from the waist down—his legs stick out in front of him like two boards. They gave him a shot in his lower back to kill the pain from his busted nuts. He can move his legs if he tries, but he really doesn't have much reason to.

He's listening to the podcast *Tymko's Times* on his laptop. He's got a love/hate relationship with Adam Tymko. A so-called man's man, A.T. preaches traditional masculinity, arguing that cultivating a macho attitude leads men to success in business, sports and sex. The host chalks up much of the craziness in today's world to the abandonment of traditional male/female roles.

Irwin thinks A.T.'s deadass right. Problem is, Irwin is twenty-seven and hasn't gotten laid since he did it with Becky Sue Langley as a junior in high school. And that didn't really count since he came all over her panties before he could get them off her. He hadn't gotten any more pussy until he met Natalie McMasters last week. She wanted the dope about her parents from the New Horizons Fertility Clinic where Irwin was working, and she made a deal to fuck him if he helped her get it. He carried out his end of the bargain, but when he got a little carried away during their tryst afterwards and tried to get some anal, she accused him of rape and went all Hong Kong fooey on him and crushed his nuts. Now he's sitting in the hospital dead from the waist down, scarfing down ice cream and waiting to find out if he'll ever be able to get it up again.

When Irwin was in college and most of his friends were getting laid on a regular basis, he gravitated towards the online community known as the manosphere, where he could get tips on shit like great opening lines or where to find babes who were truly desperate. Irwin dutifully followed most of the advice he got from these blogs and podcasts, but was still unable to score (fancy that!). At the time, the manosphere was fragmenting into two camps—one made up of the so-called alpha males who were fighting to preserve traditional male privilege, and a second faction, guys known as incels or involuntary celibates, who were growing increasingly misogynistic and desperate. Irwin found himself attracted to the latter group and entered a death spiral by euphemistically *taking the black pill*, a concept derived from the hit movie, *The Matrix*. In the film, one could either swallow a *blue pill* and exist in a state of contented obliviousness, or a *red pill* and become woke, accepting harsh reality. The incels conceived a third pill, the *black pill*, which caused the taker to descend into nihilism, believing that womankind (aka. the Stacys) would see then as eternal losers and forevermore reserve their sexual favors for the alpha males (aka. the Chads).

A.T. is the self-proclaimed king of the Chads. Along with his brother Taras, he's forging an Internet empire based on training other men how to assert their masculinity, surround themselves with male companions who are doing the same, garner wealth and attract women who want macho men to fuck them. Even though Irwin is mostly convinced that he's a *schlemiel* with no chance of ever joining the ranks of the Chads, he's still red-pilled enough so Adam's misogynistic rhetoric gives him a modicum of hope.

On *Tymko's Times* today, A.T. is on a rant about the trannys, a fave subject.

"Regardless of the lies people tell about me, I'm not a homophobe," says A.T. "I'm no trannyphobe, either."

"Is trannyphobe even a word?" asks Taras.

"Shut up while I'm talking, dumbass. And yes, it's a word because I said it." A.T. takes a long pull on a cigar the size of a baseball bat. Irwin knows that A.T. considers his cigars a symbol of his masculinity.

A.T. goes on, "I don't give a damn who you fuck, Bambi or Bob, it's all the same to me. And I don't care if you cut your dick off or grow a pair of tits. Just don't tell me that you're a woman if you do that shit."

"Right on!" says Irwin to the laptop.

"Of course, these dickless wonders ain't real men either," says A.T. "They're fuckin' nuts, is what they are. I mean, if you grow a beard and hair down to your ass, wrap yourself in a bathrobe and cruise down Main carrying a cross, sayin' you're Jesus Christ, what do they do to you?"

"They lock your crazy ass up," says Taras.

"That's what they do!" agrees Irwin.

"Damn right they do," says A.T. "But if a tranny says he's a ho because he cut off his dick, they let him join the girls' softball team or share the bathroom with my six-year-old daughter.

"You haven't got a six-year-old daughter," says Taras.

"Doesn't matter," replies A.T. "Point is, motherfucker ain't no woman. And he isn't really a man no more, neither!"

"No, he ain't!" says Irwin, making a fist and punching the air.

The door to Irwin's room rattles and he looks up in alarm like a guy caught watching porn by his mom. It's the doctor, a slight little Indian guy in lime green scrubs and huge black glasses, whose name is Veejay somethingorother. He's carrying a clipboard. Irwin hits the button to turn off the podcast and pulls out his earbuds.

"How are ve this afternoon, Meester Irvin?" The doctor asks.

"Fine." Says Irwin, shortly. "And it's Irwin, not Irvin." He glares at the doctor. A.T. promised he'd have a big announcement at the end of his show today, and Irwin hopes he won't miss it because of the interruption.

"Dot's vhat I said," Dr. Vijayalakshimi replied. He hesitates, then, "I'm afraid I have some bad news."

Irwin's blood runs cold. "What news?"

"I am sorry to say dot ve cannot repair your testicles. De ultrasound ve did dis morning shows dey are crushed. I am going to recommend you undergo a subcapsular orchiectomy."

Now Irwin's really scared. "What the fuck is that?"

"It means ve remove your damaged testicles t'rough a small incision in your scrotum. Vhen ve are done, no vun vill even notice you've had any surgery."

Irwin opens his mouth to speak, but no words come. Finally, "Then I won't be a man anymore."

"Sure you vill," says the doctor. "You vill just be sterile like you are already. Lots of men are. Ve can even put you on a course of testosterone so you von't show any loss of masculine features. No vun vill know unless you tell them."

This can't be happening! "What if I say no?" asks Irwin.

"Den your testicles will atrophy and could become necrotic. Dat would mean you could lose your genitals altogether, or it could even kill you. You really don't vant to do dot, Meester Irvin." He extends the clipboard to Irwin. "I have the consent form right here. You sign it, and ve can schedule you for surgery tomorrow."

Irwin slaps the clipboard away so it flies out of the doctor's hand and clatters on the floor. "Get that fucking thing away from me!" he grates. "And get the fuck out of here!"

The doctor, who has seen such a reaction many times, moves to pick up the clipboard. "You just t'ink about it, Meester Irvin. I come back in the morning for your answer. Ve can probably still get you scheduled tomorrow if you say OK." He goes out, closing the door softly behind him.

Irwin sits there, letting the enormity of what he's just heard consume him.

He isn't really a man anymore, neither, A.T. just said.

Irwin's just had the whole fucking bottle of black pills jammed down his throat.

After a moment, he puts his earbuds back in pushes the button again to get back to the podcast.

Taras is speaking. "So what's this big announcement you've got for us, brother?"

"I've decided to run a beauty pageant!" A.T. smirks. "A real one, where the girls are all smokin' and no trannys are allowed. I'm calling it the America's First Sexy Lady pageant. We're going to feature women with traditional values—none of them fuckin' woke bitches for us! We'll have all men judges and the girls will be evaluated on how good they are at housework and what they like to do in the sack. None of this fighting for world peace shit. And instead of a swimsuit competition, which nobody does anymore anyhow cause it ain't woke, we're gonna have a nude competition!"

"You won't get that on TV!" says Taras.

"Don't bet on it. I've already reached out to some of the streaming services, and they're interested."

"When is this gonna happen?"

"Believe it or not, I think I can get it to come off by early September," A.T. grins. "No pun intended."

"How can you do it so fast?" asks Taras.

"Because I've been working on it ever since that tranny Rex told us about a he/she winning *Miss Cosmos USA* back at Christmas time. And I've got friends, dude! Friends who owe me. *Tymko's Times* has an audience of ten million, you know. You just watch. I'll make it happen."

Irwin pulls the earbuds out again. Normally, he would be psyched beyond measure by something like this, but not today. Today, all he can think about is that they want to cut his nuts out tomorrow.

I won't really be a man anymore…

And it's all Natalie McMasters's fault!

Chapter 3

It's Tuesday before I can catch up with the OB/GYN—Monday was Labor Day. I'm in luck. They had a cancellation and I'm able to get in this afternoon.

I feel like a criminal sneaking out of the house, avoiding Danny and Lupe cuz I'm quaking that they'll ask questions I can't answer if they catch me.

The twin scents of perfume and perspiration reach my nostrils as I open the door to the reception room at Capital OB/GYN, and a low buzz of convo fills the air. A sign on a table tells me to *Please take a mask,* so I pluck a pink one out of the boxful and put it on. There are multiple docs at this office—half a dozen women are waiting. Most are about my age and in various stages of pregnancy—not showing at all, to just a bump, like me, and one who looks like she's gonna drop the kid in the next five minutes. Their eyes are all smiling and animated, just happy AF to be adding to the burden on the planet. Not me!

I've already checked in on my phone, so I don't need to talk to the girl behind the sliding glass doors who's wearing the rose colored scrubs with teddy bears. I avoid eye contact with the other moms in the waiting room, make a beeline for a corner chair, and grab a magazine to discourage any convo.

In just a few minutes another pink-clad female appears and calls my name. Guiltily looking side to side, I follow her into an inner office that looks like a hospital corridor, walk past a nurses' station and step on a scale. 105 pounds. High for me.

"How tall are you?"

"Five-one."

She leads me down the hall into a room the size of a large closet where she waves me to a pink armchair, clips an oxygen monitor on my finger, takes my BP (105/70), my temperature (normal) and my pulse (I'm alive). Then she hands me a clipboard holding about five pounds of paper.

"We'll give you some time to fill out those forms. Just press the button on the table when you're done and someone will come and get them."

The paperwork is worse than what I usually get at the doctor's. They want a complete health history, and a lot of info about shit like diet, exercise, smoking and drinking history, drug use, etc. I'm sure whoever reads it will be appalled that somebody with all my nasty habits is preggers. I'm only halfway done when a white girl with turtles on her scrubs comes in, pushing a cart with a tray on it, holding a bunch of test tubes, and long thin, opaque thingee with a pointy things on both ends.

"I'm here to take your blood," she says unnecessarily.

I extend an arm, and turn my eyes away as she slides a needle into my vein with practiced efficiency, then punctures the rubber tops of the tubes in turn, filling each one with the thick, red fluid that keeps me breathing. When she's done, she pulls the needle out of my arm and replaces it with a piece of gauze. "Hold that," she says, then she wraps some Velcro tape around it to keep it in place. She hands me a small plastic container with an orange screw cap saying, "You know what to do with this?" I nod. "There's a rest room down the hall. Leave it behind the little metal door when you're done."

When I come back, a tall, thin black woman holding a clipboard meets me. She holds out a hand to invite me into my room, then follows me, closing the door behind us. "I'm Shalyka," she says. "I'm a nurse-practitioner." She checks the clipboard. "May I call you Natalie?" I nod. "So tell me about you and your baby." The moment of truth has arrived.

I just blurt it out. "I need to know who the father is." Tears begin welling from my eyes.

She raises her eyebrows over the mask, but her tone is non-judgmental. "We can certainly help you with that," she says. "Can you tell me more about your situation?"

I haven't really thought out how I'm going to approach this. I don't want to use the r-word because I don't want the law involved. They couldn't do anything about it anyway, because it happened months ago and the motherfucker who did it is dead.

"Why don't we start with when you had you last period so we can tell how far along you are," she continues.

We play with numbers and dates for a while and settle on about sixteen weeks. She tells me the baby is about the size of an avocado and looks like a tiny human. "We can do an ultrasound if you'd like to see…"

I cut her off. "I just need to know who the father is."

" M'kay," she says. "I'll need a blood sample from you and one from the alleged father…"

"That's not going to happen," I say sharply. I guess my tone causes her to raise her eyebrows. "Look, what I tell you here is confidential, right?"

Now she's looking at me way sus. "Within reason. I'm bound to report anything to the authorities that may indicate imminent danger to you or another person…"

"That won't be a problem. What I need to know is if me and the baby's father are related. Can that be done without a blood sample from him?"

Shooters!

I can see that she's struggling to keep her expression neutral. "Yes. There's a type of DNA assay called an SNP test that can tell us that."

"Will you need to get blood from the baby to do it? Like with an amnio…" I hesitate on the big word.

"You mean an amniocentesis. No, we don't need one. There's a small amount of the baby's DNA circulating with your blood that can be amplified with PCR, so all we need is a blood sample from you. The two DNAs can be separated, then we can get the data we need." She frowns.

"What?"

"The bad news is that there are only a few places that do that kind of testing, so it could take a while. Do you have plans to terminate if the test shows that you and the father are related?"

I hesitate before answering. Catholicism dies hard. "I guess so."

Her expression is serious now. "After the Supreme Court overturned *Roe*, our state legislature imposed a twenty-week cap on abortions," she says in a bitter tone. "You don't want to run over that or you'll have to go out of state to get one. And they're even talking about making that a felony if they catch you. To top it off, Congress is considering a nationwide cap."

"You don't know if you can get the results back in a month?" I ask incredulously.

"It could be tight," she says. "A lot of clinics have closed recently, so the waiting time has gone up." Her tone becomes super-clinical. "If you think incest is likely, it might be wise to go ahead and make your decision right away."

But what if it's Danny's? "I can't do that," I tell her.

She looks at me tight-lipped. "Okay. We can get the blood sample today. We'll see you back here in a couple of weeks, and if we don't have results by then, we can revisit this." She pauses, then, "Can you assure me that you are in no danger of being victimized again?"

"Yes. If the baby's father is my… relative, he's dead."

"Okay. Get an appointment for two weeks from now on the way out."

"Will you call me if the results come in sooner?"

"Yes."

Chapter 4

Eduardo Ibáñez has the world by the balls.

Sitting at his desk in middle school, he's ready to blow this chickenshit dump and get on with his life. At the tender age of twelve, he's already killed a man (the notorious serial killer Tommy Burke) and had sex (of a sort) with a thirteen-year-old hottie. What's left for him to learn in this lame-ass place? Besides, the other students are keeping their distance and looking at him funny. His kidnapping a few months ago was all over the media—of course, they couldn't use his name, but they did mention his fam, so it wasn't too hard to figure out who "the minor child involved" was. The guy who took him had a rep for kinky sex, so naturally, everybody's wondering exactly what did happen. Eduardo tells himself he doesn't give a shit about any of it, but that's a lie.

Unfortunately, *Máma* Lupe must have scoped his 'tude, because she's gotten herself appointed as a teacher's aide and assigned to his seventh grade classroom. She's sitting quietly at her desk up front next to Ms. McCurdy, ready to assist her teacher in any way she can—handing out papers to the students or collecting them, running the PC to project AVs while teacher presents the lesson, or even taking over a breakout group if McCurdy lets her. She's trying to treat Eduardo just like the other kids—he knows that's BS because he can see the way she checks him out when she thinks he's not looking. If McCurdy calls on him and he doesn't know the answer, *Máma* Lupe makes sure to bring it up after they get home, asking him the same question again and again until she's sure that he knows. It sucks! He's being smothered—there's no place he can just *be* without her all up in his shit.

His newly adopted sister Shannie is no help either. "You should be grateful you've got a mommy who loves you and wants to make sure you're OK," she says. As a formerly homeless child, Shannie knows what she's talking about.

Before, he could go to *Máma* Nattie when he felt like *Máma* Lupe was coming on too strong, and she'd talk to *Máma* Lupe and get her to back off. But since she found out about her new baby, *Máma* Nattie doesn't listen to him like she used to. *Pápa* Danny never was much help—it actually seems like he's scared of *Máma* Lupe—he just tells Eduardo he'd better do what he's told.

The only one who seems to understand his problem is his new friend, Martin Castro. Martin is fourteen and still in the seventh grade. He's always getting in trouble for talking in class and cracking jokes—he even brought a copy of *Penthouse* to school one time and was suspended for a couple of days. McCurdy said the magazine demeans women. If that's so, Eduardo wonders why all those hot chicks have their pics in it. Martin is also on the outs with the other seventh graders because of his age and his size (he's six-four and thin as a starving zombie) and the fact that everybody thinks he's weird AF (they call him Cray Cray Marty). His normal dress is a light grey hoodie over gray city camo fatigue pants. It's natural that the two outcasts would hang together.

Eduardo has told Martin about his killing Burke and getting laid, but he doesn't think the older boy believes him.

Because he's been acting out, McCurdy has moved Martin to the front of the classroom. It hasn't really helped, because Martin doesn't really care if he pisses off McCurdy.

Eduardo turns his attention to a girl sitting in the front row, with long, curly blond hair cascading down her back. She's Ellie Schultz—easily the prettiest and most popular girl in the class—Eduardo fell in love the second he laid eyes on her. She's got a rep as a snob though, but the word around school is that she's already done it with a couple of eighth graders. Surely an experienced *hombre* like Eduardo should be able to get her to do it with him too. If he can, then maybe Martin will show him more respect.

He finally worked up the nerve to talk to her before class. She was hanging with her friend Allison Davies, who gave him the stink eye when he walked up. But Ellie looked right at him and said, "You're Eduardo Ibáñez, aren't you?"

He nodded.

"I've heard of you. You're the one that helped the police arrest that bad man last month, right?"

She's heard of me! Eduardo's chest swelled as he said, "Yes, I did that."

Ellie looked at Allison, who gave Eduardo another evil glare before she walked away.

She wants to be alone with me and Davies doesn't like it.

Eduardo and Ellie had a nice convo about things they had in common—music, movies, video games. He got up his nerve and told her the joke about the difference between a snowman and a snowwoman, and she slapped him lightly on the face before she laughed and laughed. Then she told him the one about the difference between "ooh" and "ahh" and he felt his face burning.

When the bell rang and the had to go into the classroom, she invited him to her birthday party this Saturday.

"It's going to be great! My parents even hired a DJ."

Shooters!

Eduardo's face fell. "How great can it be with your 'rents there?"

"Oh, they won't be. They trust me. They're going to Vegas for the weekend." She paused then smiled at him. "Maybe we can see if you can make me go 'ahh'," she said, and his face got hot again.

As he walked away, he looked back and saw Ellie pointing at him, saying something to Davies, then both of them were laughing.

She must have told Davies my joke about the snowman!

Ellie notices that Eduardo's looking at her, and she smiles at him, sending a cold jolt down his spine. Then she takes her phone out and holds it down at her side, her thumb tapping the screen. A muted *ding* sounds from the other side of the room and Eduardo looks that way just in time to see Martin pull out his phone.

WTF? What's she texting him for?

The older boy scowls and looks Eduardo's way, then his thumbs start hammering the screen.

Eduardo's phone dings in his pocket. He pulls it out just far enough to see the text.

She mine man. Better leave her be.

Eduardo grins at Martin. Finally he's got the upper hand.

Out of nowhere, *Máma* Lupe appears next to the older boy's desk, reaching down to pluck his cell phone out of his hands.

Martin jumps in his seat. "Hey! Whatchoo think you're doing, bitch?"

A few weeks ago, Lupe would have lambasted Martin upside the head for talking to her that way, but Eduardo knew she had to go to an orientation session before coming in the classroom. Doubtlessly that explained her newfound self-control. "You can get this back from the vice-principal," she says. "Come on. We're going to see her now."

"The fuck you say!" says Martin, but Lupe ignores the profanity and turns to Eduardo.

"You too," she says, holding out her hand for the phone he's openly holding in his hand.

"*Máma...*" Eduardo begins, but one look at her face tells him it will do no good. Too late, he realizes that he's screwed up yet again. She's told him to call her Ms. Ibáñez at school.

She heads out into the hall, still in possession of the phones. What can the boys do but follow?

Eduardo feels the eyes of the other students burning into his back as he leaves, their silent mockery ringing in his ears. McCurdy just continues on with the lesson like nothing ever happened, as harmony and order settles upon her classroom once again.

Lupe directs the boys to straight-back chairs outside vice-principal Drayton's office and goes in to explain the situation. When she returns, she gives Eduardo a look that tells him this will not be over after Drayton has dealt with him. He will face her at home, later.

Eduardo knows that Drayton is renowned for letting students stew outside her office for fifteen or twenty minutes before calling them in to face the music. The vice-principal has been heard to say that such time is necessary to allow the offenders to fully consider the gravity of their sins before she deals with them.

Martin has other ideas.

"Fuck this shit, man!" he says. "Fuckin' Drayton ain't gonna give us back our phones, she's just gonna bitch us out before she makes our 'rents come in and get them. I ain't playin' her fuckin' game." The older boy gets up in preparation for leaving. "You comin', Ibáñez? Or you gonna just sit there like a little pussy?"

Eduardo is torn. He knows that Martin is right. But he also knows he'll get it at home ten times worse if he leaves. Leaving will fall into the category of *embarrassing his mother in public*, a mortal sin if there ever was one.

"C'mon, Ibáñez," Martin says again. "Have some *cojones.*"

"I better not," says Eduardo, looking at the floor.

"*Cobarde!*" Martin spits on the floor. "Pussy! I thought you said you killed a man. You don't act like it to me." He stalks off, head held high.

Eduardo watches him go down the hall.

Reaching a side corridor, Martin tuns to hurl one last insult. "Wonder what Ellie's gonna think when I tell her about this?" He disappears from view.

Eduardo hesitates another two seconds, then jumps up and runs after Martin.

Chapter 5

It's nearly 4 p.m. when I get home from the doctor's. As I pull into the semi-circular driveway in front of Hyacinth House, I see that everyone is here—Lupe's bug, Danny's truck and M.B.'s sports car are all parked outside.

I walk right into the kitchen and major drama. Eduardo's not home from school yet and Lupe's way triggered. Lupe, Danny and Shannie are in the kitchen. Danny and Shannie are sitting at the table with cookies and milk while Lupe's marching back and forth in front of them on an epic tirade.

"He got sent to vice-principal Drayton's office for having his phone out in class!" Lupe rants. "It was all that Martin Castro's fault. I have forbidden Eduardo to hang around with him but does he listen? Of course not! That Castro is almost an adult and should not even be allowed around twelve-year-olds. Who knows what terrible things he is filling Eduardo's head with? Then vice-principal Drayton called me to her office to tell me that Eduardo left school without even talking to her. She is suspending him! For the rest of the week!"

Poor Danny just sits there tight-lipped, and Shannie looks scared AF. Danny won't confront Lupe when she's like this. He just leaves it all to me.

Not today, people. I've got enough my own shit going on.

The back door bangs and in slinks Eduardo. He probably heard his *Mamá* shouting a hundred yards away. It's not been that long since he ran away and was kidnapped by Jay Ellis. After we got him back, Lupe tried to clamp down on him like a prison guard, but me and Danny fought her, telling her that was the perfect way to get him to take off again. It was about then that the announcement came out about the school looking for teacher's aides, so we managed to push her in that direction. We didn't think that they would actually assign her to her own son's classroom, but they totally did. It's no wonder the poor kid is way shook.

Lupe wheels on him, hands on her hips, and he directs a pitiful glance at me and Danny.

No way, José. I'm not getting involved in this unless she starts beating on him.

"What have you got to say for yourself?"

"Nothing that you want to hear," he says defiantly.

Lupe takes a step toward him, cocking her arm back as she does, but I cough and throw her a shady glare. Me and Danny have told her that we won't stand for her hitting Eduardo any more. She backs off, lowering her hand. Her total disgust evident in her tone, she tells Eduardo, "You are grounded."

The poor kid looks like she just kicked him in the stomach. Lupe smiles wickedly. She knows she's hit a nerve.

The poor kid quivers like a mouse in front of a cat. "For how long?"

"Until you start doing right!" Lupe spits.

"But I've been invited to a birthday party on Saturday."

Now her face lights up. She's totally enjoying herself way too much. "Well, you are going to miss it," she says. "Think about that the next time you decide to misbehave in school."

Eduardo opens his mouth to clap back, then he thinks better of it. I can feel the hate towards his mom coming off him in waves.

I wonder how everyone would look at me if I tell them I my father raped me?

Where did that thought come from?

Danny can't take it anymore. "Don't you think you're being a little hard on him?"

"Not nearly hard enough," she tells him. "If I ever spoke that way to my *Máma*, I would be picking myself up off the floor."

Uncle Amos comes rolling into the kitchen, followed by M.B. He's obviously heard what Lupe said. "Well, I agree with Danny. I think y'all are bein' too hard on the boy, too. It's a wonder I ever got a edgycation. I used to be in the shit with them teachers all the time when I was his age."

Lupe seems to deflate like a punctured balloon. While Uncle has made no secret that he disapproves of our polygamous marriage, he has taken a particular shine to Eduardo, treating him like the son he never had. The two of them spend a lot of time together in Uncle's office, where he tells the boy stories of his time in the Marine Corps, his adventures as a detective in the early years, and shares his wisdom about life in general. He had Danny set up a shooting range on the property where the two of them are teaching Eduardo the finer points of gun handling. Lupe wasn't thrilled with that, but she's totally anxious that Uncle should like her and she treads carefully around him.

"Eddie's had a hard time at school since that bidness last spring," Uncle goes on, referring to the abduction. "Let him go to his party, *Máma*. We can find some other way to punish him for that mess at school. Maybe I can give him some work to do for me."

Eduardo smiles at Uncle. Maybe he's gonna get out of this after all!

Shooters!

Lupe takes a deep breath and straightens her shoulders. "No, *Señor* Murdock," she says. "What Eduardo did was disrespectful to Ms. McCurdy and Ms. Drayton. I am now a staff member at the school. What message would it send if I let my own son get away with that kind of behavior? I am afraid I must ask that you honor my decision."

Amos frowns. "I guess I'll have to." He turns to Eduardo. "I tried."

"Go to your room," Lupe orders her son. "I do not want to see you again until dinner time."

Eduardo leaves with head bowed and shoulders hunched. After a moment, Shannie gets up and follows him.

"Do not comfort him!" Lupe snaps at her. "He should suffer for what he has done."

Shannie's face says she doesn't like it, but she'll obey.

Lupe looks way too satisfied with herself. Is this all about what Eduardo did, or is there something else going down?

"I totally hope you're pleased with yourself." I tell her.

She looks at me with fire in her eyes. "Why should I be? I will be embarrassed to go into school tomorrow with him not there, and everyone knowing that he is suspended."

"Just what I thought. It's always about you, ain't it?"

"Nattie…," Danny warns. I glare at him and he shuts up fast.

"What? It's true!" I continue. "She's always coming down on the poor kid for something!" I turn back to Lupe. "Just because your life has gone to shit doesn't mean you get to take it out on him!"

I can almost see the waves of heat rising from her as she claps back, "What do you mean that my life is shit?"

M.B.: "Natalie, don't …!"

"What the fuck you think I mean? You whine and cry about everything all the time and nobody can do a fucking thing to please you. You can barely hold your own shit together, but you're all over the poor kid, all the fucking time! And he's a good boy! No wonder he ran away!" Now I'm on a roll. "If anybody says anything to you about your 'tude, you go crawling off to NA to cry to your sponsor about it. Why the fuck won't you talk to us? Oh, I know! It's because you're a fucking addict, and we just can't understand you! I think it's because you're fucking selfish AF!" I stop because I've run out of breath. Then I take a good look at Lupe.

27

Her normally café au lait skin is a washed out tan and tears are streaming down her cheeks. Her eyes are wide, her mouth is open, and she looks like she's about to heave.

She spins and tears out of the kitchen. I start to follow, but M.B.'s voice stops me. "Not now, Natalie. You'll just make it worse. Give her some space."

Fuckin' A! What the fuck did I just do?

Chapter 6

Irwin cautiously eases one eye open. The medistink in the air tells him that he's still at Mt. Saini Beth Israel. The spinning room gradually slows and comes into focus, but the bedstand and the lamp still seem to rise and fall, like flotsam on the waves. Holy shit, man! He's as high as an Airbus sailing through the clouds on some seriously good shit. Then he remembers.

My balls! The bastards cut out my fucking nuts!

He feels nothing at all from the waist down, but his stomach is a hollow sphere of ice.

I'm not a man anymore. Goddamn you motherfucker Natalie McMasters!

His gorge rises as he feels the tears straining to burst from his eyes.

No! Nobody's gonna see me crying in this fucking bed.

With a supreme effort of will, he swallows the bile, takes some deep breaths until the heat drains from his face and his gut relaxes. The furniture gradually ceases whirling and he starts to feel normal—that is, as normal as a dude can feel with half of his body numb and no nuts.

He notices his laptop on the bedstand.

I need somethin' to get my mind off this shit, or I'll go fuckin' cray.

He grabs the computer and hauls it into the bed. The metal is cold on his belly, causing him to shiver. He raises the lid, wiggles his fingers on the touch pad and the screen pops to life. He moves the cursor to the icon for his podcast app and selects latest episodes. He's in luck! The newest ep of *Tymko's Times* is on in real time. He clicks the link.

The screen flickers. Suddenly, A.T.'s voice is in his ear.

"…pageant is all set for September. The venue will be the Rutledge Memorial Convention Center in Capital City. Right now, we've got thirty two of the finest bitches in the U, S of A ready to strut their shit on the runway for the title of America's First Sexy Lady."

"And where can all of our fans get in on the action?" asks Taras.

"Right here on *Tymko's Times*," says A.T. "and we're also taking bids from Netflix, Hulu, Amazon Prime and other streaming services to make it available nationwide. We should know who'll get the contract by the end of the month." Adam pauses, then, "And now, the most fired-up announcement of all!"

"What is it?" asks Taras.

"You may be asking yourself…"

"Or you may not," Taras interrupts.

"STFU. You may be asking yourself, other than the totally incredible bragging rights that will come with the title of America's Most Sexy Lady as bestowed by *moi,* why would a ho even want to enter a nude beauty pageant?"

"Yeah, why would she?"

"I'll tell ya. She would want to enter because we've got the most kickin' first prize ever offered in pageant history!"

"What is it?"

"It's…" Another pregnant, pause. "One…Million…Dollaaaaaarrs!"

"Holy shit!"

"Holy shit indeed! The lucky girl who wins the pageant will be presented with one million dollars cash money right on stage just after her name is announced!"

The set goes quiet as A.T. allows time for the news to sink in, then nods to Taras.

"Why don't we take some calls from the *Tymkoverse* and see how the fans are reacting to all of this?" Taras begins repeating the call-in number, which Irwin knows by heart. He's been trying to get a call into the podcast for at least a year, but can never seem to make it. Almost automatically, his hand snakes out and snatches up his phone from his bedside table, his fingers punching in the number.

Suddenly, A.T.'s voice is in his ear. "Hey Dude, congrats! It's your lucky day! You made it onto *Tymko's Times."* It's a point of honor with the host that he has no call screener, preferring to rely on his wits to deal with whomever he gets. "Tell us about yourself. What's your name?"

"Irwin."

"Irwin what?"

"Irwin."

A.T. raises his eyebrows at Irwin's answer.

"I get that your name is Irwin. What's your last name?"

"Irwin."

Shooters!

"You're telling me your name is Irwin Irwin?" A.T. asks. Taras covers his mouth with his hand to stifle his laughter.

"That's right," says Irwin.

"Don't tell me your middle name is Irwin, too," says A.T.

"That's right," says Irwin again.

Taras can't help it—he erupts in gales of laughter.

"Jesus, your dad had a wicked sense of humor," says A.T. "So tell us about you, Mr. Triple Irwin. Where are you?"

"I'm in the hoshpital," says Irwin, slurring his words because of the drugs coursing through his veins.

"In the hospital? You sick? What's wrong with you?"

Irwin doesn't know why he says it. "They cut my nuts out, man," he whines.

"Cut your nuts out? Really? What'd they do that for? You're not some kind of tranny, are you?" A.T. asks in a suspicious tone.

"I ain't no goddamn tranny!" Irwin yells into the phone. "That bitch stepped on my nuts! Crushed 'em."

Taras is laughing so hard he can't breathe.

"Some bitch stepped on your nuts and crushed them? You must have a helluva sex life, Irwin Irwin Irwin. How did she manage that?"

"I was on the floor on my back," Irwin says. "She stood on my nuts and crushed them." Suddenly he's crying. "They cut them out, man! I ain't got no balls no more!"

"No balls at all, no balls at all, she married a man who had none at all!" sings Taras. He continues, "He's a tranny, A.T. Maybe a reluctant tranny, but a tranny all the same."

"I ain't no fucking tranny!" Irwin screams into the phone.

"Well, you might as well be," says A.T. "Only way you're getting fucked anymore is if you get a pussy yourself."

"I ain't no fucking tranny!" Irwin screams so loud he starts coughing, throwing up mucus.

The door to Irwin's room bursts open and a nurse enters. "What's going on in here?" she says, then she sees Irwin in the bed, blue in the face, sucking in air in big gulps. She runs to him, snatches his phone from his hand and attempts to push him back on the bed. Irwin backhands her across the face and she crumples to the floor.

"It was Natalie!" Irwin screams again, totally not realizing he no longer has a phone. "Fucking Natalie McMasters!" It doesn't matter, because by this time, A.T. has hung up.

"That Irwin Irwin dude was one seriously fucked up motherfucker," says A.T.

"Totally," agrees Taras.

A.T. says, "Hey Dude, congrats! It's your lucky day! You made it onto *Tymko's Times…*"

Chapter 7

The vibe in the house is *trés* cringy Wednesday morning. Lupe, Danny and M.B. are in the kitch when I come down to breakfast. As usual, the morning news is on the TV in the cabinet above the microwave.

Lupe bolts before I can even get out a "Good morning." I'm totally tempted to chase her down and try to patch things up, but M.B. shoots me a shady glare, stopping me cold. She's right. It's totally too soon. Maybe I can talk to Lupe when she gets home from school this afternoon.

Lupe was the primary cook in the house before M.B. moved in, but the older lady has taken over most of that now that Lupe's got a real job. "You want eggs?" she asks me as I reach for the coffee pot, and I shake my head. "You sure? You're eating for two now, you know?"

Christ! I don't know how much of this I can take…

"I'm sorry. My stomach is kinda flippy this morning."

"That happens," M.B. says. "You might notice more gas and cramps, too. The secret is to eat less, more often. Let me get you an egg and an English muffin."

WTF ya gonna do? "I'll take an egg McMuffin like Danny's got."

As she gets up to fix it for me, I turn my attention to the TV.

"…Capital City has had a hard time of it since the sexual assault and police corruption scandal revolving around the rogue billionaire Jerome Ellis a few months ago," a male anchor's voice intones. "Many events have been cancelled because the parties involved are fearful of guilt by association with the heinous activities that occurred on the Ellis Estate. But now, things may have changed. YouTube influencer Adam Tymko, aka A.T., is bringing his beauty pageant, America's First Sexy Lady, to Capital City's Rutledge Convention Center, starting on September 19. As of right now, thirty-five women from all over the U.S.A. will be competing." A helicopter shot of the downtown convention center serves to illustrate the commentary.

A female anchor's voice breaks in. "Tim, some folks are saying that this pageant may be a curse rather than a blessing for the city's status. Mr. Tymko has a less-than stellar reputation—some people call him a misogynist and he's had multiple sexual harassment allegations lodged against him. Furthermore, there are rumors that the contestants in this pageant are expected to compete in the nude *in lieu* of swimsuits."

"I've heard those rumors as well, Jill. Mr. Tymko has promised a major announcement about the pageant that might well address that."

"I've listened to A.T.'s podcast a time or two," says Danny. "He's an interesting guy. He's got traditional ideas about men's and women's roles, not too different than what it was like in the Corps." He picks up a shooter of OJ and chugs it.

"He's a total MCP," I say. "He thinks women are good for nothing but keeping house and fucking."

M.B. tosses me a shady glare at that last—she's trying to get me to clean up my language, but there's totally no other way to talk about A.T.

"It's no wonder a bunch of social media sites are banning him," I go on.

"I didn't think you were woke," says Danny.

"I ain't. But A.T. is totally the CEO of misogyny and homophobia."

Danny's face is like he's modeling for a Marine Corps poster. Don't tell me he's getting salty over this shit!

He replies, "While he might be a little off-base on some things, he just thinks that some of the old ideas about relationships aren't wrong. So do I." He raises his McMuffin to take a bite.

"Funny that, coming from one-third of a throuple," I counter. "Of course, you are the only guy. Maybe you think of me and Lupe as your harem."

The McMuffin stops in mid-air, then Danny puts it back on his plate. Without another word, he gets up and stalks out of the kitchen.

"You are just batting a thousand these days, aren't you, Nattie. First you alienate Lupe and now Danny," M.B. says from the stove.

I turn to look at her—she's wearing a smug look.

"What? I'm right about A.T. and you know it," I tell her.

"And you can keep right on being right and push away your whole family." A pause. "I was going to tell you to apologize to Lupe for last night after she gets home from school today. Now you can add Danny to the list."

I can feel the redness blooming on my face. "Don't tell me what to do."

"Somebody sure needs to."

The toaster pops, and she plucks two halves of an English muffin on to a plate, then steps to the stove to add Canadian bacon, egg and cheese. She brings it over and sets it in front of me with an expectant look.

"Thanks," I say grudgingly.

"You're welcome." She goes to the coffee maker, pours a cup and brings it to me, then replenishes her own. "Look. I know the pregnancy has got you stressed out. Raging hormones are a real thing. And I also have a feeling that a lot of this has to do with something that happened when you were held by Jerome Ellis. Am I right?"

Now I know my face is like a stoplight. You can't keep much from someone that's spent nearly forty years in the FBI. I look at my plate and nod.

"You need to come clean with your spouses," she says. "They love you and will honor your decisions. Don't drive everyone away because you're ashamed of yourself. You have nothing to feel guilty about."

Tears are welling in my eyes, but I resolutely shut them down.

I will not cry in front of her!

"Ok. You're right. I'll do as you say."

Mine and M.B.'s phones ding simultaneously. It's a text from Uncle.

Meet in my office in 15 minutes.

***

When me and M.B. get to Uncle's office on the first floor in the north wing, Danny and Leon Kidd are also waiting for us. Uncle's in his wheelchair behind his desk and the other two are in chairs facing him.

Kidd is the third partner in the 3M Detective Agency. He's a fiftysomething black man who could be mistaken for a retired NFL player. He's a Marine lieutenant and a former CCPD lieutenant who quit the department over corruption before signing on with Uncle.

He smiles at me as I walk in the door. "Hey, Nattie! Amos was just telling me the great news."

Shit. I try to smile back, but I don't think I quite make it, because his smile vanishes. He turns to Uncle. "Anyway, Amos, what's this news you have for all of us?"

Uncle's glowing-up more since his wedding. "C'mon and sit a spell, y'all." After we've taken the remaining seats, he continues, "We've got us a job!"

So that's why he's so lit up. "What is it," I ask.

He looks at a paper on the desk. "A Mr. Adam Tymko wants to hire 3M to provide security for a beauty pageant he's holding in the convention center downtown."

35

For a few seconds, no one says anything, then Danny speaks up. "Isn't that an awful big job for the five of us?"

"Yer darn tootin'," says Uncle. "That's why we've got to hire us some extry hands to git 'er done." He waves his arms like he's conducting an orchestra. "This is a five-figure payout. It's gonna pull 3M right out of the red. As of now, I'm thinkin' that Kidd is gonna be the overall straw boss down at the site and Danny will be boss of the extry security guys we hire." He looks at M.B. "Sweetie, I want you to vet all of our prospective hires. Your FBI experience makes you perfect for that. I'll stay back here at the office and coordinate ever'thin'."

"And what do I do?" I ask him.

"You're our free safety down at the site, doin' whatever anyone else says they need."

Great. I'm the lackey again, as per usual.

"Mr. Tymko wants to meet with us on Monday at ten to finalize the deal. So clear your calendars. Any questions?"

"When do we start?" Danny asks.

"Not sure when Mr. Tymko wants security on site. He'll tell us Monday. But I'm gonna start huntin' people and settin' up interviews as soon as we're done with this meetin'."

"I'll start my backgrounding as soon as you get me some names," M.B. says. "You want me to do the interviews, or do you want to?"

"Prolly both of us," says Uncle. "I'd like to tell Mr. Tymko on Monday how many people we can have on site how soon."

"How many will we need?" asks Danny.

"Ask me after I see the site on Monday." Uncle looks at all of us in turn. "That all?"

Nobody says anything.

"OK. See y'all at the convention center Monday at nine-thirty."

We all head out into the hall to go our separate ways when M.B. says to me, "Nattie, can I see you in my office for a minute?"

Oh shit, what did I do now to get called to the principal's office? I thought she had enough to say while we were in the kitchen.

M.B.'s office is catty-corner to Uncle's. As I come in, M.B. is just sitting down and pulling a file folder from the organizer on her desk.

"Close the door and have a seat," she says.

Shooters!

Close the door? Now the vibe I'm getting is totally cringy. I take the chair in front of her desk, facing her.

"After Amos and I got married, we all agreed I'd take charge of the family's finances," she begins.

That's right. Neither me nor mom has ever had a good head for numbers, Lupe is preoccupied with staying clean and Danny and Uncle are wrapped up in 3M. So M.B. was the natural choice.

"I've been going over our books and things are not looking great," she continues. "Dr. Feiner left you a nice little chunk of change along with this estate, but we've had a lot of expenses lately. The agency's business has tanked since the Ellis affair, so Amos and Danny aren't bringing in anything. Ditto for you, since you're not currently working either. Lupe is making $1400 a month as a teacher's aide, and I'm bringing in about $12,000 a month, but that will go down by more than half when I retire and get my pension. Your mom is unemployed too, and we're not charging her rent for the guest house. So between me and Lupe, we'll barely be covering our monthly expenses, and we're looking at a $100,000 bill for property taxes on this estate this year, which is now worth about $25,000,000. Then there will be expenses for your pregnancy. You don't have any health insurance, right?"

I nod. I feel my belly tightening and my breathing getting short. "So why are you telling me all this?"

"Because you are the one who has control over the money you inherited. With forty years working for the government, I've got a hefty 401K too, so we'll probably be OK this year, but with that $75,000 Jeep you're paying for, your nest egg is going down fast."

Yeet! "I haven't really thought about money lately…"

"I'm aware. That's why I'm bringing it to your attention." She pauses, then goes on, "You might want to think about getting a job, and I don't mean waiting tables or some other minimum wage gig. You do have a college degree, you know."

Yeah. In history. That and a couple of bucks will get me a bus ride.

"I was hoping to work for 3M…"

"I know you were. And if this job with Adam Tymko works out and the agency gets back on its feet, we can talk about that. But right now, 3M's income also covers the estate's expenses. So paying you is a liability. It would be great if you could bring in something independently."

WTF! How dare you say I'm not pulling my weight? How about the fucking mansion you're living in, lady? If you're going to lose half your income if you retire, how 'bout not doing that? If it wasn't for me, this fam and 3M wouldn't even have a place to be. Not bad for a fucking liability, am I?

"I'll see what I can do," I say between clenched teeth.

Don't hold your breath.

Chapter 8

Eduardo has been in hell all week.

His *máma* is well aware that the worst thing you can do to a young, active boy is to keep him locked up with nothing to do. Since he was suspended from school last Wednesday, he's been allowed out of his room only for meals and the bathroom. Lupe confiscated his phone, unplugged his computer, removed the cord for his PlayStation, took away his comic books and his TV. She even removed his rock collection so he couldn't divert himself with that. He tried to sleep as much as he could, but now he's awake both day and night because he's all caught up.

This morning Lupe reminded him that it's Saturday, and he will not be going to Ellie's birthday party. As if he didn't know. Ever since he was kidnapped by Jay Ellis last spring, his fellow students have looked upon him as damaged goods—the rumors that circulated about what went on in that mansion were horrific, and not far from the truth. Getting an invitation from the prettiest, most popular girl in the class seemed like a blessing from heaven, with the added attraction of a another possible sexual encounter. His first one left a lot to be desired, but some web surfing since has taught him what to do. If Ellie would only let him…

It isn't fair! I didn't do anything wrong! I'm a man, not a boy—I had sex with a girl and I even killed somebody. That shit makes you a man, right? A man doesn't stay in his room because his mamá tells him to!

He looks at his bedside clock. It's 11:30. Lunch is in half-an-hour. It will take fifteen minutes to eat it, then it's back to jail. The birthday party starts at 2:00 this afternoon. Everyone will be there. Everyone but Shannie, that is. She told him she wouldn't go because he couldn't. He told her she should anyway, but she shook her head with tears in her eyes.

Martin will prolly be there. He's trying to get into Ellie's shorts too, or so he says.

Eduardo makes up his mind.

***

The party's in full swing when Eduardo walks into the Schultz's back yard at 2:30. The trees around the pool are festooned with balloons, and there's a smoky haze in the air accompanied by a vegetal odor and the sweet smell of alcohol. About fifty kids are listening to the music and dancing.

He looks for Ellie and spots her and Allison standing near the DJ, vibin' to the tunes. Ellie's wearing a lacy white top that leaves her shoulders bare and short-short cut offs. He catches his breath.

Eduardo surveys the crowd for Martin. He won't be hard to spot, as he's a couple heads taller than everyone else.

A thrill goes through him. *He's not here! Either she didn't invite him or he didn't come!*

He makes his way through the dancers, lightly touching Ellie on her naked shoulder. He stops breathing again when she turns around.

OMG! You can see right between her boobies!

"You made it!" she says, throwing her arms around his neck and giving him a kiss on the cheek.

Allison looks disgusted and stalks off.

"Never mind her," Ellie says. "She's jealous because I've got you." She takes his hand and leads him to the dancers.

The tune is *Sete* by Blond:ish and Francis Mercier, fast with a driving rhythm, and Eduardo about loses it waiting for Ellie's titties to fall out of her top as she bounces around, but unfortunately, they never do. Then the DJ mellows it out with *Someone You Loved* by Lewis Capaldi, and she puts her arms around his neck and pulls him close, burying her face in his shoulder. The sweet scent of her hair almost overwhelms him. As the song comes to an end, she raises her face and whispers in his ear.

"Want to see if you can make me go 'aah'?"

He's so excited he can't even answer!

She pulls him out of the crowd.

"Look, we shouldn't be seen going in the house together," she says. "People will talk. Go up to the second floor to my room. It's easy to find— my name is on the door. Take off your clothes and get into bed. I'll sneak up in a little while."

It takes all the willpower Eduardo can muster not to make a mad dash. He passes through a family room furnished in black leather and stainless steel into the center of the house, where a long staircase leads up to a balcony overlooking a vast living room. Going down the corridor, he spots a white door decorated with *appliqué* flowers, with *Ellie* in a curlicue font in the center. He opens the door and goes in—the scent of flowers, the same as in Ellie's hair, brings tears to his eyes in the pink and white bedroom. He sheds his clothes on the floor, pulls back the frilly white coverlet on the bed and slips between the soft sheets, pulling the coverlet over him, trembling with anticipation.

Time crawls by. He can understand that Ellie does not want their date to be common knowledge—after all, a girl's got her reputation to think about.

Is she ashamed to be seen with me? No, she can't be. She wouldn't do it with me if she was.

It's got to have been at least ten minutes. It's warmish in the bed—Eduardo feels himself getting drowsy as the tension drains out of him. He dare not fall asleep! As he throws the covers off and the chilly air causes his skin to tighten, the bedroom door busts open and people begin streaming into the room.

OMG! Like everyone at the party is here, cheering, laughing, holding cell phones high, from which beams of light play over his naked bod. He rolls over and sits on the side of the bed, but somebody—oh no!, it's his archenemy Freddie Hall—gives him a strong push so he falls back into the bed again, his legs splayed wide. This time he just rolls so he falls out of bed onto the floor, on top of his scattered clothes, which he scrambles to snatch up as his ears ring with the hoots and catcalls of the crowd.

"OMG! He's totally naked!"

"Look! He's hard!"

Eduardo stumbles to his feet and thankfully, the mob parts so he can make it to the door, tumble into the hallway, struggle upright again and haul ass to the stairs, the mass of people sticking to him like a pack of dogs on a coon. Many remain on the balcony, recording all of the action as he dashes to the front door out onto the lawn, then to the driveway where he left his bike. He doesn't even stop to dress—he just climbs on and pedals madly away from this house of shame, vainly trying to hold on to his clothes.

Chapter 9

Monday morning, I'm riding downtown with Danny in his truck to the meeting with Adam Tymko. M.B. and Uncle are taking the van that's set up for his wheelchair. Kidd will meet us there.

I'm wearing a pair of cut-off jeans, a short shirt that let's my belly show and a pair of red Nikes.

The air in the truck hovers just above freezing. Me and Danny haven't talked much since our spat.

Maybe it's time to mend some fences.

"I just wanted to tell you sorry for what I said," I start.

He's keeping his head straight, but his eyes flicker towards me.

"You know that I love you and Lupe," he says. "Our relationship is not just about sex."

"I do know it. I don't know why I said what I did."

Danny goes on, "Adam Tymko can be a polarizing figure, especially for women. But like I said before, part of his appeal to guys is that he's a voice for a lot of the traditional principles we were raised with, which I don't think are all wrong. That doesn't mean I believe all the misogynistic shit he spews. I honestly don't think he does either. A lot of it's for show— being controversial to draw an audience. And by the way, I respect you as my partner—I don't think of you as a subordinate. Or as a sex object."

"I get that, babe. I'm sorry that I accused you of that. M.B. says my hormones are raging. And I've got a lot on my mind these days."

His eyes drift down to my belly. "I know you do."

"We're good?"

"We're good."

The temperature in the cab warms up considerably.

MLK Plaza, a pedestrian mall in the heart of downtown, is anchored by a major shopping center on the north end and the Rutledge Convention Center on the south, with a multi-story parking deck for each. However, the shopping center has been struggling lately, what with Covid and the rise of retail on the 'net. That's why many are expecting this pageant to revitalize the area.

Thomas A. Burns, Jr.

As we arrive, I notice two charter buses on the street in front of the concrete plaza filled with trees, benches and artwork, with the convention center in the middle. *Déjà vu!* The last time we were here, Danny, Lupe and I ran afoul of a gang of protestors who arrived in similar buses. We had a fracas that ended up on the nightly news and resulted with Danny going to jail. We can't afford for something like that to happen again. Not with this megajob in the offing.

After parking, we go downstairs, picking up Kidd who's waiting on the sidewalk.

"Wait till you see," he says. "The transgenders and the feminists are here. Both of them are p.o.'d about A.T.'s pageant for different reasons, but they can't seem to stop dissing each other and get together. Even so, they'll be a security issue for us."

We cross the street and enter the plaza. A scrolling illuminated sign in front of a reflecting pool and fountain advertises in bright green letters, *#Am1stSexyLady - Adam Tymko Presents America's First Sexy Lady Pageant...* A cool breeze brings the faint sound of chanting to my ears. As we near the building, the words become clearer.

Two groups brace each other on either side of the building entry, a blue-clad CCPD contingent separating them. The transgenders—a scruffy band of about a dozen twentysomethings wearing everything from business suits to Halloween costumes—are shouting "Trans women are women! Trans women are women!" and wave signs with the same slogan, as well as *No Hate Pageants,* and *LGBTQIA2s+ rights are human rights.* That acronym gets longer every time I see it. They're likely here because of Tymko's well-known transphobia, and because he's banned trans women from the pageant.

The other crowd is smaller—all of them are women maybe a decade or two older than the trans people. Their attire is more mainstream, like you'd see at a PTA meeting or at church on Sunday. Their signs urge us to *Save Women's Spaces* and proclaim that *Trans women are men!, Trans = Anti-lesbian!, and Women are more than breasts and a vagina!* They don't seem to get it that the last slogan supports the transgenders' arguments too. The TERFs are ostensibly here because they see the pageant as sexist and exploitive of women, but maybe also because they heard that the trans group would be protesting also, and they didn't want to give them the entire stage.

Both groups seem to be expending more energy fighting with each other than against Tymko, their common enemy.

M.B. and Uncle are watching the show. As we walk up, Uncle's eyes run over me, taking in my outfit.

44

Shooters!

"That's a helluva way to dress," he says. He's had something to say about my wardrobe choices since college, so I ignore him.

M.B. stands behind Uncle's wheelchair. It's motorized, but M.B. likes to push him, and he doesn't complain too much about it. The two of them lead off toward the convention center entrance.

A police officer holding a clipboard approaches as we draw near, saying, "Pardon me, Ma'am, but do you have business here?" Her nametag reads Lester and she's got two stripes on her sleeve. I remember her! She was at the riot outside our townhouse a couple of years ago.

M.B. replies, "We're the 3M Detective Agency, to meet with Mr. Adam Tymko."

She checks the clipboard. "Yep. You're on the list. You can go in."

M.B., Uncle and Danny go around to the wheelchair ramp next to the stairs to the main doors, while the rest of us walk up the stairs. Both groups of protestors berate us with hoots and catcalls. Yeet! Neither has any idea of our business here, yet they're hating on us all the same.

The activists' insults are cut off like someone flipped a switch as the glass and stainless double doors close behind us and we enter the cavernous lobby. The smell of coffee and baked goods makes my stomach flutter and my mouth water. A twentysomething dude, about Danny's size but stockier, is waiting for us beneath two giant, swirling, scintillating mobiles dangling from the thirty foot ceiling next to the second floor balcony. He's dressed in a tan checked sport coat over a white shirt with a large collar and no tie, and jet black slacks. His black hair is in a military cut and he sports a well-coiffed five o'clock shadow, something I've always thought is phony AF. He holds out a hand to Danny.

"Hi, I'm Taras Tymko. You're Amos Murdoch?"

Danny takes the hand, shaking his head. He indicates Uncle. "This is Mr. Murdoch."

"Howdy," says Uncle, extending a hand.

Taras looks down at Uncle in his wheelchair with an uncomfortable smile, then reluctantly takes his hand.

"I thought we were meetin' Mr. Adam Tymko," says Uncle.

"You are. He's my brother. I'm just the reception committee." He looks over the rest of us, his eyes settling on me. His smile brightens again. "Well! Who are you, now, pretty lady?"

"I'm Natalie. Natalie McMasters."

He lets his eyes slither down my bod, lingering on my tits, stopping when he reaches my baby bump. His leer gets even broader. Seriously? This dude totally creeps me out.

I think Danny notices. "Why don't you take us to your brother," he says, taking my arm possessively.

Taras gives the two of us a smirk that says *game on*. "Sure. Follow me."

He leads us along a corridor that runs the length of the building, with a two-story glass wall on one side and several sets of double doors on the other. We pass the *Exhibit Hall/Palmetto Room* and a single door, the *Forrest Conference Room*. We take a left at the end and follow the around the other side of the conference room, arriving at a glass door with a sign that says *Media Center*. A red light glows over the door, and Taras raises a hand to stop us.

"A.T. is on the podcast. He'll turn the light off when we can come in."

Looking inside, I see the infamous A.T., wearing headphones with a throat mic, sitting at the side of a long table, stacks of books and papers in front of him. Across from him is a wall of TV monitors, each showing a different view of the interior and exterior of this huge venue.

A.T. is almost a doppelgänger of Taras—a little older and even burlier. Waving his arms about, he passionately preaches to his invisible disciples. He glances our way and holds up a hand, says something else, then reaches over and hits a switch on the table next to him. The red light goes out. Taras opens the door, waving us into the room.

Wired up as he is, A.T. doesn't get up as we enter, nodding a greeting instead. Danny moves to the table across from him to remove some chairs and make a place for Uncle's wheelchair. Uncle gives M.B. a look and she lets go of his chair, then he works the joystick and guides himself into the vacant space.

"Mr. Tymko, I'm Amos Murdoch. I'm pleased to meet y'all."

"Yeah, me too," says A.T., sounding like he doesn't mean it.

Uncle goes on, "These are my partners Leon Kidd and Danny Merkel, my wife Maribeth, and my niece Natalie McMasters." Adam looks to each of us in turn, a brazen smirk lighting his face when he gets to me. OMG! Are both these dudes leches?

Danny reaches across the table, extending a hand to A.T. After a moment, tearing his eyes away from me, he takes it.

"It's a real pleasure to meet you, Mr. Tymko," says Danny. "I just want you to know that I think you're right on about a lot of things."

Shooters!

OMG! Danny sounds like a total fanboy!

"Yes, I know," says A.T. He drops Danny's hand and shifts his focus back to me. Noticing where my eyes have focused, he makes a fist and holds it upright so we all can admire his watch.

"It's a Patek Phillipe *Grand Complication*." He says the last two words in a bad French accent. "Cost me 350K. The face shows the configuration of the stars over Geneva at the time and date on the watch." He extends his chin a little at that last statement, preening like a peacock.

Uncle clears his throat with a moist *harrumph*.

A.T. turns back to him. "I wasn't aware that your agency was so small, Mr. Murdoch," he says, looking over his nose. "Are you sure you can provide security for an event this size?"

"Oh sure," Uncle says. "We'll hire all the folks we need."

"Well, what relevant experience do you have directing a large security staff?"

"I was the supervisor of the Marine Corps brig at Camp Lejeune North Carolina."

A.T. looks puzzled, as if he's not sure what Uncle has just told him.

"That means he was the NCO in charge of over 200 prisoners," Kidd adds.

"That was a while ago right?"

"1985. But the great thang about experience is that it doesn't go away once you get it," Uncle says.

A.T. is silent for a moment. Then, "I was planning on offering you fifty thousand for the job. But you'll have to pay any staff you hire out of that."

"All that does is give me incentive to hire less people to make more money," says Uncle. "We'll take the fifty as our fee, and I can give you a list of the personnel I think we need for good security. Y'all can decide how many of 'em you want to shell out for. If it's not enough, I'll tell y'all, and if y'all don't like it y'all can hire somebody else to provide shoddy protection."

A.T. frowns—apparently he's not used to someone talking to him like that.

"You got a deal," he says, finally. "I'll email you a contract this afternoon. When can you get me your staff requirements?"

"How many folks are involved with this thang?"

"We've got about thirty people on the pageant staff, and thirty-five contestants. That doesn't include the media people."

"I'll need lists of everyone allowed in and out."

"We're also going to have a live audience for the competitions. We could have up to two thousand for the nude contest."

A flicker of disgust appears on Uncle's face at that, but he squelches it. Money will do that.

"What about the contestants? Where are they staying?" Uncle asks.

"At the Capital City Plaza Hotel."

"All on the same floor, I hope."

"Yes. Two to a room."

"You'll want security there, too."

A.T. frowns like he's going to say no, but then looks up at the ceiling. "I guess," he says. "When can you get me that list?"

Uncle squints like he's got a gas pain. That means that there's something he's got to say that he doesn't want to.

"Now, about that million dollars…"

"What about it?

"I heard tell that y'all are gonna have it here in cash?"

"That's right. It'll make for great publicity."

Uncle's squint gets tighter. "Seems to me it'll make y'all a great target. Y'all gonna keep it on site?"

A.T. assumes a pained expression. "I'm not that stupid, Mr. Murdoch. It won't be here until the last day of the pageant. We're planning a televised segment during the nude competition that will show it being picked up from the bank by an armored car, brought here, and delivered to the stage by armed guards, who will remain with it until a winner is crowned. The money will be delivered to the winner by me while she's on stage, completely nude, then we'll take it back and secure it until she's made arrangements to formally accept it." He pauses, then, "I'll expect you to arrange for the guards and the armored car."

"I can do that." Uncle squints again. "It will help if y'all'll tone down the publicity as much as y'all can."

"That would defeat the purpose of a publicity stunt, wouldn't it, Mr. Murdoch?" When Uncle has no answer, he continues, "So when can I get your list of the personnel we need?" he asks again.

Shooters!

"How 'bout first thing in the mornin'? I'd like to look around the facility a little bit and talk to the po-lice about what they're going to do about your visitors outside."

"Oh, those losers are harmless," says Taras.

"You're likely right about that," says Uncle, "but they'll still have to be watched."

"OK," replies Adam. "Taras can take you around for a tour, then I'll see you in the morning."

"No, you won't. I'll manage things remotely from my office. After today, Mr. Kidd will be in charge on site. In case you're wonderin' about his qualifications, he used to be a lieutenant for the CCPD, and he was a platoon leader in the Marines. And Danny will be head of the security staff here."

"Let me guess. He used to be a Marine, too," says Taras, rolling his eyes.

Uncle smiles. "We're the 3M detective agency for a reason."

Adam grins at me. "Does this little lady come along with the deal?"

Who are you calling little lady, asshole?

"Nattie'll be our gal Friday on site, yes," says Uncle. "Anything you need, you tell her, and she'll git 'er done."

Adam's smirk gets way broader. Taras looks daggers at him, but Danny's still got a sappy grin on his face.

Holy shit! What did you get me into, Uncle?

Adam turns back to his paperwork, signaling that our audience is over. Taras leads us back into the hallway, and the red light over the door goes on once more. A.T. has returned to the Tymkoverse.

Taras leads us back to the escalator in the front hallway and we go up to the second level. Uncle and M.B. take the elevator.

"All of the events will take place in the ballroom." Taras says, pointing out two large entrances off the second floor balcony that runs the length of the building. "We've got interviews and a talent show on the days before the all-nude finale. Everything's on the schedule posted online."

"You'll be using the earlier competitions to make a cut?" Danny asks.

"Oh, hell no!" says Taras. "We want all the ladies nude on stage at the end with the spotlights on them."

Is it my imagination or does that bring a grin to Danny's face?

49

We go into the ballroom. It's huge and filled with rows of moveable chairs. The stage that stretches across the front is hidden behind a plush maroon curtain.

"This is all reserved seating," says Taras. "The front seats are the most expensive. You can buy tickets for the day or for the whole pageant. We'll need people to check those as people come into the room, making sure they get the seats they've paid for."

We go back to the first floor, following Taras to the Exhibit Hall near the entrance and going inside. It's a large room that has been set up as a cafeteria with chairs and tables of various sizes, and there's a counter in the back where you can get breakfast and lunch, but it's way expensive. I start to feel nauseated—food smells do me that way, now.

"We can feed a few hundred people in here," Taras says.

I have got to get out of here before I hurl. I head for the door. Taras notices and puts on a snarky grin. "I think somebody doesn't feel so good."

Asshole!

The group follows me out into the corridor, where the front doors open onto the plaza.

"We'll want metal detectors at this door and any other from outside," says Uncle, "And we'll likely ban large bags and packages. You should update your website with that information."

"Will do," says Taras, phone in hand.

"I've got to get away from here," I say, the food odor still heavy in my nose. I glance outside, but the two protesting groups are still going at it hot and heavy, so I retreat toward the back of the convention center instead. After a moment, Danny follows.

There's an alcove in the corner in back by the escalators where there's a sofa, some upholstered chairs and low tables. I flop down on the sofa and bend forward, putting my face in my hands to block out the light. I've broken out into a cold sweat, and my churning belly is a nanosec away from spewing my breakfast all over the carpet.

Danny says, "Are you OK?"

I can't help myself. "Sure. I always look green in public at fucking ten-thirty in the morning. You should try it sometime."

His tone doesn't change a bit. "Is there anything I can do for you?"

I am so totally pressed! "Go simp over your bruh A.T. and tell him what a pain in the ass it is to have a pregnant woman around."

Shooters!

A slight change in the air pressure on my skin tells me he's walked away.

Now WTF did I do that for? Fuckin' hormones!

Chapter 10

"Waddayamean, I gotta leave? My nutsh still hurt real bad, man!"

Irwin has been in the hospital for a week since the surgery that emasculated him.

"Now that is not true, Mr. Irwin," says Dr. Vijayalakshimi, consulting the tablet he holds in his hand. "You vere given ten milligrams of oxycodone, and vhen you complained that didn't relieve your pain, you vere given another ten. It is not safe to give you any more."

"If you're gonna put me out of here, you gotta give me a script, man!"

"I have to do no such thing," Dr. Veejay says. "I can require you to come here to get your medicine, and that is vhat I'm going to do."

"But I live all the way down in the Village, man! How am I s'posed to…" Irwin stops speaking because the Doctor is leaving the room.

Two hours later, Irwin is on 1st Avenue, staring at the large brown buildings of Stuy Town across the street from the hospital. He's floating from all the oxy in his veins—as doctor Veejay surmised, he was lying about hurting just so he could get even higher. He hasn't got the money for a cab, so he has to walk all the way back to his flat on St. Mark's Place.

Reaching the green metal door of his apartment, he slips the key into the lock and tries to turn it. It doesn't budge. He looks at the keyring stupidly—has he got the right key? It has to be, it's the only one like it on the ring.

He turns in frustration and stomps downstairs, stopping in front of another metal door near the front of the building. The twin scents of soy sauce and scallions hang heavy in the hallway. He clenches his fist and bangs forcefully on the door.

"Mr. Wong!" he shouts. "Ah Wong, open up!" He pounds the door again until his hand hurts.

After a moment there's a click from inside and a crack appears. An old Asian face peers out beneath the chain that keeps the door from fully opening.

"Watchoo want? You go 'way. You no stay here no mo'. "

"Goddamnit, old man, you let me into my apartment!"

"Not your 'partment no mo'. You no pay rent. You 'victed."

Irwin can't believe what he's hearing. He'd called work while he was in the hospital to tell them he wouldn't be in for a while, and found out he didn't have a job anymore because they found out he'd helped Natalie McMasters break in to the office. Another thing to hate that bitch for!

"You can't do that!" he says to Ah Wong. "The governor said nobody can be evicted while Covid's around!"

"Governor no here. You 'victed, You go 'way." The door closes again, and several clicks from internal locks sound as the old Chinaman secures it.

"Fuck!"

Irwin stomps upstairs again and begins kicking on the door to his flat to no avail. In a drug-fueled rage, he backs across the hall, lowers a shoulder and runs into the door as fast as he can, with predictable results.

He's picking himself up from the floor as he hears approaching footsteps. A hand grabs his collar and hauls him to his feet, then slams him into the plaster wall across the hall from his doorway.

Snick! His eyes focus on a shiny steel blade hovering a millimeter from his right eye. Beyond it is another Asian face, a young man with a scraggly beard and dead black eyes.

"Hey, motherfucker! Did you not hear what Mr. Wong said to you?" The point of the blade pricks the inside of Irwin's left nostril. "You get the fuck outta here or I make you look like Jack Nicholson."

Irwin is not so drugged up that he does not see the wisdom in the young man's suggestion.

***

Irwin has changed greatly over the ensuing fourteen weeks since his eviction. Formerly slightly chubby, he's now gaunt to the point of emaciation, because of the combination of a poor diet and oxy, when he can get it. He's nearly succumbed to the lure of heroin a time or two, which is much cheaper, but so far he's found the willpower to hang tight until he's accumulated enough money for his drug of choice. His once pink, healthy skin is now pale yellow and translucent, resembling a piece of desiccated fat, festooned with tiny scabs. His curly blonde hair has grown out into a mop-like Afro clinging to his head like a dead poodle, but he can't see it in the mirror, because some lowlife stole his glasses right off his nose while he was asleep on a bench in Stuyvesant Square Park.

This particular Monday morning his slumber is rudely interrupted by many voices chanting in unison:

Shooters!

"Hey hey ho ho, psychiatry has got to go!
We are trannies, fags and dykes,
And we all hate the fucking psyches!"

"Ouch, goddamnit!" Irwin curses as he rolls off his bench onto the pavement. He struggles to pull himself to his feet so he can go and see what has woken him.

The hot, smelly Manhattan air clings to him like a blanket as he peers through the woods toward the park's central plaza, where people in multicolored clothes are waving signs. As he weaves unsteadily towards the demonstration, a new chant fills the air.

A single voice cries out:

"How many years on the motherfucking list?"

The crowd roars its answer:

"Seven long years, chop off my tits!"

The mantra continues:

"How many years on the motherfucking list?
Eight long years, sew up my cunt!
How many years on the motherfucking list?
Nine long years, cut off my dick!

How many years on the motherfucking list?
Ten long years, time to get me fixed!"

By now he's reached the plaza. He can't read the signs, but their dress and other accoutrements makes it apparent who these people are. Men in women's clothing, women in men's, some in outlandish costumes more appropriate to Halloween than to August in Manhattan.

Fucking trannys!

The crowd noise winds down like someone turned a knob as a speaker ascends a platform. His topic is gender-affirming care. Apparently the state legislature has just passed, and the governor has signed, a bill to make its denial illegal to those who simply ask for it.

Since his banishment from his apartment, Irwin has tried to get himself readmitted to the hospital several times, ostensibly for his addiction to painkillers as well as other diverse ailments stemming from exposure to the elements. He really just wants three hots and a cot. None of these attempts were successful. But if what the speaker says is true…

"I want to be what I truly am!" he says to the admissions nurse at Mount Sinai Beth Israel. "A woman!"

"Come right in, Ma'am," the nurse replies.

Chapter 11

"Ima gonna kill him!" Lupe says to no one in particular.

M.B. silently eats her breakfast. She's heard it all before.

"He doesn't feel well, Máma," says Shannie. "Can't he stay home today?"

Lupe doesn't answer her. Instead, she hits the button for Eduardo's room on the kitchen intercom. "Eduardo! Get down here now! I swear to God if you make me late for school..." She does not finish the threat.

Upstairs, Eduardo sits on his bed, half doubled over, sick to his stomach. Of course, he's told no one in the fam, including Shannie, about what happened at the party. But half of his class was there. The whole school probably knows about it by now. And Máma Lupe will find out just as soon as they get there. Then it will really hit the fan.

He knows it will only be worse if he makes her come up and get him. He stands, grabs his backpack and dejectedly trudges downstairs.

Eduardo is silent on the ride to school while Lupe delivers a diatribe about how lucky he is to be getting an education in America, and how his actions in the classroom directly reflect on her. She's even beginning to have aspirations to become a real teacher someday, a lofty pinnacle indeed for someone born into squalor in a Mexican village dominated by the cartel. Her success will depend on getting good recommendations from the teachers she assists and her other co-workers, which in turn will depend on how they perceive her as a mother, which will definitely be influenced by her son's behavior and success.

"He's trying, Máma, he really is," says Shannie.

Eduardo is definitely considering rolling down the car window and diving out into oncoming traffic. At least it would be over quickly.

They park in the lot behind the school, and Eduardo miserably follows Lupe and Shannie, through the metal detector at the main entry, then to home room, McCurdy's class.

"Good morning, class," Lupe says cheerfully as they enter. She's puzzled when the students do not answer her as they usually do.

Eduardo slinks to his seat. He knows why they didn't answer. Every head in the room is turned toward him, watching his every move.

Electronic twittering suddenly fills the air as every phone in the room registers the delivery of a text. As the students check their screens, surprised exclamations ensue, followed by gales of laughter.

Eduardo touches his message app and a picture appears. OMG! It's worse than he thought! There he is in mid-air, leaping off Ellie's bed, with everything he owns blowing in the wind.

Shannie has a horrified look on her face and Máma Lupe stares at him slack-jawed as he rises from his desk. .

"Mr. Ibáñez!" shouts McCurdy. "Ms. Drayton's office! Now!"

***

Once again, Eduardo finds himself on skid row, the chairs outside the vice-principal's office. He watches as a stream of people enter—Ellie Schultz, who smiles at him saucily as she passes, her friend Allison Davies, and Freddie Hall and Buddy James who were also at the party. On his way in, Buddy stops in front of Eduardo, leans his head back and draws his index finger across his throat.

Thanks, asshole.

A little later, a well-dressed thirtysomething couple pass by. He's got on a gray pinstripe business suit, and she's wearing tennis clothes. The man glares at him while the woman doesn't look at him at all.

After a while Eduardo realizes that no one who has gone into the VP's office has come out again. Either there's a crowd gathering in there or there's another way out.

Principal Stickley arrives and bestows a doleful look on Eduardo before disappearing inside.

Finally, Lupe appears in front of him. Her face is tinged red and her eyes are swollen and puffy. The look she gives him is indescribable—he's never experienced it before—a combination of rage and disgust. It makes him feel like he's been punched in the stomach.

"Get up," she grates. "They want to see us both."

Mierda! This cannot be good.

She grabs his wrist and yanks hard, nearly catapulting him off the chair. Before opening the office door, she rearranges her features as best she can into an expression of innocence and concern.

Inside, the room smells of old books and sweat, but there is a sharp undercurrent in the air. Later in life, Eduardo will come to identify it as rage.

Shooters!

Drayton is sitting at her desk with Principal Stickley behind her and to her right, his hand on the back of her chair. There's only one chair in front of the desk. Sure enough, there's a second door on the back wall.

"This will be short," Drayton begins, "so I won't ask you to sit." She looks down at her desk and shuffles some papers, obviously reluctant to say what she has to.

"After talking to a number of witnesses to the incident on Saturday night, I have determined that Mr. Ibáñez perpetrated a sexual assault on Ms. Schultz at her birthday party." Both Eduardo and Lupe open their mouths to speak, but Drayton stops them with an upraised hand. "Please let me finish. If either of you has anything to say after I'm done, I will listen. However, I strongly suspect that it will not change my decision in this matter."

She goes on, "Initially, I was going to refer this matter to law enforcement, but the Shultz's asked in the strongest terms that I refrain from doing so. They want their daughter to begin to put this unfortunate occurrence behind her as soon as possible. I understand and agree with their sentiment. So I have decided that, effective immediately, Mr. Ibáñez will no longer be a student at this school."

No! I didn't do anything wrong!

"Of course, procedures exist that allow for an appeal of this decision, however, should you choose to do that, there will be no reason that I should not get the district attorney's office involved." She looks directly at Lupe. "Also, Ms. Ibáñez, I want to reassure you that as of *right now*," she emphasizes the last two words, "your son's actions have no bearing on your status here. Now, do either of you have anything you would like to say?"

Again, Eduardo opens his mouth to reply, but Lupe takes his wrist and squeezes it as hard as she can, and his jaw snaps shut.

"I will only say that I am very sorry for my son's actions, and I understand why he can no longer attend school here," Lupe says. "But I would like to know what we are going to do from now on so that he can continue his education."

Eduardo is crushed. *All of these people have lied about what happened, and my own Máma doesn't even want to hear my side of the story!*

"Eduardo's expulsion from the public school system is effective for one year," says Drayton. "After that, he can apply for admission to an alternative school for students who have these kinds of issues. If he's successful there, I see no reason that he cannot get his diploma, albeit a year late."

"That's very kind of you, Ms. Drayton." Lupe says.

"As for today Ms. Ibáñez," says Drayton, "I'm sure you are very upset, and will need time to process this, so you may take the rest of the day. Eduardo can remain here while you go to your classroom and get yours and his things, then return to take him home." She pauses then continues, "I am truly sorry this has happened. I wish you the best, and I hope that Eduardo can get the help that he clearly needs."

Lupe leaves, and Ms. Drayton indicates a couch against the wall. "You may sit there until your mother returns for you." She then turns her attention to some papers on her desk, ignoring Eduardo completely.

As he rises, Eduardo is becoming increasingly angry. He stares at Ms. Drayton, who doesn't appear to notice. "I did not do what they say I did," he says. She does not answer him. He tries again. "I said that I did not sexually assault Ellie Shultz."

This time she looks at him. "I heard you the first time. What else would you say?" She goes back to her paperwork.

"It's not fair to take other people's words for something like this," Eduardo continues. "I should have a chance to defend myself."

Now her face radiates anger. "You want a chance to defend yourself? Fine. I can call the district attorney and have you arrested. You can get a lawyer when they put you on trial. If you lose, they will likely send you back to Mexico. Your mother too." She puts a hand on her phone. "Shall I call them?"

He feels the words *Fuck you* rising in his throat, but he swallows them. Lupe has told him countless times how afraid she is of being deported. And he would probably never see *Máma* Nattie or *Pápa* Danny again, if that happened. He looks at the floor. "No," he says.

"No, what?" Drayton spits.

"No, ma'am." He answers.

She goes back to her papers once again.

It's about fifteen minutes later when there's a knock on the door. Drayton raises her voice. "Come in."

It's Lupe, wearing her windbreaker with the school logo and carrying hers and Eduardo's backpacks. "Let us go," she says.

He gets up and follows her out to the parking lot. The whole time, she doesn't say a word to him.

It's worse than her screaming at me.

Shooters!

Lupe is silent for the entire ride home. When they pull into the garage at Hyacinth House, she finally speaks. "You will go right to your room. I do not want to see you again until I come for you. Understand?"

"Yes, *Máma.*"

He trudges upstairs, opens the door to his cell and goes inside, throws himself face down on his bed and cries his eyes out.

Chapter 12

The fam is gathered in the kitchen at Hyacinth House, supposedly to help M.B. get dinner together, when Lupe drops the bomb that Eduardo has been expelled from school for a year.

"Sexual assault?" says Danny, wide-eyed. "Eduardo? You've got to be kidding me!"

"That is what Vice-principal Drayton said," says Lupe.

"What even qualifies her to make such a judgment?" M.B. asks. "A charge like that is in the purview of the district attorney, not some public school functionary."

"We have to fight this," says Danny. "Get a lawyer. We can't just let them expel him!"

"No!" shouts Lupe. "The vice-principal said she will turn it over to the district attorney if we do that!"

"Maybe that's a good thing," says M.B. "We'll find out where things stand. He's twelve, for God's sakes. What the hell could he have done that's so terrible?"

"They have pictures!" shouts Lupe. "Naked pictures of him, all over the school! I am so ashamed!"

"Has anybody asked him what happened?" I want to know. They all look at me stupidly. "Gotten his side of the story?"

"We really don't have the time to be messin' with this right now," says Uncle Amos. "We've got about fifty people to get hired in the next few days."

Now I'm totally triggered. "I can't even! There's nothing more important than Eduardo right now." I turn and leave the room.

"Where are you going?" hollers Lupe.

"Up to talk to him!"

"I'm coming with you," says Danny.

"No. The poor kid doesn't need everybody up in his shit right now. I'll let you know what he says."

Upstairs, I knock lightly on Eduardo's door. There's no answer. I hope he hasn't run away again. I open the door quietly and go inside.

Eduardo is passed out, face down on his bed. He doesn't move as I sit down beside him. I ruffle his hair, and his eyes slowly open.

"Hey, dude. How are you?"

"Máma Nattie." Tears well up in his deep brown eyes. "I'm so sorry."

I gather him up in my arms and hold him against my chest, rocking him back and forth. His hair smells sour from all of the tears and sweat. We stay like that for a few minutes before I push him away so I can see his face again. "What happened?" I ask him.

It takes him a good ten minutes to tell me all about how those bitches set him up. When he's done, I want desperately to go over to this Ellie Shultz's house and kick the living shit out of her. "You poor guy!"

"Please don't tell everybody else," he says. "Especially Pápa Danny and Uncle. I am so ashamed!"

"I have to tell Danny, and maybe Miss M.B. We have to fight this, dude. We can't let those mother…, ah, we can't let them get away with this."

"But Ms. Drayton says they will put me in jail if we do that!"

"Don't worry, hon. I won't let them put you in jail."

Back downstairs, I wait until Uncle has returned to his office before sharing what Eduardo told me with Lupe, Danny and M.B.

"We need to call Gary tomorrow," says Danny. Gary McDougall is the fam's lawyer.

"No! If we fight them it will just be worse," says Lupe. "I could lose my job! Besides, it is all Eduardo's fault. If he had not wanted to have sex with that girl…"

"…he wouldn't be a normal adolescent boy!" finishes M.B. "The little bitch set him up! We might even have a basis for a civil suit."

"I just want to get him back in school ASAP." I say. "His life got totally tore up because of what Jay Ellis did to him. He needs to get back to normal."

Lupe gives me one of her smoldering looks. "No," she says. "I am his mother. I forbid it. He must learn responsibility for his actions."

As I open my mouth to blast her, Danny lays a hand on my shoulder. "Maybe it would be best if Eddie stays out of school for a while to let things settle down," he says. "I think we need a break, too, before we decide what to do."

"I do not need a fucking break," Lupe counters. "My mind is made up." She strides out of the room, heading for the stairs.

Shooters!

Danny squeezes my shoulder hard enough to hurt as I open my mouth again. "Belay that, Nattie," he says in a low voice. "This isn't over."

I know he's right. When Lupe digs her heels in like this, arguing just makes it worse.

"I'll call Gary on the QT tomorrow and see what he says. We'll carry on with Lupe again this weekend."

"Ok. I guess."

We head toward the living room "Want to watch a little TV?" he asks.

"I don't think so. I'm going to call it an early night."

I leave him and head upstairs to my room. I'm tempted to check in on Eduardo, but I don't want to run into Lupe again. I'm scared of what I might say.

As I reach my bedroom door, my cell starts playing *The Marines Hymn*—that's Uncle's ringtone. I grab it and hit the button.

"Watcha want?"

"Jest got a call from Adam Tymko. He says he wants you to take point on providing security for the contestants."

Holy shit! "What did you tell him?"

"I finally said yes. He wouldn't take no for an answer. He wants you to meet him at eight tomorrow in the ballroom of the Convention Center so he can introduce you."

"Yeet! I'll be there, but Uncle…"

He cuts me off. "Don't worry, Nattie. You'll have Kidd and Danny to help you out."

That just hits different in a bad way. "Who's worried? You tell A.T. I've got this."

Chapter 13

"This is *Tymko's Times*, coming to you from the kickin' America's First Sexy Lady pageant in Capital City."

"Have you heard the latest?" Taras Tymko asks his brother. "A trannie just won a high school girls track meet in upstate New York. Just blew all the other competitors away."

Irwin is lying in his hospital bed, listening on his earbuds. Some of the nurses complained that he was producing a hostile environment by having the podcast on speaker, so someone donated the 'buds to avoid a ruckus about it.

He's been in the hospital receiving estrogen treatments for three weeks. While Dr. Veejay said that it's too early for him to be experiencing physical effects, Irwin's nevertheless convinced himself that he's transforming into a woman. His skin has lightened and softened, and the scars are healing. His nipples ache from the chafing of the hospital gown. Hell, he even smells different—less gamy, sweeter even. He never considers it might be from regular bathing.

"I've told you before that I don't have anything against trannies." A.T. replies to Taras. "You want to cut off your dick, that's on you."

"Or off of you, as the case may be," Taras says.

"STFU, baby brother. But I do think that you just need to leave other people's kids alone. Don't read to them, don't tell them how great it is to not have a dick, and for sure, don't ruin a girl's chances to compete fairly with other girls."

"I thought you didn't like competitive women," says Taras.

"I don't like bitches who think they can compete with me. Obviously, they can't, or they wouldn't be losing all these track meets and such against biological men. But I don't care if they compete with each other. Shit, that's the whole point of the America's First Sexy Lady pageant. And what red-blooded guy wouldn't like a bunch of women fighting over him?"

"So are you gonna let trans women in the pageant?" Taras asks. "Some of them got some serious T and A, I hear."

Fuck no! You know he's not.

"Fuck no! They don't qualify. They're men. Dickless men, but men just the same."

Irwin's skin burns as his blood rises to its surface. *I am not dickless!*

"These trannies don't want to compete with real men," A.T. goes on, "because they know they can't win. Hell, it's just a massive inferiority complex that's convinced them

to cut off their dicks in the first place. They don't want to go to the gym, work out, eat right, live right, do all the things that make a man strong and virile. They're afraid of failure. Better to go up against your biological inferiors and kick ass, than put in effort only to fail. They're just a bunch of losers with no hope."

I... am... NOT... a loser!

"On that note, let's go to the Tymkoverse, see what they think," says Taras, giving the call-in number.

Irwin is so worked up he nearly drops his phone punching in the number. The drone of a busy signal assaults his eardrum. He kills the call, punches in the number again. Busy. And again. Busy. Once more. Busy! Frustrated, he hurls the phone across the room, where it hits the wall and separates into several pieces.

What the fuck did I do that for? He hasn't got the money to buy another.

"Ve don't trow cell phones in deese hospital, Meester Irwin." Irwin didn't even notice Dr. Veejay come into the room. "I'm afraid I've got some bad news for you."

Now what the fuck?

"Today is your last day here. Ve need your bed for more serious cases."

"What? You can't! The legislature said..."

"The law says ve have to provide you gender affirming treatment, and ve vill. You can come in every day for your buprenorphine and your estrogen."

"But I haven't got anywhere to stay!"

"I vill have the social vorker give you a list of shelters. You can go to one of them."

***

Shooters!

"Hey man! Get outta there!"

A hand grips Irwin's ankle, and another slides under the waistband of his pants near his spine. Seconds later he's pulled from the dumpster behind a restaurant where he's been scrabbling to get a meal.

Sitting on the concrete in an alley reeking of soy sauce, Irwin looks up at a twentysomething guy dressed in kitchen whites, his curly blond hair peeking out of a black skullcap.

"You don't have to do that, man!" the guy says. "I'm not supposed to, but let me go back in the kitchen and bring something out for you." He holds out a hand to help Irwin up.

Irwin takes the hand, and as the guy pulls him to his feet, smashes him in the nose with his fist. The guy collapses to the pavement, and Irwin begins savagely kicking him in the head.

***

In another alley a few blocks away, Irwin rifles through the guy's wallet. Jackpot! A hundred and sixty-four bucks, two credit cards, a New York State ID from DMV and a metro card.

Now I'm on my way!

***

Irwin's standing at a ticket counter at La Guardia airport. He's got on a black halter top decorated with large red roses over a leopard skin sarong and white, ankle-high strappy sandals, all of which he picked up in an East Village thrift shop. He's had his blonde hair curled at a beauty shop and his face done up with pancake, eyelashes and ruby red lipstick.

He offers the clerk the stolen ID and the Visa card. The clerk looks at the ID, then at Irwin, and of course the two look nothing alike. But in this time of wokeness, the clerk knows better than to point that out.

"I want a ticket on the next flight to Capital City," Irwin says.

"Yes, ma'am," says the clerk.

Chapter 14

Eduardo's dreams are filled with chaos, a cinematic montage of everything bad that's happened to him over the past few months. In the midst of them, he feels a sharp pain in his ribs driving him to wakefulness. He opens his eyes to see Mamá Lupe looming above him. The sharp object that woke him was her finger, and she's about to poke him again.

"No! I'm awake."

She lowers her hand. "Get up!" She grates testily.

"What for?" he grouses. "It's not like I have to go to school or anything."

He brings his hands in front of his face as she draws back an arm to slap him, but she thinks better of it, so he lowers them again. "I will not have you laying around in bed all day just because you got *expelled*." She spits out that last word like it creates a bad taste in her mouth. "Get up and come to breakfast. And do not dare go back to bed when you are finished."

"What am I supposed to do all day? Will you give me back my things?"

"Absolutely not! It is probably all that online garbage that's made you this way. Go outside and play like a normal boy." A beat. "When I get time, I will get you some homeschooling work that you do not need a computer for." She turns to leave the room. "I want you dressed and downstairs in five minutes," she says as she goes out the door.

He makes it to the kitchen in the requisite five minutes. Everyone is there—Mamá Nattie, Papá Danny, Shannie, Miss M.B., and Uncle Amos. A chorus of "Good mornings!" comes from all of them.

He doesn't answer.

"Say 'Good morning' to everyone." Lupe orders.

"Good morning," he says, looking at the floor.

"Would you like tacos for breakfast," M.B. asks.

He doesn't really want anything, but he's afraid he'll draw Mamá Lupe's ire again if he refuses, so he says, "Yes, thank you."

M.B.'s breakfast tacos are usually very good, but they taste like straw in his mouth this morning.

"Nattie, I want you and Danny to leave for the convention center right after breakfast," Amos says. "Tell A.T. I'll have that list to him before lunch." To M.B.:

"Sweetie, you'll need to help me find people to fill all these positions, and get them vetted ASAP."

"Relax hon," replies M.B. "We all know what to do. We'll be good to go before the pageant starts."

The only one paying any attention to Eduardo is Shannie. She mouths "I'm sorry."

He looks away from her and wolfs down his breakfast as fast as he can. Then he tugs on Mamá Lupe's sleeve.

"Can I be excused to go outside now?"

She glares at him again. "Drink your milk and get out of my sight," she says.

He chugs the half glass remaining, then gets up to head for the door.

Mamá Nattie calls him. "C'mere, dude."

He goes to her and she puts her arms around him and kisses him on the forehead.

Looking right into his eyes, she says "You have a good day today, OK?", then she throws a shady look at Mamá Lupe, who scowls right back. "We'll talk tonight."

"I'll see you after school, too," says Shannie, and Lupe's stink eye moves to her.

Eduardo feels the tears welling up inside, so he turns away. *Real men don't cry!* As he hurries through the kitchen toward the back door, Mamá Nattie calls after him, "You got your phone, right?"

Lupe answers for him, "No, he does not. I have taken away all of his things."

Nattie claps back, "Well, he should have it. He could get hurt out there in the woods, and he'd have no way to call for help."

Eduardo's heart leaps. *Maybe Mamá Nattie can get my phone back for me!*

"You are right," Lupe says. "So maybe he should not be allowed outside after all."

Eduardo crashes and burns.

"You can't keep him locked up in his room for a whole year with nothing to do," Papá Danny says. "They don't even do that in prison."

"It could be considered child abuse, Lupe," M.B. agrees.

Shooters!

"All right!" Lupe yells. "He can have his damned phone!" She stomps out of the kitchen and returns in a few minutes with the phone. Handing it to him, she says, "I have deleted all of the games. And I will check it every night to make sure they don't come back."

Eduardo tries not to smirk as he takes it from her. At least he can surf the net and play games online. He runs to the back door and goes outside before she can change her mind.

It's a glorious fall day in the South, about seventy-five degrees. It's still early morning, so the sun is low in the sky. The wind is blowing from the north, the humidity is low and the usual morning patchy ground fog is absent. Hyacinth House occupies a twenty-five acre lot on the outskirts of Capital City near Green Lake State Park. The main house itself is on the edge of a five acre pasture that also contains the guest house where Judy McMasters lives, about a hundred yards away in a copse of trees. There's a boat dock on Green Lake on the northern edge of the property, and the rest of the lot is mostly forested and wild, home to squirrels, rabbits, deer, and wild turkey. Beavers, mink, muskrats and river otters all can be found near the lake shore, and even an occasional black bear has been reported. Eduardo has encountered many of these critters and has taken their pictures on his phone.

Maybe I can add to my collection today.

Several months ago, Danny and Kidd built a shooting range in a clearing a couple of hundred yards from the main house. There was already a small cabin there, so the boys installed new doors and locks, put bars on the windows, refurbished the interior and moved in safes for the guns and ammo. They installed an alarm system that would sound in the main house if anyone tried to break in. They also built a roofed firing point and plowed up a berm for a backstop to provide a range of 50 yards. They installed benches and a picnic table. Eduardo has spent some happy hours there with Papá Danny, who has been teaching him about gun safety and how to shoot. Eduardo decides to head there now, where he'll have a place to sit and surf the 'net.

Once he arrives, Eduardo opens a browser so he can re-download some of the games Mamá Lupe deleted.

I'll take them off again before I go home. She'll never know.

He does not feel guilty about deceiving her—he's totally ratchet that she has condemned him without even asking for his side of the story, like *Mamá* Nattie did.

A picture of Ellie Schultz pops into his head.

That bitch! I'd like to shoot her like I did that Tommy Burke guy! Teach her not to fuck with me!

Eduardo's phone titters. A text!

Today 09:45

From MAC

Martin Castro!

    wassup u k

Eduardo's thumbs pound the screen.

expelled life sux want to kms

(KMS = "Kill myself")

The screen shimmers, then Martin replies:

    me

Eduardo scratches his head. He texts back:

u expelled too?

    y

howcum?

    told that Karen Drayton she FOS

FOS? He told the vice-principal she's full of shit!

Howcum?

    I said hos did u bad dude

Holy shit! Martin went to Drayton to defend me?

    wya

(Where you at?)

home

    can I cm ovr

Eduardo thinks about it. Mamá Lupe would be p.o'd if she knew. *But she's not here.*

y

    how get thr?

He has no idea where Martin lives. He texts:

wya

    home

whr home

Shooters!

Martin tells him.

don't no whr is tell u frm school

   k

Eduardo texts Martin the directions to get to the estate from school, ending with:

meet u on road in front k?

   k cys

See you soon. Bitchin!

Eduardo puts up his phone and starts the long hike out to the road

.

Chapter 15

Because I don't know when Danny will get off work today, we take separate cars. I park in the deck like before and walk over to the convention center main entrance. The transgender and the feminist demonstrators are still out front, each totally doing their own thing. I guess that's good—if they paid attention to each other, there'd prolly be bloodshed.

I decide to stick closer to the feminists than the trans people—not sure why, except I find the former less threatening. As I approach, a women carrying a sign that says *Pussy Grabs Back* steps out of the crowd, blocking my path. She's a fortysomething, wearing a blue-and-white striped blouse and a gray pair of slacks you could go to work in. Her outfit totally conflicts with her sign. Out of the corner of my eye, I see a cop heading our way.

The woman says to me, "Why do you want to demean yourself like this? Don't you have any pride as a woman?"

She thinks I'm one of the contestants! It's predicted to be in the eighties today, so I'm wearing a white tank top and nice jeans with a silver chain belt instead of the distressed pair I usually favor. And I traded out my combat boots for white sandals.

I just stand there and say nothing—I'm afraid that any reply will just escalate things. The cop arrives—it's Officer Lester—saying, "Ma'am, you need to step back and not impede anyone's entry into the venue, as you were told when you were issued your permit to protest. Otherwise, I'll have to revoke it and ask you to leave."

The woman frowns at Lester and opens her mouth to reply, then thinks better of it and steps back into her peer group. I nod my thanks and go inside.

A.T. said that today's meeting would be in the ballroom, so I head up to the second level. I look around for Danny, but I don't see him. Upstairs, the double doors to the ballroom are closed—I peek through the narrow window and spy a group of about two dozen women in front of the stage. The maroon curtain is still down, but A.T. is standing in front of it holding a mic, addressing the ladies like a college prof. I open the door and go in.

A.T. is saying "…all of the pageant events will be held here, but this is the last time you'll be on this side of the stage—these seats will henceforth be reserved for the paying customers." Taras is standing off to one side, looking at the girls like a kid in a toy shop.

The women are occupying the first three rows of chairs in front of the stage. There look to be nearly fifty of them—applications for the pageant went off the charts after A.T. announced the million dollar prize. Most of them seem to be twentysomethings and they're all drop dead gorgeous. They're dressed in everything from tank tops and cut-offs to party dresses, but they do have some things in common. All of them are focusing on the Tymko bros like baby birds on mama with a beakfull of worms, and each has on a bright red sash showing her pageant name in gold lettering. Most of the names are based on locations. There's a *Miss Montana*, a *Miss Manhattan* and a *Miss Brooklyn,* for example. But I also notice a *Miss Pussy*, who's even got on cat ears. I take an open aisle seat on the fourth row. Most of the girls ignore me, but a stunning Asian woman in front of me turns to me and mouths, "Where's your sash, sweetie?"

"Haven't got one," I say.

Noticing the convo from the stage, A.T. says "Excuse me, I'm talking," then he sees that it's me and switches gears. "Oh, good. All of you turn around and meet Miss Natalie McMasters, who will be providing security for you during the pageant. Nattie, come on up here so everyone will know who you are."

I do as he asks, feeling the heat of the ladies' eyes on me as I get up on stage. As I'm mounting the stairs, I hear someone say, "That shrimp is our security?" I look to see who said it, but I can't tell.

A.T. extends his hand with the mic. "Say hello to everyone, Nattie."

I cringe inside as I take the mic. I totally hate this kind of bullshit, but A.T. is the client and this job is super-important to Uncle, so I do what he wants.

"Hi, y'all," I say. "You can call me Nattie."

"Are you pregnant?" Somebody asks. Again, I don't catch who.

"Yes," I answer, hoping the subject will go away.

A girl in the front row says, "Excuse me, but y'all don't look like you'll be much good if somebody threatens us." A burst of giggles erupts from the crowd. The speaker is a white girl a little taller than me (isn't everybody?) with huge ta-tas and long, flaming red hair. Her sash reads *Miss Southern Belle*.

I'm sorely tempted to draw the Sig in response to her jab, but I resist. I can hear Daddy's voice in my head. *Never draw a gun unless you're going to use it.*

"Seriously," agrees another contestant, a stunning blonde who's even shorter than me, calling herself *Miss Hot Bod* (she totally is!). "We need a couple of big strong men watching us." She smiles at the brothers. "Oh, look! We already have them."

Shooters!

"Now ladies, don't be that way," says Taras. "I'm sure little Nattie here has some tricks up her sleeve. Don't you sweetheart?"

I know it shouldn't, but his arrogant tone just pisses me off. "Totally," I say, turning to face him. "Try and grab me," I invite.

Taras gives me a patronizing grin, then suddenly reaches out with both hands, obviously intending to snatch me up bodily. I slide into horse stance as I take both of his wrists, rotating my hips to redirect all of that energy down and away from me. I help him out with a kick to his ankle as he goes by, taking his legs out from under him. One half of the World Tag Team Champions sails across the stage into a group of chairs, scattering them like bowling pins. The gasp from the audience is distinct.

OMG! I hope I didn't hurt him! I did not expect him to put that much energy into his assault.

As a former pro wrestler, I guess he knows how to fall, because he rolls and gets to his feet, mad as a wet cat. He comes at me fast and I step into *gong bu*, rotating my hands in front of me and hoping I can stop him again now that he's ready for me.

"Hey little brother, let up," A.T. says, LHAO. "She got you fair and square!"

Taras slams on the brakes, glaring at both his brother and me with hate in his eyes.

I'd better try to patch things up.

"I'm sorry, Taras, that wasn't fair. I totally set you up. You didn't know what you were walking into." I hold out a hand and give him my best smile. "Friends?"

I'm not sure this is a smart move. If he squeezes my hand as hard as he can, he'll prolly break every bone in it. No amount of Tai Chi training can save me from that. As he reaches for me, A.T. warns him, "Taras, be nice…"

Taking my hand, Taras squeezes just hard enough to make me wince. "Yah, you suckered me, bitch," he says. "It won't happen again."

I'm not sure if that's a promise or a threat. "No, it won't," I agree.

I note that he didn't say we were friends.

"OK," says A.T., "enough fun and games for this morning." He turns back to the contestants. "Originally, my brother and I were going to be the only judges for the pageant. However, there was some criticism that this was sexist, even though I say that a man is the best judge of whether a lady is sexy or not. But don't ever let it be said that I don't listen to my critics. After due deliberation, we decided to include a female judge, and I'd like to introduce her to you now." He raises his voice. "Annie, come on out here!"

The curtains ruffle and a woman steps out on stage. The air conditioner is stirring up a breeze so I can smell her powdery cheap perfume from fifteen feet away. She's blonde, with big hair like Dolly Parton's piled high on her head and hanging half way down her back. She looks to be nearly six feet tall, but it's hard to say how much is her and how much is hair and heels. She's dressed in a skin tight, black dress with silver bands that shows her ample cleavage and she has on black silk stockings with seams down the back. She's heavily made up, her lips bright red—she's wearing so much pancake and eye shadow that she'd work as an extra on the Evil Dead. The skin on her face has that pale tightness that comes from multiple lifts and repeated Botox injections.

"Let me introduce you to Miss Annie Starnes, proprietor of Annie's Aerie, one of the oldest licensed brothels in the state of Nevada. I think everyone will agree that Annie knows a sexy lady when she sees one."

A ripple of laughter and polite applause arises from the crowd.

Now I recognize her. Annie's been a fixture on the late-night TV circuit for years and a frequent guest on my friend Roderigo Hernandez's talk show from New York City.

"I just want to say I'm pleased to do this for my good friend A.T.," says Annie. "I want to wish all of you the best of luck, and if you don't win, come and see me about a job afterwards."

More laughter, sounding forced and somewhat hesitant this time.

A.T. reaches into a box and comes out with a bunch of red folders, which he hands to Taras, then grabs more, giving them to me. "Hand these out, you two." Now I'm his flunky?

"These have your daily schedules in them," he tells the girls. "Like other pageants, we will have interviews, where you'll get points for how sexy you come across. The talent show is a pole dancing competition that will start out with all of you on stage simultaneously, and you'll be eliminated one-by-one until only a winner is left."

Miss Pussy has her hand up.

"Yes?"

"What if you don't know how to pole dance?"

"If you look at your schedule," A.T. says pointedly, "you'll see we have a practice session with an instructor the evening before." He goes on, "On the next-to-last day, we'll have a party in here, where you'll interact with sponsors, the media, and ticket holders. Finally, instead of a swimsuit competition, the last event on the final day will be the nude competition, where you'll appear on stage one at a time to show us what you've got, then remain there until everyone has had a chance. After that, a winner will be chosen and awarded the one million dollars in cash."

Miss Montana has a question. "How come everything is in the daytime? Most beauty pageants do their thing at night."

"We're streaming this internationally," A.T. replies. "Europe is five to eight hours ahead of us, so they'll see everything in the afternoon, and in the evening in India."

India? OMG, this thing is totally international.

Taras is behind me as I go down the stairs at the side of the stage. A push in the middle of my back that sends me sprawling on the floor and all of my folders and their contents scatter. Another burst of embarrassed laughter comes from the women. I roll over on my back to see Taras looming over me, a huge grin on his face. "Ooops!" he says. "Sorry." He doesn't reach down to lend me a hand up.

I get up and brush the dirt off my nice clothes, then collect my folders and their contents. I guess I deserved that, but it doesn't mean that I'm not p.o.'d at the big thug. I hand out stuff to the girls who didn't get it. There's a couple left over, so I keep one for myself.

"Brunch for everyone downstairs in the coffee shop," A.T. says. "See all of you there in a few minutes."

Oh, shit, I hope my stomach is up to that. I file out with the girls.

Someone behind me says, "The way you threw Taras across that stage was badass. He was a real jerk for doing what he did."

I turn and see little *Miss Hot Bod* smiling at me. She's really tiny, but her fine blonde hair looks totally natural. "You should be in this pageant," she says. "You're way cute! By the way, I'm Gracie."

The Asian woman who asked about my sash is right behind Gracie. Hers reads *Miss San Francisco.* "I'm Miko," she says in a voice like dark honey. "She's right. You're gorgeous."

Why do I get the feeling she's hitting on me? I thought all the girls in the pageant were supposed to be straight. "Thanks, but I really am just security," I tell her. "And I did embarrass Taras in front of everybody. I should have expected payback."

We're riding down the escalator and I smell the food from down the hall. Oh shit! Then my mouth begins to water, and I suddenly realize I'm hungry. Go figure.

81

Heading down the hall toward the cafeteria, I notice some guys setting up a metal detector at the main doors. Danny, his back to me, is supervising. I don't say anything because I don't want to bother him while he's working.

Inside the cafeteria, the aroma tells me that they're still serving breakfast. I've already had some at home, but my stomach is growling like I haven't eaten all day. I get in line to get me a ham biscuit and grits. I notice that none of the other girls are getting in line with me—they're all getting drinks and sorting themselves among various tables. Reminds me of high school cliques.

I look for a seat and spot Gracie at a big round table over by the window overlooking the plaza. There's a chair next to her balanced on two legs with the back resting against the table—did she save a seat for me? She did! She's waving at me to come over. As I approach, she pushes the chair down and back so I can just put down my tray and sit. On the other side is *Miss Brooklyn*, a dark-haired beauty with Asian features. She holds out a hand and I take it. "Hi, Nattie. My name is Ni," she says in a contralto voice.

"Hi," I reply, then I reach for my biscuit. I'm suddenly famished! Because all of the others are watching me, I try not to snatch it up and eat half of it in one bite. I do take a pretty big bite, though, and reluctantly set it down.

"Wow!" says Gracie. "I guess you're eatin' for two. When is your baby due?"

Shit. I so do not want to talk about my condition with these ladies. "Sometime in February, I think." I look at the other girls. "So what are your names?"

Next to Ni is a black woman in a black sweatshirt that reads *Catalina Island*. Her sash says she's *Miss Fresno*. "I'm Tata. That's short for Taisha."

"I'm Angel," says the lady beside Taisha, who's got a cowboy hat on the table in front of her. She's wearing a faded plaid man's shirt and jeans. "I really am *Miss Montana*. I was a runner-up for Miss America."

"You won't be for long," says *Miss Pussy*, who's next to Gracie. She's a brunette with long, straight hair and enormous breasts which she's showing off by wearing a skimpy halter top. "My name is Sallie, Nattie." Back to Angel. "When they find out you're in this pageant, they'll kick your butt out of the Miss America organization."

"I'm counting on it," says Angel. "The lawsuit I hit them with when they do should get me great publicity."

"That's cold, Angel," says *Miss Manhattan*, a tall black-haired beauty sitting beside the cat lady, who's also quite well endowed. I'll bet that A.T.

Shooters!

and Taras hand-picked these girls. "I'm Bee, Nattie. I want you to teach me that move you used on Taras."

"I'd love to," I say, "but it took about three years-worth of Tai Chi training for me to get to where I could do that."

"I thought Tai Chi was what old farts did in parks," says the redheaded *Miss Southern Belle*, who's taken a seat next to Angel. She has on a pastel green party dress that's totally out of place in this venue.

"It's really a martial art," I tell her, "and it's great if you're not very strong. I used all of Taras's strength to throw him like that, not mine."

"Bet he won't let you do it again," says Gracie.

"Don't want to do it again. But I hope it will teach him to keep his hands off me."

"He can put his hands on me anytime he wants," says Sallie.

"Now, no fair fucking the judges for points," replies Ni. A wave of high-pitched giggles goes around the table.

I'm suddenly uncomfortable. This fucking does remind me of high school, a place I totally didn't fit in, and I was way depressed because of it. College was better, because I didn't have to associate with anybody I didn't want to. I'm also way mad at Uncle for sticking me with this gig. WTF does he expect me to do? I know some Tai Chi and I'm pretty good with my gun, but a bodyguard I ain't. And how am I supposed to keep up with thirty-five girls? I think he sent me here just to satisfy A.T., who I'm pretty sure wants to get into my shorts. Just like he does for every other woman on the planet. Well, the young and pretty ones, anyhow.

Unexpectedly, I feel a pair of hands on my shoulders. I tense up—turn, expecting it's one of the brothers. But it's Danny!

"Hey, sweetie," he says. "Are you going to introduce me to your friends?"

He's got a goddamn kid-in-a-candy-store look on his face too. Men! I put my hand on one of his and say, "Ladies, this is my husband Danny."

I'm secretly pleased as I see most of their eyes get wide. Danny is six-two, wears a blonde, high-and-tight Marine haircut and skin tight t-shirts that show off his muscles. He's a hunk and brother, does he know it.

Several of the girls get up and hold out hands for him to take, telling him their names. His grin gets even broader. Oh, just wait till I get you home, dude!

I cast a glance at Miko next to me and OMFG! She's totally giving Danny a shady look. That settles it. She's a lezzie for sure, and she's got the

83

hots for me! I wonder if she can tell that I like girls too? She's totally out of luck, because I've promised not to mess around on Danny and Lupe, or at least not unless they know about it ahead of time.

"Can I talk to you for a minute?" Danny says. "In private?"

"Sure." I get up and go with him out into the hall. "What's up?" I ask.

"Amos called. He says that forthwith, he wants you to stick with the beauty queens. If you see anything that looks hinky going down, tell me or Kidd ASAP."

I roll my eyes. "Oh Jesus," I say. "Most of them are total pick me girls. I'm gonna be bored out of my mind!"

"Hey, that's why we're paying you the big bucks," he smiles.

"Not." I turn to go back in with my new charges.

"Good luck," he says.

I am so going to give it to him when we get home!

As I come into the cafeteria again, I see A.T. across the room. He notices and waves at me. The dude is totally cringy, but he is the boss. I'd better see what he wants.

"Hey, Nattie," he says as I approach. I wish he wouldn't call me that. "I've got a proposition for you."

"What is it?"

"How would you like to be a contestant in the America's First Sexy Lady pageant and be in the running for the million dollars?"

WTF!

Chapter 16

A soft *ping* sounds as the seat belt sign comes on, but the old woman sitting next to Irwin never misses a beat.

"Now this is my grandson Concord," she says, swiping the screen of her cell phone to bring a pic of a tall, gawky kid into view.

Concord? They named their fucking kid after a grape? Suddenly the name Irwin Irwin Irwin doesn't seem so bad after all.

"He's seventeen. He wants to be an artist, he says. Cain't draw a lick, but that's no mind. A lot of them so-called artists are in the same boat. And what's college for, if not to learn how to do things?"

The old bitch has been jabbering at Irwin since the plane took off. Here it is nearly three hours later and she still hasn't run out of grandkids.

"What did you say you're going to Capital City for, Miss Irving?"

Irwin doesn't bother to correct her mispronunciation of his name. "A beauty pageant," he replies.

"Really!" She runs a practiced eye over Irwin. "You don't seem like the beauty queen type, if'n you don't mind my sayin' so."

"Oh, I'm not a contestant. I'm going to write it up for a magazine."

"Y'all are a writer! Land sakes, so is my granddaughter Adelaide! She's named for me, you know. I think I've got her picture right here somewhere…"

***

Later, Irwin and Miss Adelaide are walking down the concourse toward the exit of the parking garage. She's dragging her rolling suitcase, while Irwin's got only a shoulder bag that matches his halter top.

"It's so nice of you to offer me a ride into town, Miss Adelaide." Irwin says.

"Think nothing of it, Miss Irving," she says. "Why, after the all the time we've spent together, I feel like you're another one of my grandkids

They arrive at Miss Adelaide's car—a deep blue 2020 Lincoln Continental. She fumbles in her purse and brings out her fob, presses the button and the cavernous trunk pops open.

Irwin looks around, and seeing he's unobserved, doubles his fist and brings it down hard at the base of the frail old woman's neck. She falls forward so her upper body is in the trunk. Irwin grabs her ankles and heaves the rest of her inside. He rolls her over on her back, wraps his hands around her neck and squeezes. She's already unconscious, so gratefully, she never knows when the life leaves her body. Irwin throws the rolling bag in with her before slamming the trunk lid shut. He makes sure to take her fob and purse with him into the car.

He pops the glove compartment and rummages through it, coming up with the leather folder that contains the owner's manual and the vehicle documentation. Holy shit! The old bitch has saved every piece of paper she's ever gotten since buying the car, including the registration and the title!

***

Driving down a lonely country road toward town, Irwin spots a likely gully. He pulls to the side of the road, and when he sees no traffic coming from either direction, he drags the body from the trunk and rolls it into the ditch, and her suitcase after it.

***

CASH FOR YOUR CAR!!!

The bright red letters march across the sign twenty feet above a lot full of cars of every make and model. Irwin pulls the Lincoln into the driveway, stopping in front of a squat wooden building with a row of fluttering American flags across the front of its shingled roof. A red neon sign in the plate glass window facing the rows of cars alternately flashes $$$!!, then OPEN.

Shooters!

A short, round guy in a straw hat, seersucker jacket and tan dockers pops out of the shack as Irwin exits the car. He does a double take at Irwin's outlandish getup, but he's much too seasoned to say anything. A customer is, after all, a customer.

"What can I do for you, sir?"

Irwin fixes him with a baleful glare.

"It's ma'am!"

Shit! You can never tell, these days. "I'm so sorry ma'am, no offense intended."

"None taken," says Irwin. "I need to sell my car. I can get cash?"

"Absolutely!"

Twenty minutes later the salesman is calling Irwin an Uber after making the best deal of his life.

***

The Uber drops Irwin off at MLK Plaza in the city center. His eye is drawn to the fountain where the bright green sign ripples, "Adam Tymko Presents America's First Sexy Lady Pageant…" Hate rises in his gorge. He strides into the plaza between metal sculptures that resemble cars that have collided with concrete walls, towards the muffled chanting carried on the breeze.

Further on, he spots the transgenders and the TERFs opposing each other. He gravitates toward the former, snarling at the latter. A person wearing a red and white German dirndl that accentuates their enormous breasts, with long, blonde braids on either side of their black-bearded face steps out of the trans crowd to greet him, handing him a sign that reads *We're coming for your kids!* Irwin takes it and the person who gave it to him hugs him and kisses him on both cheeks before joining in the chant once more.

"Two, four, six, eight! Fuck your pageant, fuck your hate!"

Irwin fixes his gaze on the glass doors of the convention center behind which the hated Tymko brothers are making a mockery of himself and everyone like him. Red heat blooms in his belly, wells up into his chest and flows downward into his loins, giving him a feeling akin to sexual arousal, which he hasn't experienced since that bitch Natalie took his manhood.

87

Maybe she did me a fucking favor. I haven't felt this great ever in my life!

Chanting loudly, he pumps his sign up and down like a piston, glaring at those doors like he expects bolts of energy to spring from his eyes, blasting them to smithereens. The volume of the chanting doubles as the doors open and a crowd of young women comes out, the blue-shirted pigs interposing themselves between the girls and the protestors on both sides. Irwin's hatred becomes nearly palpable as he sees the beautiful women who willingly serve as pawns of the Tymkos, women whom he can no longer have (like he ever could!), women who enable the brothers' oppression of him and his new comrades.

Irwin stares in disbelief as a short, blonde emerges from the crowd. No! It can't be! It is! It's her!

Natalie McMasters!

Chapter 17

Eduardo and Martin are sitting at the rifle range picnic table. Martin's car is parked in the woods near the road.

The older boy's signature hoodie and tactical pants are covered with dirt and leaves.

It looks like he's been sleeping outside.

Martin has flipped back his hood and his unkempt black hair hangs from the sides of his head like weeds sprouting from an embankment. A sour, goat-like smell emanates from him. Eduardo tries not to shy away.

He's the only one who cares about what happens to me now.

"So what did Drayton say when you told her she was FOS man?" Eduardo asks.

"Not fucking much. She said get out. I said I'd be happy to."

"I wish I'd done that."

"Yeah, well, your *mamá* was there. You don't talk that way in front of your *mamá*."

The boys are silent for a minute. Then Eduardo asks, "So whatchoo gonna do now that you're expelled?"

"Dunno, dude. My dad says I should get a job, but I'm not gonna. He'd just put my money right up his nose even though he's got a ton of his own." He looks down at the ground. "I'm not going back there, anyhow. He started beating on me when I said I was expelled, so I knocked him down. He said go and don't come back."

"What did your máma say?"

"Nothin'. She lets that sumbitch do whatever he fuckin' wants."

Eduardo hesitates—he really doesn't want to ask, but he figures he has to. "So where you staying?"

"Around, man. Where you think?"

Eduardo hesitates, then just says it. "When was the last time you ate?"

"Day before yesterday, maybe."

"Shit, dude. Come up to the house and let's get you something."

"Don't wanna come to the house. Don't want nobody to see me like this. Don't want your 'rents to call CPS on me." Martin points to the cabin. "What's this place?"

"It's our gun range, dude. My *papá* and my uncle are detectives."

"You got guns in there? Cool!"

"Yeah, but they're all locked up."

Martin looks at the cabin again, then back at Eduardo. "Anyway, can I stay here for a while? Would beat sleeping in the woods. I won't make a mess or anything. I promise."

"They keep it locked and there's bars on the windows…"

"You get the key? It would only be for a night or two."

"I guess. They gotta big job downtown right now and won't be using the range for a while. Let me see what I can do."

Eduardo gets up and starts walking toward Hyacinth House.

"You bring back something to eat, too?" Martin calls after him.

***

Eduardo is peering around the corner into Uncle Amos's office. The old man is at his desk in his wheelchair, peering intently at his monitor. He raises his voice. "How long before you can okay those last five hires?"

M.B. answers from her office across the hall. "I told you I've submitted the names. The reports will come back when they come back."

"I told Tymko I'd have him that list this morning. It's nearly noon now."

"Just send him the list of positions. He doesn't need the names of the people who'll fill them. I doubt he'll care. And we don't have to have everybody on site for a couple of days yet."

Eduardo slips into the office. Amos is so intent on his work that he doesn't even notice. The file cabinet behind him is unlocked--Eduardo can tell because the top drawer is cracked.

He keeps the keys in the bottom drawer.

Eduardo sidles over to the cabinet, carefully watching the old Marine. He gently pushes the top drawer shut, then squats down. The bottom drawer is closed—he needs to work the latch at the base, then use the handle to pull it open.

Shooters!

If it makes any noise when I open it, he'll hear. What am I gonna say if that happens?

Eduardo doesn't know, but he doesn't have a choice. He pushes the latch to the side and applies a little pressure to the handle. The drawer doesn't move.

Shit.

He tugs harder and it gives a little.

Amos hollers, "Hellfire! You got his email address? I cain't find it!" Eduardo nearly jumps out of his skin, pulling hard on the drawer in the process. It makes a rumbling sound as it pops open.

"I'll send it to you," M.B. hollers back. "Again!"

With all the shouting, he didn't hear!

Looking into the drawer, Eduardo sees the key ring. He snatches it up. Beneath it is an index card, strings of block numbers printed on it in black ink He takes that too.

He drops the keys into his pocket, and slides the drawer shut almost noiselessly. He steps away from the file cabinet.

"Hey Uncle," he says.

Amos's wheelchair jerks as the old man jumps. "Tarnation! Where did you come from, boy?"

"I wanted to see if I could sneak up on the famous detective," Eduardo says.

"Well, you done did it," Amos says, not unkindly. He works the joystick on his chair, turning it around so he faces Eduardo. "Look son, I don't have time to talk to you right now. Come back later this afternoon and maybe we can spend some time."

I feel bad about taking his keys, but I'm not really doing anything wrong. Martin just needs a place to stay for a while.

"OK, Uncle, I will do that. See you later."

"See ya," Amos says, turning back to his computer.

Eduardo goes into the hall. "See you later, Miss Maribeth," he hollers.

***

91

Back at the gun range. Eduardo hands Martin a bag containing three bologna and cheese sandwiches. The older boy takes one out and wolfs it down.

"Did you bring me a drink?" he asks.

Eduardo produces a bottle of water from a pocket.

"Next time make it a beer," says Martin, taking the bottle. "What about the keys?"

Proud of himself, Eduardo takes them from another pocket and dangles them in front of Martin.

Indicating the cabin, Martin says, "Whatchoo waitin' for, dude? Let's go inside."

Eduardo opens the door.

SCREE! An electronic howl fills the air.

WTF?

Eduardo steps inside and sees a white keypad on the wall near the door.

Shit! I forgot about the burglar alarm!

Numbers flash across a bright blue screen on top.

10, 9, 8…

The code! I have to put in the code or the alarm will go off in the house! They'll find out I took the keys!

"Dude, you know the code, right?" asks Martin.

"I don't…" Eduardo begins.

The card! The one with the numbers!

He fumbles in his pocket and drags out the card:

07231950

47228916

23011684

Eduardo is becoming frantic.

Which numbers do I use?

6, 5, 4…

Shooters!

He's got one chance. He steps up to the keypad and inputs the top string of numbers.

The twittering stops. The screen flashes:

SYSTEM DISARMED

Thank you, Jesus! Eduardo lets go of the card, which flutters to the floor.

The cabin contains a huge gun safe and a large chest for ammo storage, both with keypad locks. There's also a workbench against one wall with a tool cabinet on it, and a small table and four chairs. Eduardo pulls out one and sinks down on it to wait for his heart to stop pounding.

Martin picks up the card and studies it.

"Give me that." Martin does, and Eduardo crams the card back into his pocket.

Martin is standing by the safe. "There are guns in here? Let's see!"

"No way, dude! *Pápa* and Uncle would kill me if they found out we were messing with the guns."

"How they gonna find out if you don't tell them?"

"Isn't gonna happen, dude."

Martin gives Eduardo a look that combines pity and disgust. That cold ball begins growing in Eduardo's stomach again, but he shrugs it off.

"So I can stay here tonight?" Martin asks.

"I guess so," says Eduardo. "I doubt if anyone will come here before the weekend." He pauses, then, "But you totally need to find yourself another place, dude. You can't stay here forever."

"I know it. I will. You're a good friend, Eddie."

The cold ball dissolves into a comforting warmth. "I'll try and bring you something else to eat tonight," he says.

Abruptly, Martin steps up and gives Eduardo a big hug. The younger boy tenses, not knowing how to handle the sudden intimacy. Martin lets him go, then says, "Dude, you totally did not deserve what fucking Schultz and Davies did to you. You need to get even, man. That goes for the rest of those kids, and Drayton too."

"What do you mean?"

"It simple, dude. Somebody hurts you, you hurt 'em back."

That sounds just fine to me!

Chapter 18

I can't believe that A.T. wants me in the pageant!

"You got to be blowin' smoke, dude!"

"Not at all. You're gorgeous and you're sexy. I think you've got a good chance to take it all."

"But I'm pregnant!"

"So? Plenty of guys think pregnant women are the sexiest of all."

I'm actually thinking about it! A million dollars is a lot of bread, and Dog knows I need bread. But what will Danny say? And Uncle?

"I'll have to talk it over with my fam."

"Why? You can't make decisions on your own?"

Ouch! Dude sure knows how to hurt a girl. "That's not the way we do things in our fam. I'll talk to them and get back to you."

"Better hurry. We start the prelims tomorrow a.m."

"I said I'll get back to you, dude."

A.T. shrugs and walks away. A thought occurs. A.T. is one of the judges. And he's telling me I've got a good chance to win if I enter? What's he gonna want in return? OTOH, a million dollars would more that solve all the money problems that M.B. brought up the other day. She couldn't accuse me of not pulling my weight, then. Maybe a BJ and a fuck is not too steep a price to pay. Nobody but me has to know.

"Attention contestants!" A.T. is now wearing a headset with a mic that's apparently bluetoothed to speakers in the room. "We've organized a shopping trip and a tour this afternoon that will leave from the hotel. Dinner will be at a local restaurant this evening. Be upstairs in the ball room at 8 a.m. for the interviews."

The girls are getting up and picking up their bags prior to leaving. I guess I'm going with them. I'll have to talk to Danny and Lupe tonight about entering the pageant.

I join the group and we leave the cafeteria and go outside where the protestors are still going strong. The cops move to flank us as we go down the stairs to the plaza. My eyes catch movement from the transgenders and I turn my head to see a person carrying a sign that says "We're coming for your kids!" break from the crowd and charge us with a piercing scream. I totally don't get these people—as much as our fam has been subjected to all

kinds of discrimination and abuse, I'm totally for equal rights for everybody,but tell me you're coming for my kids or my spouses, and I'll damn sure get you first. Anybody would

I turn toward the person who is rushing us (I can't tell if it's a dude or a girl), stepping into *gong bu*, but two of Capital City's finest intercept them before they get to me, so I don't have to defend myself. The rest of the cops hurry us away from the.protestors. The last thing I see is the assailant being hauled off by Lester and another cop.

We leave the convention center plaza in a group and cross the street into the MLK pedestrian mall. It's after noon, so most of the shops and restaurants are open and a lunchtime crowd is building. The Capital City Plaza Hotel is a twenty story glass and steel building in the middle of the block—it's got a marquee in front with "Welcome America's First Sexy Lady Contestants" marching across the screen in wavy white letters. We enter the lobby through revolving doors. The contemporary motif is continued inside with glass, silver and gold and artfully-placed mirrors making the entire area seem to be twice as big as it actually is.

At this point I'm unsure what I should be doing. If the girls are going to their rooms, I'm surely not going with them and I'm not going to just hang around in the hotel lobby, either. So I head back to the convention center. I need to talk to Danny about joining the pageant.

When I get back to the cafeteria, I find him sitting at a table by himself, making entries into a spreadsheet on a laptop. He doesn't even look up as I approach.

"Hey," I say. "What's shakin?"

"Oh Nattie, it's you." He looks back to his screen.

"Can we talk?"

He keeps his attention on the screen. "Now is not a great time. I've got twenty-five new hires showing up this afternoon and I've got to figure out how to allocate them. Can it wait until tonight?"

"Yeah, I guess so." He acts like he didn't even hear me.

What was I gonna ask him anyhow? I know just what he'll say if I tell him I want to join an all-nude beauty pageant. Hell no! Uncle and M.B. will

Shooters!

hate the idea too. Lupe prolly won't give a damn, though. But WTF, it's my decision, nobody else's! And it's always easier to get forgiven than to get permission.

I look around the cafeteria for A.T., but he's no longer here. I head on over to the Media Center, where I find the door closed and the red light on. I peer through the narrow window in the door and see the brothers seated at a table, wearing their headsets. A.T. spots me at the window. He waves me inside.

Something tells me it's a bad idea, but I go on in anyway.

"Hey, Tymkovites!" says A.T. "Look who's here! It's Natalie McMasters, the sexiest detective in the 3M Detective Agency, whom we've hired to provide security for the America's First Sexy Lady Pageant. Come on in, Nattie!" He pushes the chair next to him away from the table so I can take a seat.

Now I'm sure it's a totally bad idea. I go over and sit next to him.

He claps a beefy hand on my thigh. "I wish you could see her. She's totally gorgeous, guys!" He continues, 'I asked Nattie an important question a little earlier today, and I'll just bet she has an answer for me now." He turns my head to look me in the eyes. His are deep, deep brown. His beard and moustache form a circle around his mouth, his cheeks are shaved clean to accentuate his sharp nose and high cheekbones, and he wears a high-and-tight military haircut like Danny's. The dude just radiates animal magnetism—just looking at his smile makes me tingle down there. "So tell me, Nattie. Are you going to try to become America's First Sexy Lady?"

"Yes, A.T. Yes I am!"

A.T. breaks out in a broad grin. "There you have it, Tymkovites! I knew I could count on her!"

He flips a switch and says, "Okay, we're off the air. There's just one thing…"

A shiver goes through me. "What's that?"

"I'm afraid that I'm going to have to insist that you move into the hotel with the rest of the contestants. And as a contestant, you will no longer be part of the security team. That means you can't carry a gun." He smiles again. "But given what you did to my brother earlier, that shouldn't be a big problem."

Shit, I'm never comfortable when I'm not carrying. But I guess I don't have a choice if this is what I want to do.

"That's Gucci with me, A.T. Is it OK if I move in in the morning?"

97

"The girls are having breakfast at nine before the interviews start at ten. I'd like you to be at the breakfast, so I'll meet you in the lobby at eight."

"I'll be there."

***

That evening, Danny and me are alone in the living room at Hyacinth House.

"You did what?" He hollers when I tell him my news.

"You heard me. You didn't have time to talk about it at lunchtime today, so I just made my own decision. We could really use that million bucks." I give him a quick summary of what M.B. said the other day. "I wanted to let you know before I tell everyone else."

"I don't believe this!" He rants. "You're pregnant, and you're gonna parade around naked on a stage on international TV? For money? What even makes you think you have a chance of winning?"

Now you're walking on dangerous ground, dude. "What makes you think I don't?"

"You're pregnant!" He says again.

"A.T. says a lot of guys think pregnant women are sexy."

"What are Amos and M.B. gonna say?"

"I don't care. Besides, they'll get over it real fast if I win that million."

His face is flushed and his eyes are slits. "A.T. and that creepy brother of his are the judges. You know what they're gonna want from the winner."

"They're not the only judges." I don't tell him that they're the only two that count, though. "Besides, all I have to do is make them think I'm gonna have to win for them to get what they want. I got way good at that shit when I was a stripper."

He throws up his hands and walks away, saying in a disgusted tone, "Do what you want, Nattie. You always do."

I tell the rest of the fam at supper. The reactions are predictable. M.B. shakes her head, saying, "That's not what I had in mind when I said you should look for a job."

Lupe says, "I do not see how you can be concerned with a beauty pageant when we must think about what to do with Eduardo."

Shooters!

Uncle doesn't say anything—he just looks at me with disappointment all over his face. I think that hurts most of all.

Later, I lay awake in my room, staring at the ceiling. I've done it again—everyone I love is totally ratchet with me. Hopefully that will change when I bring home that million dollars!

Chapter 19

The sight of Natalie McMasters, the one responsible for all of his present ills, is just too much for Irwin. He lets loose a primal scream and breaks from the crowd, wielding his sign like a battleaxe with which he hopes to behead his mortal enemy.

A couple of the other transgenders follow him, not to join in the assault, but to rein him in before the cops decide to clear out all of them. Unfortunately, they are too late. The vigilant Officer Lester alerts the other cops to get between the charging Irwin and the pageant contestants. Poor Irwin doesn't have a chance—he's so blinded with rage that he runs straight into the blockading police. Lester grabs the haft of his sign and tears it from his grasp while two more cops get hold of his arms and wrestle him to the ground. Before he knows what hit him, he's handcuffed on his belly, spewing vituperation.

The other trans people raise their hands in a gesture of surrender and back off to rejoin their fellows. The cops haul Irwin to his feet and hustle him off toward the periphery of the plaza where squad cars await. By the time they arrive, Irwin has largely run out of steam, and it's beginning to penetrate his addled brain that he might be in real trouble.

A waiting policeman opens the rear door of a squad car and the two officers holding Irwin move him in that direction.

Lester speaks up. "Hey guys, hold off a minute." She approaches Irwin, who now has an anxious expression.

"You look like you've calmed down some," she says.

Irwin, scared shitless, just nods.

"If we let you go, do you promise not to cause any more trouble?"

"Hey, Corp, what are you doin'?" asks another cop.

"You know if we haul him downtown, the D.A. is just gonna cut him loose anyway." Lester answers him. "Shit, we can't even keep muggers and carjackers in jail. Why not just let him go now and save some paperwork?"

"You're right about that," the cop agrees.

Lester turns back to Irwin. "What about it? Will you behave yourself if we turn you loose?"

"Yes, officer," says Irwin.

"Don't you go back to the convention center or we will haul your ass in," Lester tells him. Irwin nods again. Lester looks at the officer again. "Unhook him." The cop wields his keys, and Irwin is free. He rubs his wrists and stretches his shoulders.

"Get a move on!" says Lester.

Irwin begins walking randomly away. Suddenly, a cramp hits, almost taking him to the pavement. He looks around for a minute to see how much attention he's drawn. He spots a city park a couple of blocks away, and the thought occurs he might find some oxy there—just what he needs to calm him down after seeing the hated Natalie. Now that he knows where to find her though, he needs to get revenge.

As he enters the park, a slight odor of excrement is apparent–he's not totally sure if it's canine or human. A squirrel sits in his path—he spies its naked tail. That's no squirrel! To his right is a park bench containing a shapeless form covered by newspapers. Further down, two more homeless people, a man and a woman, sit side-by-side. The homeless guy spits Irwin with a glare. He's a big dude, black, with several days' growth of beard, wearing a Navy pea coat and a stocking cap despite the heat of the day. The woman is white with long, dirty brown hair, dressed in what used to be a nice flowered house dress. She studiously avoids looking at Irwin, inspecting her nails instead.

They oughta know where I can find a couple of 80s.

"Whatchew want here, ofay?" The black guy says. "This here is Legends turf."

"WTF is Legends?"

"The Urban Legends. This here is their park."

"Yo! Y'know where I could score some oxy?"

"Well, you ain't the law, that's fer sure," the guy says. "But why you think information is free?"

"I don't, dude. Tell you what, if I score, I'll give you some."

The guy gives Irwin a sour look. "No thanks. I don't do that shit. I'd as soon get paid up front."

Irwin scrabbles around in his pocket and comes up with a ten, which he holds out to the guy.

"That all it's worth to ya?"

Irwin's starting to get pissed at this fucker, but the dude looks big enough to take him apart. He's got to be careful. If he's seen to have a lot of money, things could get ugly.

Shooters!

"It's too much, man, but I got no change. I need to save the rest of my cash to get well."

The guy gets up and snatches Irwin's ten. "Jest you keep walkin'," he says. "Go little ways an' you'll see a brother wit' a neckfulla bling sittin' by hisself. He da man."

Dude could be scammin' me, but what're ya gonna do?

Irwin raises a hand in farewell, and heads off.

The guy he's hunting occupies a bench near the middle of the park, just where the homeless guy said he'd be. He's a big black dude—looks like he could play tight end for the Jets or be a color commentator. Several strings of golden chains glisten against his black turtleneck and a black wire dangles from an earplug in his right ear. The benches that surround his are unoccupied, although the remnants of newspapers and empty wine bottles show they used to be.

"S'up,?" he says as Irwin approaches. "Y'all lookin' me?"

Irwin gets right to the point. "I'm told you can get me some 80s."

"Eighty migs is a powerful mess of oxy. Sure y'all can handle it? I don't wanna be up on no murder rap."

"You can get it, I can handle it. Can you get it?"

"I can get anything."

"How much, and by when?"

"Two 80s is two bennies. I can have 'em in an hour."

"That's steep, man."

"It's the real shit, man. OxyContin by Perdue. No fentanyl, guaranteed." He reclines and drapes his arms across the back of the bench. "You want it?"

Irwin licks his lips.

I got plenty of cash. I just hate gettin' ripped off by a nigger.

He tries again. "It should only be one-sixty, dude. A buck a mig."

"It's the real deal, dude. Perdue Pharma. No poison. That costs these days."

"OK, OK."

The banger holds out his hand. "Gimme."

"You said an hour. No pills, no cash."

Now the banger looks hurt. "Dude. Anybody tell you that LeBrowne's word be gold. I gots to pay my source. Now gimme, if you want a taste."

A film of Natalie McMasters is playing in Irwin's head. *I got to get that cunt outta my mind!* He digs in his pocket and comes out with a roll of cash, peels off two hundred, hands it over.

LeBrowne raises his eyebrows at the wad. "Thank you kindly, my man."

"I ain't no man!"

LeBrowne smiles, showing several gold teeth. "Hey, no offense. You be what you need to be." He extends an arm and consults a silver Rolex. "It be two-thirty now. Be back here at three-thirty and I'll have your shit." He gets up and swaggers off.

Irwin sits on the bench, holds his belly and doubles over.

What I want to do is find that bitch and kill her. Irwin frowns as he remembers how Nattie beat the shit out of him in New York. Then a light comes on in his eyes.

Irwin has no other place to go, so he just hangs out on the bench and waits for LeBrowne to return. The seconds crawl by, each one seeming like an hour. Finally he spots the big black man approaching.

LeBrowne takes a seat, reaches in his pocket and holds out an envelope to Irwin. He snatches at it.

It takes everything that Irwin has not to tear into the envelope then and there. LeBrowne looks at him with a little half-smile. "You be needin' anyhin' else, dude?"

"Yeah," Irwin says. "A gun. Can you get me a gun? One of those scary black ones. And a bulletproof vest, too."

LeBrowne gives Irwin a golden smile. "I can get anything, ma'am." he says. "Gimme some mo' bread."

Chapter 20

"I do not see how you can be concerned with a beauty pageant when we must think about what to do with Eduardo." Mamá Lupe says to Mamá Nattie at dinner.

"What to do with Eduardo." She talks about me like I'm not even here! Not a person, not her son, just a thing to be dealt with.

Nobody else is looking at him either. Since this new job came up, nobody has time for him. Even *Mamá* Nattie, who doesn't seem to blame him for what happened, is all wrapped up in this beauty pageant, and now, everybody is all pissed off at her too.

When he was in school, Eduardo was never Mr. Popular. A Mexican kid in a class full of whites, he didn't experience any overt racism or bullying, but he sure didn't fit in. Nobody seemed to care about him unless he fucked up, including McCurdy, his teacher. That's why he was so elated when Ellie Schultz noticed him and invited him to her party. It never entered his mind that she would go to so much trouble just to humiliate him. On top of that, she accused him of something he didn't do just to save her own ass. Now he feels the same way around his own family as he did in school. It sucks!

Eduardo eats his food without tasting it, trying to get away from the table as fast as he can.

After escaping, Eduardo goes into the kitchen. He gets a paper plate from a cabinet and loads it with the leftovers from the stove, then covers it tightly with aluminum foil. After putting a knife, fork and spoon from a drawer into his pocket, he heads for the back door. He stops when he gets there, thinks for a sec, then lays the plate on the counter, goes back to the fridge and opens it again. He scans the cans of drinks of the top shelf—there's beer and soda. He reaches for a beer.

If Pápa finds out, I'll be in trouble.

He grabs a coke instead.

Gathering up the food again, he goes outside and makes the trek to the range. He has to be careful while carrying the paper plate in both hands. Darkness is falling, and with the sun setting behind the trees over Green Lake, the sky is a vibrant montage of orange and indigo. An encroaching cold front is blowing away the heat of the late autumn day, bringing the smell of vegetation and fish from the lake. He has to slow his pace when he enters the woods, and carefully pick his way over protruding stones and burgeoning roots in the dirt path like a dancer on a stage. Finally, a patch of brightness ahead tells him he's approaching the clearing where the range is. The lights in the cabin are on, but the door is closed. He goes up on the porch, steps up to the door and kicks the bottom of it to knock because his hands are full. The door is unlatched, so it swings open. Eduardo's eyes widen and he nearly pees himself! The plate of food tumbles upside down on to the floor. The door to the gun safe and the top of the ammo box lie open. Martin is standing there with an AR-15 in his hand, sighting out of a window!

"No!" exclaims Eduardo. "How did you... Put that back!"

Martin turns so the barrel of the AR comes into line with Eduardo's chest.

He's breaking the rules! He's pointing a gun at me! And he's got his finger on the trigger!

Eduardo winces as he sees Martin's knuckle whiten as his finger tightens. Then he notices that there's no mag protruding from the bottom of the rifle.

He steps up and grabs the barrel, pushes it to the side.

"I said put that down. We're not allowed to touch the guns without an adult here!"

Martin smiles a frosty smile. But he leans the rifle against the wall beneath the window.

"Chill, dude. I was just playin' with you. It ain't loaded."

"It's doesn't matter! Rule number one is always keep the gun pointed in a safe direction!" Eduardo picks up the AR, making sure to keep it pointed away from Martin. "How did you get the safe and the ammo box open, anyhow?"

"I figured the numbers on that card you had were the combinations. I was right."

Martin just looked at those cards for a second, and he remembered those numbers?

"Put the gun away, dude. I'll go and tell *Pápa* if you don't. Then you'll have to leave."

"OK, OK. I didn't mean anything bad, dude, I just wanted to see the guns."

Eduardo puts the weapon back into the rack in the safe, closes the door, turns the latch and spins the dial. He locks up the ammo box again too, and his heart begins to drop from his throat back to where it belongs.

"If you ever do that again, dude, you're gonna have to go."

Shooters!

"OK," Martin says again. "I won't. I swear." He points to the plate lying upside down on the floor. "What's that?"

"It's your dinner, dude."

Eduardo reflects that it was a good thing he decided to cover the plate with foil, because it stopped him from making a big mess on the floor that he would have to clean up or explain. He picks up the plate carefully, inverts it and places it on the table. He pulls the utensils out of his pocket and the Coke, and sets them next to the plate.

"What is it?" Martin asks again.

"Pork chops, mashed potatoes and gravy, and collards. My aunt Maribeth made it."

"Cool." Martin sits down and removes the foil, then picks up the knife and fork and starts eating. He grabs the Coke. "I thought I tolya to bring me a beer."

"Couldn't," Eduardo lies. "*Pápa* always knows how many are in the fridge—he'd miss it."

"So next time put another one in when you take out a cold one," Martin says.

He didn't even say thanks.

There's something unnerving about watching Martin eat. It's almost a mechanical activity. He methodically empties his plate, then picks up the piece of foil and licks it with a fat, bluish tongue, getting potatoes and gravy all over his mouth. Eduardo has to turn away.

"So what do you think about getting even with those fucking bitches," Martin asks.

Eduardo turns back just in time to see Martin wiping his mouth on his sleeve.

Yuck!

"What do you mean?"

"You know what I mean. Fucking Schultz and fucking Davies. They should pay for what they did to you."

"Davies had nothing to do with it."

"The fuck she didn't. She helped Shultz plan it."

"How do you know that?"

"I heard them talking. It's all over school, how you got suckered in."

A cold rage grows inside Eduardo. "How would we do it?"

Martin smiles evilly, looking at the gun safe.

"We could take a couple of these guns and scare the shit out of them."

"No!"

Now Martin is grinning broadly, and his eyes are shining. "Maybe we could even make them fuck us. For real." He pauses. "Think about it, dude. Both of them naked on the floor. You're standing there over fucking Schultz, shoving the gun barrel right into her pussy. She'd do anything you said, man, anything so you didn't hurt her." He grins evilly. "Maybe even suck your dick!"

Eduardo is horrified, but nevertheless feels a twitch in his loins. The picture that Martin so deftly painted appears in his mind.

Schultz's eyes are wide, her mouth open. She's spread-eagled naked on the floor in front of him. "No," she begs, as he strokes her with the gun barrel. "Please," she cries. "I'll do anything if you don't hurt me!"

A warm feeling blooms down low and begins spreading throughout his body.

Then reality sets in and a frosty wave runs through him.

"No, dude, it isn't gonna happen. They'd tell what we did, and we'd go to jail."

"What if we told them we'd kill them if they told?" Martin pushes. "What if we told them we'd kill their 'rents, too?"

Ellen Schultz kneels in front of him, her face a mask of terror. She puts her hands on his jeans.

Eduardo smiles at the thought.

"Shit dude, maybe we could come back and fuck them every week!" Martin goes on. "Take pics of them on our phones that we'd show everybody if they told. Remember how it was when all of those kids came into that room and saw you naked? And how you felt when those pics of you were on everybody's phone? It's fucking Schultz's fault that you're expelled, man. What did she have to go and do that for? It was just meanness, dude. Just total meanness."

He's back in Schultz's bedroom. The taunting voices, the laughter, feelings of shock, helplessness and humiliation consume him.

It takes everything he has not to start crying in front of Martin.

"If it wasn't for those bitches we'd both be in school right now," Martin finishes. "No real man is gonna take that shit! They need to pay!"

Shooters!

He's right. Those girls do need to pay. I let down my whole family. Mamá Lupe doesn't even love me anymore. The rest of them just feel sorry for me. My whole fucking life is ruined. I'll never go to college, never make anything of myself like Mamá Lupe wanted me to. And all of those kids were laughing at me. Laughing! There's naked pictures of me online that will never go away!

"You're right as fuck, Martin. How can we make Schultz and Davies pay?

Chapter 21

M.B. is in the kitchen when I come down at 6 a.m. Shit! One of the reasons I got up this early was to slip out without seeing anybody.

"Good morning," she says, but her tone tells me she doesn't mean it. "Do you want breakfast?"

I take a seat at the table. "No, thanks, just coffee. I'll be having breakfast later."

"With the other contestants, I suppose."

"That's right."

Again she gives me the stink eye as she goes to the Mr. Coffee. "You know that you've got everyone really upset with you." Yeet! This lady does not mince words. Well, neither do I.

"That's y'all's problem," I tell her. "Just the other day you were on me for not pulling my weight. Now you've got a problem with how I decided to do it."

"Oh, give me a break, Natalie. You're better than this."

"Better than what? You know, when I was a stripper, it didn't take me long to figure out what you respectable dudes thought of us. I had a good friend who was killed and the cops didn't even want to investigate because they thought she brought it on herself. So now I've got a chance to make a million bucks by strutting my stuff. Does that piss you off because you've never had the same chance?"

Now I can feel her radiating heat from across the room. But I fucking don't care! I've dealt with this kind of bullshit for years, and I'm sick of it.

"It pisses me off because you don't care about what those who love you think."

"You can stop with the guilt trips, M.B. I've been worked on by experts. Those who say they love me can prove it by changing their damn attitude and respecting my decisions."

"So the way for people to show they love you is by approving everything that you do, regardless of what they might think? Sounds awfully damn selfish to me. And for the record, I've never felt the need to 'strut my stuff' for money, as you put it. I'm proud that I worked hard and achieved my position with the Bureau, where I was able to contribute to society by getting a lot of bad people off the street."

"So you dis sex workers because they don't contribute to society? Remember, I've gotten a few bad people off the street myself. I've got the scars to show for it.

"Yes you do. I've never said that you don't have the talent and the potential to do great things. And I'm not dissing anybody. It's sad that all some women can do to earn a living is sex work. But that's not you."

"I'm so glad I have you to tell me who I am. I'd never know it without you."

"You'll figure it out eventually. I'm just trying to save you some pain while you do."

"Thanks but no thanks." I push back my chair and get up. "You know what? There's a Starbucks downtown. I'll get my coffee there." I go back upstairs.

It doesn't take me long to pack. I grab a rolling suitcase and toss in a week's worth of socks, underwear and t-shirts, a spare pair of jeans and my hairbrush. I think a sec, then go to another drawer and find some sexy undies and nighties, a thong, a couple of tank tops, a pair of short shorts and a mini skirt. I'll bring my toothbrush from the bathroom when I'm done with it.

A few minutes later I'm riding the elevator down to the first floor so I don't have to carry the suitcase down the steps. I get off and head for the front door. It opens, and Danny comes in. He stops when he sees me.

I'm totally tempted just to blow by him, but as M.B. pointed out, I'm better than that. "I'm off," I say. "I'll prolly see you around the convention center."

He looks at me with sad eyes. "Nattie. You know you don't have to do this, right? It doesn't matter if we lose the job with the Tymkos…"

"I'm not doing this because of the job, Danny. I'm doing this because I want a chance to win a million bucks. Why is that so fucking hard for you to understand?"

His eyes harden. "I guess it isn't. You're just being you. I guess my problem is that I don't like you very much right now."

"Then get over it, dude," I say as I walk past him. "Or not," I add as I open the door and go out.

It's early, so the drive downtown is quick because there's no traffic. That's great, cuz I don't want a lot of time to think. Despite what I said to M.B., I do feel guilty. I wish these goddamn people who say they love me would understand me. I'm not doing this to hurt anybody. I'm doing it to help them. If I win the mil, the fam won't have to worry about money for a long time. Shit, it's not like I'm selling my ass on the street!

The parking deck is mostly empty so I get a space on the lowest level. I lock the Jeep and drag my bag down the mall to the hotel. The sky is bright blue and the air smells of bacon, eggs and toast—I suck in a lungful. Damn! It's a gorgeous new day and I've got a great chance to be a million bucks richer by the end of the week! It's a bangin' life if everyone would just let me live it.

The crowd in the lobby is sparse, but Starbucks is open. I get me a venti mocha latte with a triple shot and carry it into the lobby. I check the clock. A.T. said eight, and it's just seven. An hour to wait, then.

As I take a seat, poor Eduardo pops into my head. The two of us are in the same boat. I'm the only one who even bothered to get his side of the story. If I win this money, the first thing I'm gonna do is hire a good lawyer and sue the shit out of that school, and the fams of those kids that set him up. I'll use some of it to get him a tutor until we can get shit cleared up, then to pay for a good private school for him.

I'm worried about Lupe and Danny, too. I really do love them both, but damn Gina, they need to cut me some slack. Lupe's obsessed about this teaching job of hers—she sees it as a way to finally get respectable in her own head. She doesn't seem to get that I love her not for what she does, but for who she is. I hate that she has to fight her addiction every day, but she's doing it and doing it well. I just hope it doesn't kill her sweetness and innocence.

One of the things that attracted me to Danny was his single-minded sense of duty and purpose. He's a Marine through and through. I don't agree with a lot of the shit he believes, but so what? He's my rock—strong, brave, and dependable. He'd die for me, Lupe or Eduardo without a second thought. That's why I love him. I just wish he'd see my side of things.

"Hey, Nattie!"

I jump and damn near spill my coffee all over myself. It's A.T. He's got on a white tux this morning, with a ruffled shirt and a white bow tie. The man's a total jerk, but damn, he's way hot! He's holding out a hand to help me up from my seat. I take it, and he pulls me into a hug. He smells of sweat and spice as he runs his hand up and down my back. I try not to tense up. Remember, promise him everything, Nattie, but give him only a little. Just enough so he wants more.

"Ready to meet your roommate?" he asks.

Roommate? WTF?

He takes my hand and leads me to the elevator. "To save a few bucks, we've got the girls staying in pairs. We've had thirty-five contestants—you make it thirty-six. So there's one single girl for you to room with."

The elevator doors close with a hiss and there's barely a jolt as it starts upward. "Who is it?" I ask. I'm totally not comfortable with rooming with someone, but somebody like Gracie or Sallie would be OK.

"It's Miko."

Shit. That broad impressed me as somebody with a rod up her ass. And I think she's gay, and hot for me too.

The doors slide open on the twelfth floor. A man and a woman are waiting, and step back as we get out. The dude does a double take and says, "Hey, you're A.T., right? Man, I love me some Tymko's Times! You tell it like it is, bro."

A.T. nods, wearing a self-satisfied smirk. "Glad you're a fan. He reaches into an inner pocket of his jacket. "Here's a couple of passes to this morning's interviews at the America's First Sexy Lady pageant. Come on down and check us out."

"I sure will. Hey, is this one of the girls in the pageant?"

I smile and extend a hand. "I sure am. I'm *Miss Capital City*. Please come and see us."

The guy stands there open-mouthed, then reaches to take my hand, but he stops when he looks at his S.O., who's glaring at him like he peed on her shoes. "We'll try to make it," he says, as she pulls him into the elevator.

The doors slide shut, and A.T. turns to me. "Hey Nattie, just some ground rules. The guy was talking to me, not to you. Next time you just stay quiet like a good little girl."

I open my mouth to slam him, but a thought occurs.

Do you want to win that million, Nattie?

"I'm sorry A.T. I'm not used to being a celebrity. It won't happen again."

"Good. And for the record, you are not the celebrity. I am. You are just a hanger on."

"Yes sir." Asshole!

We stop at a door to a room halfway down the hall. A.T. takes a plastic card from his pocket and slips it into the slot on the lock. I don't believe it. Is that just the key to Miko's room, or does he have a passkey to every girl's room? He opens the door and hollers, "Hey Miko, I've got a surprise for you!" Shit, he didn't even tell her?

The room is warm and humid, smelling of soapy flowers. One of the beds is empty with the covers tossed aside, while the other hasn't been slept in. The bathroom door gapes wide, steam billows out, the sound of running water coming from inside.

The shower stops, the curtain swishes, and Miko appears naked in the doorway. She's skinny, nearly anorexic, with tiny, pointed titties and every rib obvious. Her shiny black hair lies flat on her head like a skullcap and her sallow skin glistens with moisture, My eyes are unavoidably drawn to her shaved cunny peeping out beneath her six-pack abs.

"Hey hon…, shit, what's she doing here?" She steps back into the steam and the door swings shut.

"Hey Miko, come out and meet your new roomie!"

The door opens a crack. "What the fuck! You told me I'd have a single."

"That was before Nattie decided to join the pageant. Come on out, Miko."

The door opens and she appears, wrapped in a white hotel towel from tits to pussy that barely covers her nakedness. Wearing a broad grin, A.T. steps forward, grabs the towel and rips it from her after a brief struggle. "You're going to be nude on stage, remember?" He smirks.

"That's different," she says. "This is my safe space." She grabs the towel in an attempt to get it back, and after a brief struggle, he relents and lets her have it.

"Not all yours anymore," says A.T., unapologetically.

I try to mollify her. "Hey Miko, I didn't know he was gonna do this. I'm sorry."

"You've got nothing to be sorry for, Nattie," says A.T. "Miko is just gonna have to get used to it. Right, Miko?"

I think about what I said to Danny earlier. *"Just get over it, dude."*

Her eyes could bore holes in concrete. "If you say so," she grates.

"Damn right," he smiles. Turning to leave, he continues, "I'll see you two in the cafeteria for breakfast." He goes out, shutting the door behind him.

I'm left standing there staring at Miko. She's wrapped the towel around her again somewhat carelessly—the hard brown points of her nipples are peeping over the top of it. "I really am sorry," I say. "I don't want you for an enemy."

"Just drop it, Nattie," she says. She lets the towel fall to the floor and stands facing me, giving me a great view of all she has. She's a little skinny, but definitely radiates a sexy vibe. She's gonna be someone to watch in this pageant.

My coffee is starting to work, so I turn toward the bathroom.

"Hey!" she shouts, barreling by me, going inside and slamming the door.

"What the fuck!" I holler.

I go from one foot to the other until the door opens a minute later and she comes out carrying a large pink makeup bag. "Sorry," she says, "When I gotta go, I gotta go now. I must have a bladder infection or something."

"It's OK." Not, but WTF.

I go into the bathroom. The toilet is on the wall farthest from the door, so I scurry between the sink on a mirrored wall and a kidney-shaped tub surrounded by a shower curtain, drop my jeans and sit just in time. It's disturbing to see myself in all those mirrors, perched on the throne—I lower my gaze to the geometrical black-and-white tiled floor. I see something in front of the sink—a pill. Miko must have dropped it. After I finish, I pull up my jeans, go and pick it up. It's wet, and starting to dissolve, so she likely won't want it back. It's a yellow oval tablet, engraved with Searle 1041. I turn it over and see the words Aldactone 50 engraved on the other side.

I get an uneasy feeling. I don't want to be rooming with somebody doing drugs. I pull out my phone and pull up Google. I type in Aldactone.

Whoa! It's a drug used to treat high blood pressure and heart failure. Could a young woman like Miko have that? Why would she enter a high-stress beauty pageant if she did?

I continue reading. Aldactone is also used along with estrogen for hormone therapy for transgender women. But that's not Miko. One look at that bod of hers has convinced me she's as much of a girl as I am. So it must be her blood pressure.

When I go back into the room, Miko is standing in front of the dresser, admiring herself in the mirror. She has on a white, V-necked blouse and black short shorts—she's not wearing a bra and I can see her nipples poking thru the cloth. She knows what the Tymko boys like.

Shooters!

She reaches for a pink teddy bear dressed in a tutu that's sitting on the bureau and scratches it under the chin. "How do I look, Frankie?" She asks it.

Frankie makes me cringy. It's good-sized, about as big as a one-year-old and has large, round eyes that seem to fix on you even if you're not right in front of it.

"Nice tits, sweetie!" Frankie says. Holy shit! It's mouth even moves!

"That's a good idea," I say, pulling my t-shirt over my head. Her eyes become riveted to my chest as I reach behind and undo my bra, let the straps slide off my shoulders and my titties hang free. They're way bigger than hers. I shake them a little, noting the hungry look on her face with satisfaction. Oh yeah, she likes girls, all right.

I address the bear. "How 'bout these apples, Frankie?"

Frankie has no comment.

"By the way, you dropped one of your pills on the floor in the bathroom." I tell her. "It was a yellow one." Her expression goes from horny to alarmed. "It got all wet and yucky, so I flushed it. I hope that's not a problem for you."

"No," she replies, getting her face under control. "Thanks for telling me."

Now I'm wondering again if she is on drugs. Oh well, if she is, that's her prob. I ain't gonna say nothing. OTOH, if it looks like she might win that mil…

I slither into a strapless pink tube top that shows off my baby bump and a pair of cutoffs with no panties. I know I'll be flashing my snatch when I sit, but that's how the game is played, no? Now Miko really can't take her eyes off me—she's running them up and down my bod just like a guy would. I pull on my bright red *Miss Capital City* sash and wiggle my shoulders so it falls in place.

"C'mon," I say "I'm starved. Let's get breakfast."

Chapter 22

Irwin's dreams are dark and chaotic. Something's chasing him, he's not sure what, but he's certain if it gets him, it's all over. OMFG! It has got him! By the ankle!

His eyes snap open. A giant has a hold of him, tugging on his leg. He lashes out with the other foot, attempting to free himself from its clutches. Oh no! Now it's got his other foot too! It jerks hard, and he sails off the park bench, the wind knocked out of him as he lands on his back on the asphalt.

Looming over him is a black banger in a black sleeveless top, wearing black jeans and a bright red do-rag. The morning sun glints off gold chains dangling on his shirt.

"Get up, honkey! Diss is da man's bench. He be heah soon, an' y'all bes' be gone when he get heah."

Irwin tastes blood as he rolls over so he can use his arms to get up, scrambling to get his feet under him, then he scampers away from his assailant like a whipped puppy. His vision is blurry, his head roaring and stomach doing flip-flops—that oxy he snorted last night is wearing off and Mr. Jones has come a'callin'.

Irwin stumbles out of the park and into the street. A horn blares and brakes squeal.

"Hey asshole! You trine to get yerself killed?"

Who you callin' asshole, motherfucker!

Instinct leads Irwin back to the convention center plaza. As he approaches, he spots a group of young women headed in the same direction, all wearing red sashes—a striking, tall brunette, a pretty black woman and a short blonde.

Is that her? No...

He rushes up to the group. The black girl reaches into her pocket and brings out a keychain with a small spray can attached, but before she can use it, the blonde puts her hand on it to stop her.

"Tata, no! This person needs help. Can I call 911 for you, sir? I mean, ma'am."

Kind words are not something Irwin is used to hearing of late, and they take him aback.

"No," he says. "I'm all right.

Thomas A. Burns, Jr.

The blond is wearing a loose white halter top that looks like it's going to slide down off those perfect titties any second now, and a diamond glints in her belly button. She's wearing a skin tight pair of pink hot pants, and a red sash inscribed with the words *Miss Hot Bod* completes her ensemble. She opens the fanny pack that she's got turned around to her front and extracts some bills. "Here. At least go get yourself some breakfast in that coffee shop across the way. You can clean up in the restroom.

Irwin smirks. *She's got no idea how much money I've got.* But he's oddly touched by her gesture.

"I will if you'll come with me," he says. *Now where'd that come from?*

Gracie hesitates. "I can't. I've got to be at breakfast inside…"

"Oh, I get it." Irwin's voice drips self-pity. "I wouldn't want to be seen with me either."

She gets a look on her face that says she's made up her mind. "OK, come with me. You can have breakfast with us. By the way, my name is Gracie. What's yours?"

"Gracie, you can't…" says Tata.

"He's not supposed to…" says Bee.

Gracie ignores them and leads Irwin up the stairs to the convention center entrance.

Officer Lester rushes over, saying, "Hey! You can't go in there!"

"He's with me," says Gracie, and Irwin swells with pride.

Lester backs off, and Gracie pulls the door open.

Things have changed since yesterday. Now a metal detector bars the way. A long table sits next to it and extends past to the other side. Behind the table is a man in a blue uniform with a gold tag on his jacket that says *Murphy*. The dude has to be eighty if he's a day—long, white hair peeps from beneath his peaked cap and he's wearing a white handle bar mustache. He looks at the clipboard in his hand and says to Irwin, "Your name, sir?"

"Oh, it's all right," says Gracie. "He's with me."

"Don't matter," says Murph. "I've got strict orders from Mr. Merkel. If he ain't on this list, he don't get in. He can buy a ticket later when we open to the public."

"Please!" says Gracie. Her face would melt an iceberg. "He's hungry."

Murph exudes sympathy, but he says, "Sorry, Miss. I can't do it. It would mean my job if I let him in.

120

Shooters!

Exasperated, Gracie looks at her companions. "You two go on. I'll be there before the interviews start."

"Girl are you out of your mind?" Tata exclaims.

"No," Gracie says adamantly. "It's the Christian thing to do. Y'all go. We're only going to the coffee shop across the street. I'll be fine."

"If we don't see you at ten, I'm calling out the dogs," says Bee Shilling, *Miss Manhattan*. Shaking their heads, the two women head for the convention center.

Gracie takes Irwin's hand. "Come on, you poor soul. Let's get you somethin' to eat." She goes outside and leads Irwin back across the plaza to the crosswalk.

The light turns and they cross and go into the coffee shop. It's still early, so the place isn't full. Irwin's still got cramps from the oxy jones and the aroma of coffee, yeast and eggs damn near throws him. The chubby middle-aged woman behind the cash register gets a look at his face and says, "Woah! You can't come in here."

Gracie just pushes ahead. "Please ma'am, he's my brother and he's not feelin' well this mornin'. I'm sure a cup of your coffee will fix him right up, though." She smiles at Irwin and gives him a little push towards the rest rooms. "You go freshen up hon, and I'll see you in that booth right over there."

Damn, she's gorgeous! How come a Stacy like her didn't notice me when I was a guy? But he knows the answer. *I might'a been a guy, but I was never a Chad.*

He stops in front of the rest room doors, momentarily confused, then finally chooses the women's. He enters a stall and tries to go, but it's futile—constipation is a common side effect of oxy. As he comes out, another older woman is coming in. She takes one look at him, turns and leaves. Irwin steps up to the sink and checks himself out in the mirror. He's a hot mess indeed, with leaves in his hair which is going every whichaways, dirt on his clothes and half-dried blood stuck to his skin below his smashed nose. He looks a little better after combing his hair with his hand and working on his face with a couple of wet paper towels. He takes a deep breath and goes back out into the coffee shop, half expecting Gracie to be gone. But she isn't—she's in the booth where she said she'd be, waiting for him with a cup of coffee in front of her and another for him.

"You can order anythin' you'd like," she says as he sits down across from her. "I'll pay for it."

Again his eyes are drawn to that perfect face—blue eyes, pert nose, perfectly kissable little mouth.

Thomas A. Burns, Jr.

Maybe this tranny thing wasn't such a good idea after all.

Then he remembers what Natalie McMasters did to his balls, and rage wells up inside him.

Gracie reaches across the table and puts her hand on his. It's cool and it's soft. "Hey now, don't be that way. Have some breakfast and it will get better."

Her sweet tone chases that rage right out of him.

"You never told me your name. You're one of those transgender people, right?" she asks. "What are your pronouns?"

"What?" *I don't give a cold shit about pronouns!* "It's Irwin. And I guess I haven't thought about pronouns yet," he says.

"Well, which one are you? A man or a woman?"

I sure wish I was a man right now. "I dunno. A woman, I guess."

"But you used to be a guy?" Her eyes widen. *God, I could get lost in those eyes!* "Hey, I'm sorry if you don't want to talk about it. I just want to treat you in a way to make you comfortable."

He feels tears welling up. *Damn it!*

"What the fuck is going on here?" A harsh male voice says from behind him.

For the second time that morning, someone grabs him, yanks him out of the booth and throws him to the floor. It's Taras Tymko, and he looks mad as fire.

"Gracie, what the hell do you think you're doing?"

Gracie comes out of her seat to rush to Irwin, but Taras's arm is an iron bar, blocking her. She turns on him, enraged. "How dare you? I'm buyin' breakfast for a hungry woman," she shouts.

"Woman, my ass! You're supposed to be at breakfast with the rest of the girls, not here encouraging these perverts! Now get your ass out of here before I tell my brother to drop you from the pageant!"

Now she's in tears. Seeing that, Irwin springs up from the floor and launches himself at Taras, but the wrestler just catches his shirtfront, picks him up bodily, shakes him like a gator shaking its prey, and throws him across the room onto a table, which overturns with Irwin beneath it.

Hands on hips, Taras says to Gracie, "What'll it be? You want a shot at that million or not?"

Shooters!

Still crying, she looks at Irwin and mouths "I'm sorry." Taras grabs her wrist and leads her from the restaurant.

"That's what I get for letting you people in here in the first place!" Says the cash register lady, the proprietor, to Irwin. "Who's gonna pay for this mess?"

"You are, bitch! Sooner than you think!" Irwin gets to his feet once more and rushes out into the street.

Chapter 23

Eduardo's radio bursts into music at 4:15 a.m. His eyes open, and he lies in bed a minute before he realizes what's happening. He set his alarm this early because he has to beat Miss Maribeth down to the kitchen to get food for Martin. He also has to put the key and the combination card back in the file cabinet in Uncle's office before the old man realizes they are gone.

He takes off his top and pulls on a t-shirt, then puts his jeans on over his PJ bottoms. He'll come back to bed after he's finished his clandestine chores and get up again at regular time so nobody's the wiser.

It takes but a moment to put the stuff back in Uncle's office—the old man doesn't keep it locked. In the kitchen, Eduardo quickly makes a ham and cheese sandwich, pours some tortilla chips into a plastic snack bag, then gets the thermos that he used to take to school from a cabinet and fills it with milk. The sandwich and chips go into a brown paper bag from the pantry, then he hides everything on a lower shelf in the mudroom where he can get it unobserved later.

Back in bed, Eduardo closes his eyes, but he's sure he won't get back to sleep. Today, he's got to get Martin out of the cabin before *Papá* Danny or somebody else takes it into their head to show up.

Claws digging into his shoulder send sparks of pain into his neck and arm. His eyes pop open and he sees *Mamá* Lupe glaring down at him.

"Get up!" she says unkindly, throwing his jeans in his face. "Just because you're expelled does not mean to get to sleep all day."

***

Later, when everyone's left for work, Eduardo retrieves the sandwich and goes to the cabin. When he gets there, he's horrified to see Martin in the outdoor shelter, sighting an AR-15 downrange. He put all of the guns away last night before he left—Martin must have the combinations memorized.

"What the fuck are you doing!" he hollers. "Put that back"

"Chill, dude," says Martin. He squeezes the trigger of the AR and it makes a loud pop. A plume of dust spurts from the earthen berm behind the silhouette target that Martin has set up. The report of the gun is muffled, and dissipates quickly in the woods surrounding the range. Danny has no wish to antagonize his neighbors with the sounds of gunfire, so all of the rifles are suppressed and the mags loaded with subsonic ammo, to avoid a loud crack from a bullet breaking the sound barrier.

Eduardo runs over to Martin and puts his hand on the rifle. "Stop, dude! They can hear that at the house!" While that's strictly true, Eduardo knows that Amos is half deaf, and Miss Maribeth likes to play classical music in her office while she's working. But if someone should hear the gunfire and come down here...

The way that Martin looks at Eduardo makes the younger boy wonder if he's going to turn the gun on him. But he lays the weapon down on the bench and steps back. Eduardo takes up the AR, drops the mag and pulls the charging lever to eject the chambered round. He points the barrel skyward so as not to sweep Martin when he turns to go back to the cabin.

Martin's voice come from behind him. "I don't know how the fuck you plan to get even with Shultz and Davies if we can't use the guns, dude."

Eduardo can't believe his ears. He turns and stares at Martin.

"You're not going to shoot them!" he says.

"What else?" says Martin. "You gonna say bad words to them? Beat them up? If you're gonna get even, man, get fucking even. Or just give it up. Is that really what you want to do?"

"I..." Eduardo begins.

"Remember, dude. Remember how you felt when you were naked in Schultz's bed, thinking she was coming to fuck you, and that door opened and everybody was there, laughing their asses off. Remember how you felt when they sent all those naked pictures of you to everybody in the fucking school. They're prolly still over there, and they're all prolly still laughing. Remember how you felt when you got expelled, when fucking Drayton made your *máma* cry. You never going back to that school, dude. You never gonna get a high school diploma and you be working shit jobs for the rest of your life. They won't even take your ass in the fucking army! Maybe they'll even put you on the sex offender list because Shultz said you tried to rape her. You know what happens to guys on that list? They can't get a job, they can't live anywhere near a school, a playground, or anywhere else kids are. Hell, the cops can arrest you for just walking past a park! Your life is so over, dude. Because of that little ho Schultz and that fucking cunt Drayton..."

Eduardo raises a hand. "Stop it, Martin. Just stop it."

Martin bores in for the kill. "What kind of man is it who lets some fucking hos do shit like that to him, and lets them get away with it..."

126

Shooters!

Eduardo raises his voice. "I said stop!"

Martin shuts up, but stands there looking at Eduardo like he's shit on his shoe.

"I'm not gonna let them get away with it, Martin," says Eduardo.

"Then watchoo gonna do about it??"

Eduardo shakes his head. "I dunno,"

"I have a suggestion," says Martin, hefting the rifle.

Chapter 24

Miko and me walk to the convention center for breakfast. There's no more convo on the way. Her stride is deliberate, her head high, not looking at me at all. Totally mad at the world. I wonder why? Oh well, it's gonna be way hard for her to win a million bucks with a 'tude like that. Way better for me.

At the end of the block near the parking deck, as we're crossing the street, I see Taisha on the sidewalk having a convo with a black dude in dreads, wearing a back-asswards red ball cap, dirty black hoodie, baggy pants and high-top kicks. Looks like banger. Seems like she could do way better. Her body language says she's hearing something she don't like. Dude points a finger in her face and walks off, and she turns and crosses the street, heading toward the convention center.

All of a sudden another dude bursts out of a coffee shop, dragging a blonde woman by the wrist. It's Taras! And Gracie! She's trying to fight him and get back inside, but he's having none of it. He gets her across the street, stops and takes her by both shoulders and gets in her face. I can't hear what he says, but she's crying when he's done. She nods, and he takes her hand this time and they head for the convention center. Miko and me follow.

The protestors are still going strong, but I ignore them. They're part of the background now.

Inside, I notice a metal detector has shown up. An old dude with white hair and a big bushy 'stache, wearing a light blue uniform, says to empty our pockets into a plastic bucket before we walk through. It doesn't beep for me, but when I get to the other side, the dude reaches into the bucket and comes up with my Swiss Army knife.

"Sorry honey, but I got to confiscate this. No weapons allowed inside."

"You can't! My daddy gave me that before he died."

The dude—his name tag says Murphy—looks at me with sad eyes. "I'm sorry. I just can't let you in with it. Best I can do is let you leave and put it up, then come back through.

Miko says, "Come on Nattie, we're going to be late. It's just a knife. You can get another one."

Shit. I left my gun locked in the Jeep because I knew I couldn't bring it in. But there's no way I'm losing Daddy's knife. I walk through the metal detector the wrong way and hold out my hand to Murphy. "Gimme." To Miko: "You go on. I'll be there after I put this in my car."

She shrugs and walks on.

It takes all of fifteen minutes to get to the Jeep, lock up the knife with my gun and get back. I'm p.o.'d the whole time. With my Tai Chi training, I can do way more damage to somebody bare-handed, than I ever could with that stupid little knife. I'm so fucking sick of people and their dumbshit rules!

It looks like most everybody is done with breakfast when I get to the cafeteria. As I'm grabbing a coffee and Danish, A.T. is standing in the middle of the room—he's got that portable mic. His voice sounds tinny.

"Everybody! Head on up to the ballroom and go backstage. We're going to be letting the public in in a few minutes and I don't want anybody to see you unless they pay for the privilege. I'll divide you into groups for the interviews after we get there. The first group will kick off at ten o'clock"

I check my Timex—it's just after nine. I follow the crowd out the door. There's Gracie, still looking shook. I sidle up next to her. Her face is red and her mascara has run—she's been crying! I tap her shoulder.

"Wassup, girl?"

She jumps at my touch, looking at me like she's done something.

"Oh, it's you, Nattie. Nothing, I'm OK."

We're going out into the corridor and heading for the escalator.

"You don't sound OK. What's happening? I saw you and Taras outside."

"It's really nothing. He caught me in the coffee shop buying breakfast for a street person, and he didn't like it. Doesn't want me associating with those people—he said it would cause image issues. He's prolly right. I told him I won't do it again."

Now I'm totally glad I threw the fucking asshole across the stage. Who the fuck does he think he is?

"Hey, girl, you did right. You got a big heart. Don't apologize for that."

She gets on the escalator with me behind her. She looks back at me sheepishly as we ride up.

"Gee, thanks, Nattie. You're all right."

We get off the escalator, and pass the double doors to the ballroom, arriving at a door labeled *Stage Door*. It opens into a narrow corridor smelling like nerves, which runs parallel to the ballroom and ends at a large open area backstage. A.T., Taras and Madam Annie are already there, and there are rows of folding chairs set up for us girls. Taras waves us to them. After we're settled, A.T. addresses us.

Shooters!

"Listen up!" I jump because his voice is a lot louder here than it was in the cafeteria. He lowers his voice when he speaks again. "So here's the POA for today. I'm gonna divide you into six groups of six each, then interview each group for thirty minutes. We'll start at ten and with breaks, we should be done by three. I'll ask questions to the group, not individually, so if you wanna be heard, you'll have to speak up. If you don't it will count against you."

I can't help but wonder if that's true, or if the winner of this thing will be the girl that gives the brothers the best BJs.

I end up in the first group, with Miko (*Miss San Francisco*), Angela (*Miss Montana*), Gracie (*Miss Hot Bod*), Delia (*Miss Southern Belle*), and Sallie (*Miss Pussy*).

A couple of techs wire us up with small radios that go on the waistband or in a pocket. Each has a mic and an earpiece so we can get instructions that the audience can't hear. There's a problem with Sallie, who's wearing a white body suit that has no belt and no pockets—they have to shove the radio underneath it from behind and run the wires inside it up to her ear. She slips the straps off her shoulders, showing us a great set of titties, and the tech, a young guy, can barely bring himself to touch her to set up the rig. She'll end up sitting on the little radio though, which will be uncomfortable AF. I can put my radio under the waistband of my cutoffs like an IWB holster and run the wires up through my tube top on my side where they'll be hard to see. As the tech approaches to do me, I suddenly decide to roll down my top as well so everyone can have a tit shot—don't want Sallie to upstage me. I smile at the tech as he stops in his tracks with eyes get as big as dinner plates.

"Quit screwing around, Nattie," says Taras. "We charge for that shit. Don't give it away."

I blow Taras a kiss as I roll my top back up. Sallie glares at me. She knows exactly what I did.

A little before ten, Taras hollers, "OK, group one, get ready to go on."

He leads us into an area that's curtained off front and back, where A.T. is perched on a tall stool, facing a semicircle of six similar chairs. When the curtain opens, we'll be sideways to the audience, so I trot to snag the seat nearest to the front of the stage, bumping into Miko in the process. I get there first, earning a dirty look. Tough titty, bitch.

As we settle into our seats, a voice in my ear says, "OK, ladies, when the curtain goes up, we want you to turn your heads and smile at the audience. In 3, 2, 1, going up…"

The curtain rises. Damn, Gina! I'm looking out at a deadass sea of people in the ballroom—there must be hundreds and most are guys.

A.T. moves to stand in the center of our semicircle, facing the crowd and holding his arms out like the ringmaster at a circus.

"Gentlemen and ladies, I'd like to welcome you to first ever America's First Sexy Lady Pageant!" He goes off into a short spiel about how the pageant came to be.

In my ear, "When A.T. calls your name, get up and curtsy to the audience, then sit down."

Curtsy? Dude, you gotta be fuckin' kidding me! How the fuck do you even do that? I struggle to remember every old movie I ever watched, but come up blank.

A.T. turns toward me, swinging both arms as a signal for me to rise.

"Here's Natalie McMasters, *Miss Capital City!*"

I stand and face the audience, smile, and bow from the waist. I get a scattering of applause. I sit down again.

"Mihara Aiko, *Miss San Francisco!*"

Miko appears as clueless as I am, repeating my poor performance.

"Angela Stratton, *Miss Montana!*"

Wolf whistles erupt from the audience at that intro. Angel, who's wearing a leather vest over a skimpy black bra and a white miniskirt with a matching cowboy hat, faces the audience and takes the sides of her skirt between her forefingers and thumbs. Bowing her head, she moves her right foot behind her left, bending her knees and slowly sinking toward the floor. She holds that position for a couple seconds, then slowly and gracefully returns to a standing position.

The crowd goes wild, and Angel turns to me and Miko, giving us a wink before taking her seat again.

Guess I just lost the first competition.

The rest of the girls attempt to mimic Angel's performance, but none comes close to her perfection. Figures, since she did *Miss America*.

When we've all finished our little puppet show, A.T. goes over the interview rules.

"I'll ask a question to the group, and you will have a maximum of five minutes to respond. I'm not calling names or recognizing hands—just jump right in and speak your mind. If the discussion dies, I'll just ask the next question."

So he's trying for a free-for-all. Should be interesting.

Shooters!

"Here's the first question. What do you think makes a woman sexy?"

Completely oblivious to the instructions, Gracie shoots a hand in the air while bouncing up and down in her seat.

"I know! I know!"

True to his word, A.T. totally ignores her.

Angel pipes up. "Men like a strong, independent woman." A typical *Miss America* answer if I ever heard one.

"What the hell ever gave you that idea?" says A.T. "That's the last thing a real man wants."

Applause from the audience.

Angel looks puzzled and butthurt. "Well…"

Sallie cuts her off. "Men like a great pair of tits and a nice ass!"

More applause, louder.

A.T. rewards her with a smile. "Sallie gets it."

"I should. I'm a paid escort."

Gracie pipes up, "Me too!"

"That's disgusting!" exclaims Angel.

Sallie snorts, "You're going to walk around on a stage totally naked in a couple of days and you're telling me that I'm disgusting because I'm an escort?"

Laughter.

"It's not the same thing," Angel says. "I'm don't fuck for money."

"I'll bet A.T. and Taras are sorry to hear that," I say.

More laughter. A point for *moi*.

"Hey!" A.T. exclaims, "We're judging this pageant on totally objective criteria."

"Sure you are," I smile, looking right into his eyes and slightly extending my tongue to lick my upper lip. His eyes widen slightly—he got the message.

"I don't fuck my clients for money," Sallie says. "I ain't no whore. I accompany them to various functions as a plus one."

"And you never end up in bed with one of them?" Angel asks incredulously.

"What happens, happens," Sallie replies. "Don't tell me you never fucked a guy after he gave you a nice night on the town."

Angel doesn't answer, which is all the answer needed.

"Here's a related question," says A.T. "How do you please a man?"

Miko speaks up. "Fuck his brains out!"

Mega applause. The audience really likes that one.

"So you're telling me that you think all guys want from you is sex?" A.T. challenges.

"Pretty much."

A.T. throws the question to the rest of us. "Is she right?"

"Yes," says Sallie.

"Absolutely," Delia echoes.

"Yes!" Gracie says.

I've got to jump into this minefield. And I've got to stand out.

"Not exactly," I say.

" Aha! A dissenter!" says A.T. "If not sex, then what?"

"A man wants to be admired," I say. "Worshipped, even. That's what will keep him coming back to you."

Applause.

"Explain that, Nattie," A.T. says.

"Look, as girls, we've been brought up not to be too free with sex, because a man will just take what we give him, then move on. The trick is to keep him coming back to us for something he can get anywhere. How? Make him feel special. He'll kill for that."

"That's only true for a man who doesn't know who he is," says A.T. "Like Taras, for instance…"

Laughter.

"Fuck you!" says Taras.

"Just kidding, little bro."

During the exchange between the brothers, I let my eyes wander out over the crowd. I spot Danny in the back. His gaze is riveted on me and he's got a look on his face like's he's stepped in something.

Shooters!

I jerk my mind back the discussion. "You're right," I answer A.T., not meaning it. "You know how special you are."

Oooooo…. from the crowd.

I give him a big smile and flutter my eyelashes. The corners of his mouth creep upwards.

Gotcha!

We go on in the same vein until the *Grand Complication* titters. "Time's up, ladies," he says, pushing a button on the watch. Standing, he addresses the audience, holding both arms sideways to present us to them. "Let's give these girls a great big hand!"

A roar of applause arises, complete with whistles and catcalls, sending shivers through my bod. I do confess that since my stripping days, I have never gotten tired of applause. It's a total drug. A.T. raises his open palms for us to get up, and the voice in my ear says, "Curtsy to the audience." We do, knowing how this time. Then A.T. motions me to lead the other girls backstage.

When we get there, Taras is already lining up the next group. He waves us to take the chairs they just vacated. As we sit, Miko says to Gracie, "You really screwed the pooch on that one, Pratt."

"What do you mean?"

"What do you think?" Miko replies. "Didn't you hear the man say not to raise your hand, just speak up? You came off looking like a real doofus, and you accomplished it it in front of a live audience. Bravo! Why don't you just drop out now, and save yourself a few more days of pain and embarrassment?"

Gracie's face is a study in emotions. First her jaw drops and her eyes widen as the impact of the cruel words hits her, then her eyes slowly close and her chin wrinkles as big tears like raindrops well up and begin streaming down her cheeks. She jumps up and tears out of there, ignoring Sallie's shouts that she has to stay. I resist the impulse to follow her. I want that mil! But Sallie doesn't—she goes after Gracie, casting a glare back at the rest of us who stay behind.

"That was a totally shitty thing to do," I say to Miko, who just shrugs.

"If you can't take the heat…"

I'd love to get up and clock her one, but I'll do nothing that will get me in trouble.

135

We can watch the next interview on a TV screen hanging on the wall. It proceeds in much the same vein as ours—the questions are somewhat different, but the theme is the same. How does a girl best please her man?

After a little while, Sallie comes back, but no Gracie. "She ran outside," Sallie tells us.

"Good riddance," says Miko.

I just can't help it. "You are a total piece of shit," I say to her.

That gets to her. She comes up out of her chair stepping towards me, cocking her right arm. I stand, stepping into *gong bu*.

Her open hand is coming for my face. I step back, grab her wrist and pull, just like I did to Taras. There's surprising power in her blow, so she goes flying. Unlike Taras, she doesn't know how to fall, so she ends up in a heap in the corner. I wheel and face her again, my arms chest high, palms open.

She slowly drags herself to her feet and limps away, giving me a look of pure hatred.

The other girls cheer spontaneously.

We break for lunch when the second group is finished. "Be back here at one sharp," Taras says. I hook up with Sallie and Angel, and we head downstairs to the cafeteria.

Going inside, the food smells assail me and I inadvertently hold my breath. Will I be overcome with waves of nausea or will my mouth water with hunger? Luckily, it's the latter. We move to the end of the food line that winds its way through parallel rails in front of the service area.

I feel a tap on my shoulder. I turn. It's Danny.

"We need to talk," he says.

136

Chapter 25

After leaving the coffee shop, Irwin turns toward the city park, but takes only a few steps before remembering the guy who rousted him from sleep that morning.

I don't want to see that nigger again!

Instead, Irwin goes to the convention center plaza. He doesn't really want to join the trans people in their demonstration today—it all just seems so meaningless. But where else to go? What he really wants is his gun, but that won't be here for a few days.

Then I'll teach people to fuck with me!

Sadly, he shuffles off to join the protestors—the closest thing to a fam that he's got.

Once there, Irwin grabs the *We're Coming for Your Kids* sign and halfheartedly joins in the chants. As per usual, the protest devolves into a shouting match between the trans people and the TERFs, with the cops threatening to haul everybody in if violence erupts.

It's nearly lunchtime when the convention center doors fly open and a woman runs out, down the steps and out into the plaza. Irwin sees a flash of blonde hair and a flash of rage burns his skin. Is it the hated Natalie McMasters? No, it's Gracie, the hottie who bought him breakfast this morning. And it looks like she's crying! Irwin drops his sign and hurries after her, heedless of the calls from his fellow protestors to stop.

He catches up with her at the plaza entrance, where she's been halted by the lunchtime traffic on the main drag. He puts a hand on her shoulder from behind, which makes her jump, but she calms down when she sees who it is.

"What happened?" Irwin asks. "Why are you crying?"

"Nothing!" she answers.

"It's not nothing!" Irwin says. "Somebody did something! What was it?"

"It was stupid. I shouldn't be this way."

"But you are," says Irwin. "Where were you going?"

"I don't know. My room, I guess."

"Well I'll come with you. You shouldn't be alone like this."

Her eyes shine with gratitude, and it sends a thrill through him that he hasn't felt in a long time. She takes his hand.

"OK. You can come."

They wait for the light to change, then cross the street into the pedestrian mall. It's teeming with people and it's difficult to stay together holding hands, but Irwin clings to her like a drowning man to a life raft. They're an unlikely pair—gorgeous Gracie in her pageant regalia and outrageous Irwin in his ragtag get-up—the pair draws more than a few disparaging stares from passers-by. Finally arriving at the hotel, they enter the opulent lobby and take the elevator up to Gracie's floor. She leads Irwin to her room, finally letting go of his hand to fumble for her keycard.

Once in the room, Gracie drops onto an unmade bed, spreading her arms behind her to prop her up, pushing her most excellent ta-ta's toward the ceiling. Irwin closes his eyes in disbelief, and breathes deeply of the scents in the air—earthy sweat, sweet perfume, the *je ne sais quoi* of the quintessential woman. Something nags inside his head, but he pushes it away. Opening his eyes again, he watches as Gracie pushes herself upright and pats the mattress beside her.

"Come on, Irving, sit here with me."

He doesn't even bother to correct her mispronunciation of his name as he sits next to her on the bed. Shyly putting a hand on his thigh, she looks into his eyes, saying, "It's really so nice of you to stay with me. I feel so much better with you here."

Her face is an angel's, bringing a smile to his, but it's also a knife to his heart. He's anticipating that familiar stirring in his loins, but it's not there Then he remembers what's nagging him. His balls... they cut out his balls... Tears well up in his eyes.

"Hey," Gracie says, "Don't you dare cry!" She reaches a hand to snatch one of his tears on a fingertip, then kisses her finger and smiles at him.

Irwin reaches out in turn, stroking her cheek with two fingers, letting his hand drop to her shoulder.

Gracie looks down at his lap, then lays her hand between his legs. Smiling at him, she squeezes his penis. Poor Irwin feels nothing but the pressure from her fingers.

Smiling angelically, Gracie says, "I knew it! You are a man! Come on, get hard for Momma..." She starts massaging his organ.

A red mist dances before Irwin's eyes. He places his other hand on her opposite shoulder, then slides both hands toward each other to meet around her neck. The hands clasp. They squeeze. Tighter. Ever tighter.

Gracie's eyes widen and bulge. Her mouth gapes and a stream of spittle runs out the side and drips onto her halter top. The sharp smell of urine suddenly fills the air. Irwin's hands tighten even more, and he feels a bone in her neck crack as she grabs his wrists, vainly trying to pry them from her windpipe. That terrible grip doesn't loosen, so she lets go and curls her hands into claws, using her last bit of strength to sink her nails into his cheeks and rake downwards. Irwin's mouth opens in a hiss of pure rage and he shakes her like a doll. She goes limp, and he throws her onto the floor like a piece of trash.

Jumping up, he dashes to the bathroom, snatching a bright white towel from the rack to mop his stinging face. He looks in the mirror and sees it—the mark of Cain—two tripartite crimson gouges running down each cheek! He scans the counter and spies a woman's makeup case. Flipping open the lid, he rifles through it, coming up with a good-sized styptic pencil and a bottle of thick, beige liquid. He takes the pencil out of the case and begins dabbing it on the scratches—it stings like a motherfucker, but between it and a washrag he manages to get the bleeding mostly stopped. He pours a dollop of the thick liquid onto his fingers and smears it on the marks. It covers them well enough so they're not immediately apparent, although a close inspection would still discern them. Diving back into the case, he finds a compact filled with pancake. He snaps it open and uses the pad to smear it on his cheeks. That's better—the marks are nearly gone, but there's still a pesky drop or two of dark red liquid that soaks through the foundation.

He finally deems it good enough and slides the styptic, the foundation and the pancake into a pocket, then he re-enters the bedroom. Gracie lies sprawled on the floor, her head at an odd angle, facing the bed. A ball of grief chokes him—why did the dumb bitch have to grab his dick like that, anyhow? He can't be held responsible his actions after she did that.

He eases the door open, checking to see that the hall is empty. Slipping outside, he heads for the stairs, hoping to find a side door so he can avoid the lobby. At the bottom, he finds a metal door that has a push bar with a sign: *Emergency Exit Only – Alarm Will Sound.*

Shit!

The alarms are disabled on half of these doors. But for others, pushing the bar can set off a loud buzzer. He looks around for a camera. Doesn't see one.

There will be cameras in the lobby though. Lots of 'em.

He makes his decision. He pushes the door open. Silence reigns. He vanishes into the bowels of the city.

Chapter 26

My Manifesto

1. My name is Martín Victor Aguilar Castro and I am a proud Mexican man. The blood that runs in my veins is the same blood that ran through Moctezuma, Cuauhtemoc, Juarez, Hidalgo, Zapata and Pancho Villa.

2. I was born a weakling, but I am taking a magic potion that will transform me into the strongest, smartest, fastest, most powerful man in the world. By the time I finish the treatment I will be the greatest hero that Mexico has ever known.

3. The meaning of Martín is warrior. The meaning of Victor is conqueror. The meaning of Aguilar is Place of Eagles. The meaning of Castro is castle. Thus I am a warrior from the Castle of Eagles who vanquishes his enemies.

4. I hate the white people of the United States of America. I hate them because they have taken all of the good things of the world for themselves. They have claimed all of the food, the clothing and the riches of the land which they have made into computers, iPhones and televisions for themselves. They control all the money in the world which they use to buy other things for themselves. They give money to the cartels in Mexico who enslave us to provide drugs for them to get high on.

5. I hate the black people of the United States of America because they are the slaves of the whites and do their bidding to oppress us, in return for drugs, electronics and gold.

6. I hate the government of the United States of America because it keeps us proud Mexicans imprisoned below their stinking border to live in squalor and filth. They finance the puppet Mexican government and the drug cartels who enslave us.

7. I want to kill all the white Americans and their black slaves who have meticulously planned the genocide of the proud Mexican race. They act together with the Mexican government and the cartels, each of them playing his part to destroy us. Their crimes are endless. They lie and deceive the rest of the world with their corrupt news media, they use their stinking banks to bury poor nations under mountains of debt and control all their money for the purpose of funding evil, they start endless wars with their despicable lies which have cost millions of lives throughout history, they distribute degenerate entertainment as video games, movies and pornography to corrupt our people, and promote feminism and transgenderism, all of which have ruined our men and women and undermined our *machismo*. Their

army, their police and their Border Patrol keep us imprisoned in poverty.

8. To my family and friends who ask me, How can you throw your life away? You made it into the United States and were adopted by a loving family who clothed and fed you. They took you to church. They sent you to school. You can live the American dream and have a family of your own someday. But what value does my life have when my brothers and sisters are imprisoned below the border in squalor and filth? Can I betray them by living a comfortable life while they die slowly in agony? No! I will not sell my soul by sitting idly by as evil grows. I'd rather die in glory or spend the rest of my life in prison than waste away knowing that I did nothing to stop this evil. I am Martín Victor Aguilar Castro, the son of Eagles and a proud Mexican man, and I am not afraid. I am not afraid of death, I am not afraid of jail. I will seek our enemies out root and branch, I will hunt them, I will slay them in their workplaces, their schools and their homes.

9. Finally, I know that I will never truly die. Like my Lord and Savior Jesus Christ, I will ascend into heaven to take my place alongside God the Father Almighty, where I will rule over the world at his side.

Eduardo lays the papera on the workbench and looks at Martin, whose wide eyes and half-smile seem to say, *Now you understand me.* He feels vaguely nervous and uneasy, not sure of the right thing to say.

Finally Martin forces the issue. "So? What do you think?"

"Yeah, wow, it's great, Martin…"

"Don't bullshit me, Ibáñez. Tell me what you really think. Are you in this or not?"

"In what?"

Martin rolls his eyes. "What the fuck have we been talkin' about for the last couple of days? We take these guns, we go down to that fuckin' school and we show these bastards what happens when they fuck with us!"

"I don't know, man…"

"What the fuck!" Martin exclaims again. "So you're just gonna let Schultz and Davies get away with what they did to you?"

"No, but…"

"But nothing! Are you gonna be a fucking man or not? You say you've already killed somebody. Is that just bullshit?"

Shooters!

A sudden anger arises in Eduardo. "It's not bullshit. I did it. Shot the motherfucker right in the heart and watched him die."

"Then you can do it again. Are you a proud Mexican man?"

"Yes!"

"Do you believe it's better to die or go to prison than to let the motherfuckers get away with what they did? Or worse yet, what they're going to do to us and others like us if we don't stop them?"

It takes Eduardo a little longer to respond this time. "Yes."

"You sure?"

"Yes!"

"Then let's get some of these guns and ammo over to my car."

Eduardo hesitates, then, "What if my *Pápa* comes down here and sees they're gone?"

"We'll take just a couple guns and three or four mags each. Maybe two handguns and extra ammo for them, too. Then we'll lock the rest back up. Nobody will notice unless they open the lockers. And nobody is gonna do that, at least till the weekend. You said they're all out on a job, right?"

Eduardo nods.

"Then it's a piece of cake. Nobody will know till we're done." His eyes shine. "But then will they know!"

The two boys begin opening locks and gathering the instruments of death.

Chapter 27

Me and Danny don't speak as we go through the lunch line. I can tell he's got heavy shit on his mind and doesn't want to air it in public. I grab a salad and a bottle of green tea, he gets a sandwich and milk, and we go looking for an empty table.

As I walk past a table where Miko and several other contestants are sitting, a girl who is drinking sweet tea through a straw suddenly stops and spits a mouthful back into her glass. "Ohmigod! That's the worst tea I ever had," she says.

Thank God I've got bottled tea.

We find a small table overlooking the plaza where we'll have some privacy. "What's up?" I say to Danny as I set down my tray and sit.

He doesn't answer until he's seated across from me. He's frowning and not looking directly at me as he begins, "Was it true—what you said in that interview?"

"Was what true?"

"That you try to make a man feel special just to get him to keep coming back to you. Is that what you've been doing to me?"

I can't even! "How could you even ask me something like that?"

He still won't look at me. "Nattie, you've changed lately. It's like I don't know whether I can trust you anymore."

"What do you mean?"

"It started after you told me about that guy in New York. That you had sex with him to get the poop about your birth. You didn't seem to think there was anything wrong with that—that I was wrong to be upset about it. You said you wouldn't do it again, and I believed you."

Now I'm getting seriously pressed. "You mean that you don't believe me anymore?"

He shakes his head. "I don't know what to believe. You've just been hard to talk to lately. And now you're in this stupid pageant! You're going to run around naked on a stage in front of thousands of people on international TV for a chance to win a million bucks? Even though you know that I'm seriously against it."

"The last time we talked about it you said that I should do what I want."

145

His jaw drops, his eyes widen and he holds out both hands palms up. "And you didn't get that I was pissed about it?"

"Oh, I got it OK. I just didn't think it was any of your business. I still don't."

Now his eyes harden and his mouth becomes a thin line. "And what else don't you think is my business? You sleeping with other guys, for instance? Is that your plan to win a million, Nattie? Screwing A.T.? Maybe Taras, too?"

It isn't, but I'm sure AF that I'm not gonna tell him that. "Maybe," I lie.

"Is that baby even mine?"

That one hits like a gut punch, because I don't know the answer. And would he even believe me if I told him about the rape?

Any thought of food is history. I jump up from the chair and stomp towards the door, not sure of where I'm even going. I almost run into one of the contestants who's blocking my way. It's the one who got the bad tea a little while ago. She's got a weird look on her face and she's holding her belly, then suddenly her opens mouth and an ocean of puke falls out, just missing me. The smell is all it takes to get me started, then several other people nearby also join in the fun.

Danny's hollers from behind me. "Nattie!"

I have to get the fuck out of here. My stomach still in spasms, I run for the door, into the hall, past old Murphy at the metal detector and into the plaza, between the ranks of cops in front of the jeering groups of protestors. All I can think about is getting to the hotel, to my room, taking off my filthy clothes, getting a shower and laying down.

It's a good long block down the pedestrian mall to the hotel. The fresh air clears my head and calms my stomach a little. Laser-focused, I weave through the crowd, uncaring of their stares. As I near the hotel, the throng thickens. I catch snippets of voices.

"Somebody's been hurt…"

"They're saying it's murder…"

"Look! They're bringing her out now."

I push through the front of the mob where a line of blue-clad cops blocks me. They're fanned out from an ambulance that's parked on the pedestrian mall, its rear doors splayed wide. White-coated EMTs huddle inside, awaiting the arrival of the patient. Other medics roll a gurney out of the hotel with a body atop, swaddled tightly in a pale blue sheet. Another

Shooters!

walks along side with an IV bag held high like a talisman that scatters the crowd. Long blonde hair streams down from the gurney towards the pavement.

Gracie? OMG! Is that Gracie?

Chapter 28

Irwin dashes out of the alley next to the hotel into the lunchtime crowd on the mall. No one pays him any mind in spite of his outlandish attire—these jaded city dwellers have seen it all. But to Irwin, every eye is fixed on him. They all know what he did! He's dreading the raising of the hue and cry.

Help! Help! Murder!

He pushes through the mass of people, frantically trying to decide where to go.

Not back to the convention center, that's for fuckin' A sure. It's the first place the cops will look. How about the park? Maybe my gun has come in.

A decision made, he moves in that direction, fighting to keep to a walk.

Once away from the mall, the crowd thins considerably. He spots a cop car approaching and it takes everything he's got not to cut and run—that would assuredly bring the long arm of the law crashing down on his shoulder.

They've got to know what I look like—there were probably cameras in the hall outside Gracie's room. And the streets around here are full of them.

He spots a pharmacy ahead.

A better disguise! That's what I need!

He goes in and buys more make-up, brown hair dye, a pair of clippers and a razor.

When I get done not even my own mother will know me.

But where to go? Since he got here, he's been living on the streets. He needs a place to hole up.

Maybe that LeBrowne nigger can help. He knows everything!

The park comes into view. Again, Irwin has to stop himself from breaking into a run. Holding his bag of purchases in two hands, he tries to saunter.

Nothing to see here, people!

Once in the park, he follows the circuitous path to LeBrowne's central sanctum. A banger suddenly appears, thick dreads sticking out from under a red ball cap worn backwards, hate in his eyes.

"Whatchew lookin' here, ofay?"

Irwin steels himself, challenges the sentinel with a hardened gaze.

"I gots bidness wit' da man," he says in an affected accent. "You want to tell him why you won't let me by?"

Apparently the banger does not, because he moves aside to let Irwin pass.

Irwin goes round the last bend and LeBrowne comes into view, sitting back on his bench, arms and legs splayed out, catching some rays. As Irwin approaches, LeBrowne levels his gaze and says, "Why you here for, dude? I tol' yew I let you know when the merch is in."

Irwin steels himself.

I gotta trust somebody if I'm gonna get help.

"I gotta situation, man. I need a place to lay low for a few days."

LeBrowne touches his earplug. "It ain't got nothing to do wit' that fracas down de hotel now, do it?"

A bolt of fear pierces Irwin's guts. "How you know about that?"

"I knows everythin' dude. Looks like you some hot prop right about now. I might can put you up, but it gonna cost."

"How much?"

"A yard a day."

"A yard? What the fuck's a yard?"

"A grand. A thou, dude."

A thousand bucks a day! Holy fuck! Even with the cash from the old lady's car, I can't do that for long.

"Yew been hangin' round that beauty pageant at the convo center." LeBrowne says. "Whatchew know aboud a million bucks comin' in down there?"

"A million bucks? Nothing, man. I ain't never been inside."

That's not true, but Mr. Nigger doesn't need to know that.

"Too bad. A little info could lower yo' bill."

"Look dude, can you help me out or not?"

LeBrowne gives him a patronizing smile. "You pay me the daily yard, I can let y'all stay at the Legends crib a few days. But you get too hot, yer out on the street, dude."

"I guess I got no choice. Can we go there now?"

Shooters!

"I get a nigga to take you directly. When you get there, you make yourself mighty small so's you don't get yer ass beat. Some of my niggas don't like ofays much. Especially he-she ofays." "Can you get me an 80, too? That will help"

"We'll see."

Maybe when I get that gun, I'll take some of you mofos out too!

Chapter 29

Martin pops the hatch of a new white Buick SUV parked in a clearing near the rifle range, places the ARs and magazines inside and throws a blanket over them. He takes a 1911 pistol, racks the slide to cock the hammer and chamber a round, before tucking it under his belt next to his spine and letting his shirt flop over it. He offers the other 1911 to Eduardo.

"It's dangerous to carry it like that, with the hammer cocked," Eduardo says.

"Huh?"

Eduardo takes the other pistol, racks the slide, then pushes up the safety lever on the side and shows it to Martin.

"This is called Condition One. You can't pull the trigger unless you push the safety down."

"But what if I don't want to use the safety?"

"The way you have it, if you touch the trigger when you draw it, you can shoot yourself. And these guns have really touchy triggers."

"How do you know this?"

"My *pápa* taught me."

Martin reaches for the gun. Eduardo says, "Don't. Let me get it."

Martin rolls his eyes, but he turns with his shirt hiked up so Eduardo can see the pistol. The younger boy grasps the stock and pulls it out of Martin's waistband, making sure that the trigger doesn't catch on his clothes. He engages the safety and hands the gun back to Martin. '"Now it's safe. Just don't forget to push the lever down before you shoot."

Martin puts the gun back in his waistband, then presses a button on the hatch door. It slowly lowers and the lock clicks. He looks at Eduardo.

"Get in," he says.

"Where are we going?" asks Eduardo.

"My folks' place."

"What for?"

"We need someplace to stay until tomorrow. We could get caught if we're here. That would fuck up everything."

Eduardo hops in the shotgun seat while Martin drives. The older boy has some trouble turning the large car around in the limited space in the clearing, but he finally manages, and drives down the dirt two-track towards the main road. Both boys are silent. Martin seems to be concentrating on navigating the tight, bumpy road, while Eduardo simply sits there and worries.

What have I gotten myself into? What exactly is Martin gonna do tomorrow?

What if Pápa Danny comes home and finds the guns gone?

Can I really shoot Schultz and Davies? I don't have to do that to get even. What I really want is to see the two of them kneeling in front of me, crying. Telling me how sorry they are for what they did. Maybe I can even get them to blow me, and take a pic of them doing it! Send that all over the school. Then we'll see!

About ten minutes later, Martin takes a right on a side street blocked by a black wrought iron gate. He stops the car and reaches up to push a button on a panel mounted in the center of the windshield near the rear-view mirror. The gate slowly swings open, and Martin drives through. Eduardo turns to see the gate close behind them.

They're on a wide thoroughfare with large, multistory brick homes on both sides. Martin enters a semicircular driveway rimmed by a low brick wall sprouting black iron spikes on top. Past a gate, the driveway forks— Martin follows the left fork around the house to a garage in the rear. Another button opens the garage door, the overhead lights and he drives inside. The door closes behind them. Martin pushes the parking brake button and kills the engine. "We're here," he says.

He opens the door and the smells of engine exhaust and motor oil invade the car. Martin gets out, leading the way to a door on the left that opens into a white utility room smelling of detergent and dryer sheets. It contains a washer and dryer, a large sink, a hot water heater and a rack of household tools. A door on the other side opens into a mud room with a bathroom on the right. The smells transform into normal household odors— food, cigarette smoke, air deodorizer, but there's an underlying funk that Eduardo can't identify—spoiled meat maybe? From the mud room they go into a kitchen that's all dark wood cabinets, black and white granite countertops and stainless steel appliances. It's as neat as a medical office but the stench is stronger there. Eduardo wrinkles his nose and says, "Wow, dude. Place stinks."

"Yeah," agrees Martin. "A rat died in a kitchen cabinet. last weekend We were at the lake, didn't find it for a couple days. *Pápa* had the place cleaned, but they said it would take a few weeks for the smell to get completely out."

"Where are your folks?"

"At the lake. They won't be back until Monday."

"Then why did you have to stay at my place the last few days?"

"They left last night, dude!" Martin huffs. "What's with all the fuckin' questions?

"Sorry…"

Suddenly Martin smiles. "Didn't nobody ever tell you to never apologize? Makes you look weak." He cocks his head toward the great room. "Let's play some video games. Get some practice for tomorrow."

Martin grabs a big bag of cheese curls and a beer from the fridge. Showing the can to Eduardo, he asks, "You want one?"

"No. It throws my gaming off. You got any coke?"

Martin opens the pantry door and pulls out a fresh, two liter bottle. He takes it to the counter and gets a Solo cup from a cabinet. "You want ice?"

"Sure."

Martin turns his back to Eduardo as he fills the cup on the counter, then faces him to give him the cup. Eduardo takes a swig. "Tastes funny."

"That's cuz it's been here forever, man. Beer's better."

They go into the great room, which features a brick fireplace on one wall and a dark wood floor-to-ceiling bookcase opposite. A cushy leather sofa faces a wall-mounted TV that's seven feet wide if it's an inch. There's a couple of video game consoles on a credenza beneath the TV with a shelf below for the controllers.

Eduardo points to a set of double doors on the fourth wall. "What's in there?"

"That's my folks' room."

Eduardo rubs his nose. The foul odor is stronger here. A fly with a green butt lands on his hand and he waves it away.

Martin powers up the TV and the PS5. A bunch of icons appear on the screen.

Handing a controller to Eduardo, Martin enumerates the games shown on the screen. "We got *Call of Duty*, *Rainbow Six*, *Zombie Army*, and *Halo*. What's your pleasure?"

"Whatever. You pick." Damn these flies! Where are they all coming from?

"*Rainbow Six* it is. Let's kill us some stinkin' ay-rabs."

Martin moves a pair of armchairs in front of the TV and set up two tray tables in front for the controllers, drinks and snacks. The boys each take a chair, then Martin fires up the game and picks the team and he and Eduardo choose their avatars. It's a first person shooter with a split screen, so the POV is a gun sight. The game commences with the two of them moving through a dilapidated building, taking out enemies as they appear. "Look! It's the vice-principal!" Martin shouts before blowing the target away. "Hey, there's Schultz! She's yours! Get her, get her!" Eduardo hits the fire button and a thrill goes through him as the target goes down. The smell and the flies fade out as he immerses himself in the game, moving from room to room, acquiring targets and mowing them down. As the images whirl on the screen, Eduardo feels himself being drawn into the game. It's soon like he's really there in the game world—he's no longer keeping count of his kills, just reveling in non-stop action.

After they've been playing for about an hour, the pressure in Eduardo's lower abdomen is noticeable as he keeps refilling his glass from the two-liter bottle. *Máma* Lupe would never allow him to drink so much coke, but screw her—she's not here. Finally, he just can't stand it anymore. He puts the controller on the table. "Hey, man. Got to tap a kidney." He got that one from *Pápa* Danny.

Now where's the bathroom? There's one in the mudroom by the back door, but he wonders if there's one closer. He's really got to go! No point in asking Martin. Dude is riveted on the game, wallowing in gore. Eduardo checks out the bedroom door. A master bedroom usually has an attached bathroom. Martin's 'rents won't care if he uses it—they're at the lake.

Eduardo pushes his tray aside and stands. The room becomes blurry and seems to spin around him. He half falls half sits back down in the armchair, rubbing his eyes to refocus them. The bedroom door comes into view again, so he rises and quickly crosses the room before it can disappear, putting his hand on the doorknob to freeze it in place. Martin catches a glimpse out of the corner of his eye, drops his controller, and opens his mouth to holler. But it's too late. Eduardo opens the door and the funk of decomp overwhelms him as a black cloud emerges and swirls around his head.

It's like a disjointed abstract painting. On the bed, two bodies, blanketed in brown blood. A man with no head—there it is! On the mattress, beside him. The woman is whole, but her face is unrecognizable, a moving mass of buzzing blackness. The drone of a million flies, hovering

Shooters!

above the bodies in a noxious cloud, fills the air, as the draft from the open door disturbs their feast.

Eduardo's and Martin's simultaneous screams blend into a mix of rage and horror.

Chapter 30

The EMTs load Gracie into the ambulance and close the doors. The siren emits a single plaintive bleat, the red lights flash and the vehicle moves off slowly to avoid running down the surrounding onlookers. Picking up speed, it weaves among the benches and trashcans on the pedestrian mall until it reaches the street, where the siren kicks in full bore as it speeds off.

I approach one of the EMTs who stayed behind, a Japanese girl even shorter than me, with long black hair, wearing a light blue shirt and navy pants. "Can you tell me who was just taken away? She might be a friend of mine."

"I'm sorry," she replies. "We don't know her name, and I couldn't say even if we did. HIPAA, you know. What's your friend's name?"

Perversely, I don't want to answer her because she wouldn't tell me. But that's way stupid. "I think it might have been Gracie. Gracie Pratt. She's a contestant in the beauty pageant going on at the convention center."

She pulls a notebook and pen from her shirt pocket and makes an entry. "What is your name?" she asks. "The police might want to talk with you about this."

I answer her question with one of my own. "Why are the cops involved? Did somebody hurt her?"

"I can't say," she replies. "Can you tell me your name, please?"

I look down at myself, realizing that I'm still wearing my bright red *Miss Capital City* sash. Turning sideways to her, I answer, "I don't think so."

I move off into the crowd as she calls after me, "Miss! Miss…" Pulling off my sash, I cram it into the pocket of my cutoffs.

The crowd thins as I approach the end of the mall near the convention center plaza. Most everyone is going the other way, toward the hotel— apparently the news has spread that that's where the action is. In front of the center itself, I notice an altercation between the cops and the protestors. As I get close enough, I hear part of a convo between Lester and a trans guy with a short green buzz cut, a spiked collar, a rainbow tank top with a white paper stuck to his chest reading He/Him.

"…your assembly permit has been temporarily suspended by the city." Lester is saying. "I need y'all to disperse, now."

"Since when can the city suspend the Constitution?" the guy retorts. "The first amendment says…"

Lester cuts him off. "Look. I'm giving y'all ten minutes to pack up your stuff and go. You can call police headquarters to find out when you'll be allowed to come back. If y'all're here after that time, we'll arrest you. Now who will that help?"

"What about them?" He points to the feminists across the way.

"That's where I'm headed next. Now please comply with my order." She turns her back and approaches the fems.

She notices me as I trot up the stairs and calls after me, "Miss…"

I yank my sash out of my pocket and show her. "I'm a contestant." She waves me on inside.

I smile at Murphy as I pass through the metal detector, then head into the cafeteria, looking for A.T. or Taras. I catch a faint odor of puke as I go in the door, and I'm afraid that I'm going to have to go outside again. But I swallow a couple of times and get ahold of myself. I don't see either of the brothers, but I do catch sight of Sallie.

"They're up in the ballroom," she says in response to my question. "A.T. is mad as hell. Apparently one of the contestants has been hurt somehow, and the cops are suspending the pageant so they can question everybody. A.T. has got to get the ticket holders out, and he doesn't want to return any money." She looks me in the eye. "Do you know anything about this?"

"Not really," I answer truthfully. "I saw a girl taken away from the hotel in an ambulance, but I couldn't see who it was. I came here to see if I could find out more."

"Well, I'd stay away from A.T. and Taras right now if I were you."

That's probably good advice, but I catch the barf smell again and realize that I have to vacate before I make my own contribution. I decide to head upstairs and see if I can find Danny. If he's still talking to me, that is.

The escalator is full of people coming down. Snippets of conversation tell me that A.T. has shut things down for the day. He hasn't returned any money, but those who paid for a ticket today will get in for free tomorrow. If the pageant is even on tomorrow.

"Natalie." It's Taras, coming down on the escalator as I go up. "A.T. wants all the contestants in the ballroom." He passes me, prolly going to tell the rest of the girls in the cafeteria.

I have to wait outside the ballroom until the crowd coming out thins. Going inside, I spot A.T. up on the stage talking to Danny and Kidd below. As I approach, Danny breaks away from the convo and comes toward me.

Shooters!

Noticing me, he makes a face and alters course to avoid me. Fine, be that way. I'll talk to Kidd.

Danny leaves the ballroom, apparently on an errand for A.T. In turn, A.T. leaves Kidd and goes back on stage. I catch the detective's eye with a wave, and he waits for me to come over.

"Wassup?" he says when I get in earshot.

"That's what I was gonna ask you. Have you heard anything about the girl who was hurt?"

"Not much. They took her to University Hospital. If A.T. has gotten a report on her condition, he's not telling me."

"What about the pageant? Is it off?"

"For now it is. The cops want to question the contestants. The poop is that what happened to the girl may not have been an accident."

"What, they think somebody hurt her on purpose?"

Kidd just shrugs. Then he says, "You know, we really could use you back on the team."

Not you too, Kidd! "I get that. But I can't as long as the pageant is on. I signed a contract."

Kidd sighs. "In that case, I hope you win." Finally somebody's on my side!

Speakers boom as A.T. taps on the mic. "Any contestants in the room, stay. I've sent Taras to fetch the rest of you, then I'll have some announcements."

I chill for five minutes as the remaining girls arrive. Taras closes the doors, then joins his brother on stage. Looking around, I see that some of the contestants are not here. Angel, for one, Gracie, for another.

A.T. taps on the mic again. When he's got everybody's attention, he begins. "You've all probably heard what happened. We think the girl who's hurt might have been Grace Pratt, *Miss Hot Bod*. The cops aren't saying much, but they think somebody did something to her, and they want to question all of us. They'll be here in a little while to get started. Unfortunately, there will be no talent competition tomorrow, because all the interviews won't be completed today. Since we've only got this venue till Saturday, we'll drop the talent show and go straight to the party on Friday with the finale on Saturday. That is, if the cops will even let us start up again at all." The bitterness in his tone is apparent at that last remark.

Shit. I was expecting to kick ass in pole dancing.

"One other thing. Apparently, we had a few cases of food poisoning at lunch. Nothing serious. We hope that everyone affected will be back on their game by Friday. Any questions?"

I raise my hand.

"Nattie?"

"How is Gracie?"

"They're not even saying if it's her. She's at University Hospital. She's not allowed visitors."

That takes care of my next question.

A.T. recognizes another hand. "Taisha?"

"Will we get any compensation if you have to cancel the pageant?"

"No." A.T. says bluntly. "The contract you signed doesn't promise you anything unless you win."

"You could use some of that million to help us out if nobody wins."

"Do I look like I've got a long, white beard and I'm wearing a red and white suit? Anybody else?" Apparently nobody wants to draw fire from A.T. "Good," he continues. "Just hang tight till the cops show up. They'll take it from there."

Almost on cue, the back doors open and the cops come in. A half dozen unis—Lester is one—an older guy in plainclothes and a thirtysomething, pretty blonde woman who I know, Detective Julia Sykes. We met during the sniper investigation on State campus, and our paths have crossed a couple times since, most recently during the Ellis affair. She proceeds right up on stage like she owns the place, drawing a dirty look from A.T. The older detective follows. She and A.T. exchange a few words we can't hear, then he leaves the stage to join us rabble on the floor. Sykes takes the mic.

"Okay, everybody, listen up. My name is Detective Sykes, and this is my partner, Detective O'Hoolihan." She indicates the older dude. "We'll be setting up some interview stations downstairs, and we'll call you down in pairs to answer some routine questions. Yes?" She acknowledges my raised hand.

"What if we don't know anything about it?"

"Then you'll be done really quickly. Actually, we hope to have all of this done with by lunchtime tomorrow." She glances at a notebook in her hand. "We ask that you do not talk among yourselves until we call you. The uniformed officers are here to be sure you do not."

Shooters!

"Oh, give me a break!" Sallie says. "What the fuck are we supposed to do while we're waiting?"

"Think about anything you may know about Ms. Pratt," replies Sykes. "We've confirmed it was she who's been injured. Anything else? Good. Please find a seat, and make sure there's at least one empty seat between you and your neighbor." She consults the notebook again. "We'll take the Tymko brothers first, then Natalie McMasters and Mihara Aiko. We'll call the rest of you when it's your turn."

Hands in the audience are still waving, but Sykes and O'Hoolihan leave the stage and exit through the rear doors. The unis start ushering girls to seats who don't go on their own, then stand around like hall monitors in high school to enforce the no talking rule.

In about fifteen minutes, Lester touches her left ear, then says, "Okay, will Natalie McMasters and Mihara Aiko follow me downstairs, please?"

I get up and so does Miko, across the room. She's walking with a slight limp, but it doesn't look like I did her any permanent damage.

I'll bet I have the honor to be first because Sykes knows me. Downstairs, Lester stops at the *Forrest Conference Room* and opens the door. Sykes is waiting inside, sitting at the end of a long conference table. There's a pitcher of ice water in front of her and a stack of small red Solo cups to one side. As I approach, she fills one and pushes it in front of the chair she wants me to take. As I sit, she says, "Natalie. We've got to stop meeting like this."

"You're right. Let's make this quick. I don't know anything about what happened to Gracie."

She frowns and narrows her eyes. "Why did you refuse to tell the EMT on site your name when she asked you?"

"Because she wouldn't tell me who it was going in the ambulance. And I didn't think she needed to know."

Sykes gives me a half-smile. "Same old Natalie. Always got to be in charge."

"I guess we've both got the same prob."

"Yes, but unlike you, being in charge is my job. Why were you outside the hotel?"

"Duh! Because I have a room there."

The eyes narrow again. "You need to drop the attitude."

"Look. You can prolly tell I'm expecting…"

163

"Congratulations."

"I was feeling shitty after lunch and wanted to go to my room to lie down. I ran into that shit storm at the hotel. When I saw them bringing her out, I thought it was Gracie. We've sorta made a connection. I tried to confirm it with the EMT and she went all HIPAA on me. So I left her on read."

"Why didn't you go to your room?"

I sigh audibly. "Because I wanted to find out if my friend was hurt. I thought somebody here might know. Can you tell me what happened to her?"

"C'mon. You should know I can't do that."

"Well, can you tell me how she's doing?"

"Sorry, no can do that either."

"Now who's got the attitude?"

She shakes her head. "OK. We'll chalk it up to hormones. We're done. You can go to your room if you want. In fact, we'd prefer that you do. We'll call you if we have any more questions."

I get up and head for the door.

The food smells hit again when I get outside. My cheeks bulge as lunch comes up, and I dash for the ladies room. I'm in there for nearly half an hour—every time I think I'm done and try to leave, I get started again.

Finally, I'm able to make it to the sink and rinse out my mouth with cold water. It helps. When I come out into the hall, I run right into Danny, who's heading back upstairs. I wonder if Sykes interviewed him right after me. He sees me and starts to walk away, then he does a double take and comes over. "Nattie! What's wrong?"

"I'm preggers. And I'm sick. I don't think I can make it to the hotel, and I need someplace to lie down."

His face is a mask of concern. "I'm taking you home."

"No. It's against the rules. I'll get kicked out of the pageant if A.T. finds out. I need someplace here. Where it doesn't smell like food."

He takes my elbow and leads me to a padded bench against the wall. "Sit here and let me see what I can do." He pats my head and goes off.

As I watch him walk away, my thoughts swirl like a whirlpool. WTF am I doing? Why did I enter a stupid beauty pageant run by a couple of dipshit misogynists? So I can run around naked on a stage, my preggo belly for all the world to see? To win a million bucks? Right. Even I know that the winner will be the one who gives A.T. and his bro the best sex. All the people I love are p.o.'d at me, but I'm doing it anyway. What the fuck is wrong with me?

Danny returns in a few minutes. "C'mon. I've got my truck out back. I'll give you a ride to the hotel and get you to your room so you won't get in trouble with A.T."

I start to cry. He hates that I'm doing what I'm doing, and still he tries to take care of me. What is that but love?

He helps me to the rear of the convention center where the loading dock is and puts me in his pickup. He drives to the back of the hotel, which is on a street parallel to the pedestrian mall. He double parks and uses my room keycard to get us in the rear door. We ride the elevator up to my room. Outside the door, I take his wrist and look into his blue eyes.

"I've got it from here, babe. Thanks."

I give him a big hug. I don't kiss him cause I taste like shit.

He waits until I get the door open, then heads for the elevator.

Inside the room, the drapes are pulled. The only light is the little bit that comes through the cracks. I stumble toward my bed and pull the cover down. I crawl in and I swear I'm out before my head hits the pillow.

Chapter 31

LeBrowne waves a hand and a banger appears seemingly from nowhere.

"Take this honkey to the crib, Rashaad, and get him a place to stay. Tell the niggas he be my guest."

The banger's eyes widen at that last, but he takes Irwin's elbow and attempts to lead him off. Irwin jerks his arm away and snarls, "Don't touch me, dude!"

Anger flashes in Rashaad's eyes, but he just says, "Come on den," and walks off. Irwin follows him to the edge of the park, where a monochromatic battleship grey Cadillac Escalade sits at the curb. Irwin starts to get in the back, but Rashaad says, "I ain't your chauffer, honkey. You ride up front."

"Whatever," Irwin replies, and takes the shotgun seat.

They drive to the southeast side of town. The buildings change from multistory concrete and brick to small single family dwellings, with fenced-in front yards that are more bare dirt than grass. Many have bars on the windows. Few folks are on the streets—the atmosphere is that of a town under siege. Rashaad pulls up in front of a square three-story dark red brick building, obviously a holdover from another age. The lower windows are unbarred and a neon sign showing Colt 45 in blue inside a yellow horseshoe hangs in one of them. Several twentysomething African-American dudes occupy sofas on a covered front porch.

"C'mon, ofay," Rasheed says, opening the door and getting out of the car. Irwin stares at the guys on the porch, suddenly thinking that coming here may not have been the best idea.

Coming around to the passenger side of the Caddy, Rasheed barks, "Whatchew waitin' on, dude? If I have to open the door fo' your ass, I'm gonna kick it all over the sidewalk!"

Irwin nervously opens the door and gets out. The bangers on the porch get a load of him and erupt in gales of laughter. He's still wearing the black halter top with red roses, the leopard skin sarong and the white sandals he bought in New York, but all are worse for wear. The beauty shop curls have come out of his hair and his homemade make-up job has made his face a caricature.

"Yo!" says Rasheed. "LeBrowne says this dude's his guest."

The boys quiet down some, but a few snickers follow Irwin inside.

If I just had my gun…

A corridor on the first floor contains rooms opening on both sides and a flight of stairs going up. The first right opens into a large room set up as a bar, with half a dozen or more bangers inside. Seeing them, Irwin hesitates, and Rasheed says "Upstairs, honkey." As they reach the second floor, Rasheed prods, "Keep on goin'", and Irwin proceeds to the third floor where there's another hallway. Rasheed pushes in front of Irwin and leads him to a room in the back. He opens the door into a dreary

bedroom that stinks of mold. Diffuse light streams through a dirty window above the backyard. It's decorated with peeling wallpaper in a flowered pattern popular a century ago and the only furnishing is a double bed with a stained, bare mattress.

"If'n I was you, I wouldn't show my face outta this room while you're here," says Rasheed.

"Hey man, I'm gonna need a shitter…"

"Down the hall. Remember what I said." Rasheed gives Irwin a shove inside and shuts the door behind him.

Irwin looks around the bleak little room as his heart sinks. It feels like a prison. Sure, he could just go downstairs and out into the street, but the cops are hunting him and will throw him in jail if they catch him, if they don't kill him first.

If I only had my gun! Then I would show everybody not to fuck with me…

He throws himself down on the filthy mattress and tries to get some sleep.

Irwin is jolted awake by loud voices.

"…I tol' you, m'nigga. Get a load of that shit!"

Irwin rolls over and his chest contracts as he finds himself surrounded by four large gangstas, pointing at him and laughing wildly.

"Hey sweetcheeks, what're you? A bizzle or a dude?"

"He ain't no dude, bro, he's a ho."

"No homey, he got him a package."

"Mebbe we oughta take off that fancy skirt he's wearin' and see what he's got."

One of the guys holds Irwin's shoulders while another reaches for his sarong. Irwin struggles, but it's no good. The gangsta pulls it down, revealing a dirty pair of tighty whities underneath.

"Toldjah! He got him a D in there, man."

Shooters!

"That ain't no D, it's too small. Here' I'll show ya!"

Rough hands grab Irwin's undershorts, stripping them off. Gales of laughter rise as his shriveled penis and missing testicles are exposed.

"See! That's no D, it's a wart or suthin'. He is a ho! Ima get me a piece of that!"

The banger grabs Irwin's ankles and pulls him to the end of the bed with ass hanging off the mattress.

"Here, grab its ankles!"

Irwin cries out as his legs are spread apart so wide that he feels like he's being ripped apart, then they're pulled toward his head, so his butt is angled up, exposing his asshole.

"No!"

The gangsta standing at the end of the bed drops his pants, revealing a rampant erection. He begins forcing himself inside.

"Nooooooo!"

The pain is like nothing Irwin's ever felt before, like a hot iron stabbing into his vitals.

The gangsta begins thrusting. Irwin's screams mingle with the cruel laughter of the rapists.

"What the fuck!" A new voice, coming from the doorway.

A gunshot explodes, deafening everyone in the room. Irwin is splattered with bone, flesh and blood as the rapist's head dissolves into a mist. His legs released, he curls into a fetal position.

"Did I not tell you this dude was our guest? I oughtta do every fuckin' one of y'all!"

LeBrowne fills the doorway, a huge chrome revolver in his hand randomly sweeping the crowd. The bangers are frozen in place, they can't vacate the room without running into the mouth of the gun. The muzzle settles on another gangsta.

"Run, motherfucka." LeBrowne orders in an even tone. The terrifying sound of metal on metal resonates through the room as he cocks the hammer.

The banger's eyes are like dinner plates. He wheels and dashes toward the window. Glass shatters as he throws himself through it. The ground is three floors below.

Better a chance at life than sure death.

LeBrowne steps aside, waving his gun toward the doorway.

"Get the fuck outta here!"

The bangers are only too happy to comply.

He gazes down at Irwin moaning on the bed as his blood trickles down his leg and onto the mattress.

"You still owe me one large for this room tonight, dude," LeBrowne says, then leaves.

Chapter 32

CRASH! Martin's tray table overturns as he leaps up from his seat and rushes over, slamming the bedroom door shut as Eduardo is frozen, paralyzed with horror. Martin takes him by the shoulders and marches him back to his chair, pushing him down into it. The front of Eduardo's jeans is soaking wet—he's peed himself!

The young boy plaintively looks up at Martin with wide, tear-filled eyes. "What the fuck, dude?"

"It isn't what it looks like, man."

"You killed them…"

"No," he says. "I killed Máma. She killed Pápa. She cut his head off."

"Why?"

"He beat us, dude. All the time. He'd get wasted and beat the fuck out of us. She couldn't take anymore, so she killed him with a kitchen knife and cut his head off. I heard him screaming. She was taking his head off when I opened the door. She came for me with the knife, saying she was going to send all of us to be with Jesus. I got it away from her and stabbed her with it. I didn't know what else to do! I put her in bed with him and I went over to your place."

Eduardo is silent, still looking at Martin, processing the story. The room behind him is a blur. Finally he says, "Why didn't you call nine-one-one? Why didn't you tell me what was wrong when you got to my house?"

"I didn't want the cops to know. They'd lock me up, put me back in the group home. I wouldn't be able to do what I have to do tomorrow. If they find out afterwards, it won't matter anymore." He looks Eduardo right in the eyes, boring inside him with his dark brown eyes. "Are you still with me, dude? We're still gonna take those *maricons* out tomorrow, right?"

"I don't know, Martin…"

"Fuck, man, you promised!"

"I don't know…"

Martin grabs Eduardo under the armpits, hauls him bodily out of the chair and lifts him up so they're face-to-face. "Don't you dare wimp out on me now! Don't you still want to get even with Schultz and Davies for making a fool out of you in front of the entire school and with Drayton for kicking you out? Where's your *cojones*, dude?"

"I…I…"

Martin throws Eduardo back into the chair with such force that he bites his tongue. He's screaming now, spittle flying from his mouth. "Fine! Fine! Run out on me when I fucking need you! You said you were a proud Mexican man. You said you'd rather die or go to prison than to let those *maricons* get away with what they did to you. Was that just bullshit? Are you gonna run away at the sight of a little blood? What the fuck you think you're gonna see tomorrow, dude?"

Eduardo's thoughts are whirling in his head like a bird in a sandstorm. He wants to say no, it's all a terrible idea, but he promised. He remembers that he promised. And a real man always keeps his…

"…promises, dude!" Martin spits. "I can't do this without you! Then Schultz, and Davies, and Drayton, they're just gonna do it again, man. They're going to do it again to some other *mejicano*. And they're gonna laugh, dude. They're gonna laugh, and laugh, and laugh, knowing they got the best of you, *ese*. And you're gonna just let 'em?"

"No," mutters Eduardo.

"What did you say?"

"No!" he says louder.

"Whatchoo gonna do about it?"

"I'm gonna kill those *maricons!*" Eduardo shouts.

His world is a riot of color, and the red is the brightest of all.

Chapter 33

Sometime later, I come to. Soft moans are coming from across the room. Turning my head, I see a dark mass on Miko's bed near the window. Looking more closely, forms begin to separate from the blackness. There's one, two, three... My first impulse is to get up and out of here, but shit, I'm still sick! I reach over and snap the light on.

Taras, totally nude, has his arms spread out on top of the headboard, his head thrown back and his mouth open. Miko lies between his splayed legs, holding his erection in her hand, her head bobbing up and down. Behind her on his knees is A.T., methodically pumping in and out. The action stops when the lights come on—they all turn, staring at me in surprise.

Taras just grins at me.

"Hi, Natalie," says A.T. "Now that you're awake, wanna make it a foursome?"

Taras reaches down and grabs Miko's head, pushing it toward his crotch, encouraging her to continue. She resumes servicing him, but I can tell she's not thrilled about it.

I start to tell A.T. I'll pass, but then I think about it. Do you want that mil or not, Nattie? Let's keep our options open. "Not right now, boys," I say. "I came back here because I'm not feeling good and I wanted to lie down. I am preggers, you know."

Taras closes his eyes and sucks in a breath as Miko does something creative with her tongue. Opening them again, he says, "Well, don't let us stop you."

He lays his head back and closes his eyes once more, a shit-eating grin on his face. A.T. puts his hands on Miko's hips and starts stroking again.

I turn my eyes away from the spectacle, looking at the dresser across from the bed where Frankie, Miko's stupid teddy bear sits like a spectator at the porno show. I so want out of here, but OTOH, I really am sick. I get out of bed and grab some clean underwear from my suitcase, then go into the john for a quick shower to rinse the puke off. After finishing, I put on the clean clothes and take the dirty ones back into the bedroom, getting a plastic laundry bag from the closet to hide the smell. The threesome is still going strong—now all three of them are upright, with her sandwiched between the two guys. I can't hardly tell who's got what going where. Disgusted, I turn down the covers on my bed to expose the pillows, and lie on my face on top of the comforter, trying to ignore the squeaking and moaning from across the room. .

I must be way sick, because I pass out again almost immediately. Later, I wake up w a hand on my ass.

Of course it's A.T. "I'm outta here now, Natalie," he says, "but I'm gonna hold you to that foursome."

I so want to kick that fucking smirk off his face!

"Maybe tomorrow." Not! "See you later."

"Later," he smiles.

After he's gone, I look around for Taras, but he's already gone. I turn to Miko, aware we still have unfinished business.

"You really hurt me this morning," she says with a pouty face.

"You totally deserved it. You were acting way ick."

"I know. I'm sorry."

"Are you pressed about something?"

"What do you think? You think I'm doing those assholes because I want to?"

I know the answer, but I ask anyway. "Then why are you?"

"That's a dumbshit question. I want that mil. If you want a shot at it, you'll do them too. We'll have to have that foursome."

I shudder at the thought.

She gets out of bed and opens the drapes to let in the evening light from the mall outside. I check out her naked bod as she faces me. She's a totally unlikely candidate for a beauty pageant. Her skinny torso, small, pointy tits and muscular abs make her appear almost boyish. But a glance at her crotch confirms she's totally female. She's staring at me, too. I'm still in my undies, and I can see a gleam in her eyes. As she takes a step toward me, I say. "Serious. I am way sick."

She stops, looks at me, then seems to make a decision. "Just a sec," she says. She goes into the bathroom, returning a moment later. "Here," she says, her palm extended in front of me. There's a small, yellow, lozenge-shaped pill in the center of it.

"What's this?"

"Zofran. It'll help with the nausea."

"I don't know. I'm pregnant."

"It won't hurt your baby. Take it. You'll feel better."

Shooters!

I take the pill from her hand and go into the bathroom for a glass of water to swallow it with. A couple of paper-wrapped glasses are sitting on the counter next to the sink. I start to reach for one, and notice Miko's makeup bag. It's open. There's a couple of panels on top that hide the contents in main compartment. There's a seam down the center—obviously, the panels flip up to give access to the inside. I open them.

Holy shit! Girl's got her a whole fucking drugstore in here. There must be a dozen bottles of pills and liquids, as well as some pump sprays and injectables. There's an amber bottle with a blue top half full of liquid. It's labeled Ipecacuanha, and there's a small squeeze bottle that looks like it contains the same thing. I find the Zofran bottle and read the label—Take one tablet as needed for nausea and vomiting. OK, so she isn't trying to poison me. I close up the case, then unwrap the glass, fill it hallway and take the Zofran. I rinse it and turn it upside down on the counter.

Something inside my head is knocking, trying to get into the light.

The label on the bottle says *Ipecacuanha*.

I'm a little girl, maybe four or five. I've gotten hold of the bottle of Flintstones gummy vitamins, which I dearly love, and am sitting in the middle of the kitchen floor, happily chowing down. Daddy walks in, takes one look and hollers to Mom, "Oh my God. Judy! Get the ipecac!"

Daddy snatches me up in his arms and Mom runs in with a brown bottle. She pinches my nose and forces a couple of tablespoons of the vile-tasting liquid down my throat. Five minutes later, I'm throwing up everything I ever ate in my life.

Ipecacuanha. Ipecac!

I open the medicine case again, get the bottle and take it out into the bedroom.

Miko, still nude, is sitting on the side of my bed. I show her the bottle, and she goes white. "I know what you did in the cafeteria at lunchtime," I tell her.

"You don't understand," she says.

"Oh, I get it just fine, Miko. You decided to take out some of your competition. What'd you do? Put some ipecac in that little squeeze bottle and hide it in your hand, squirt some in a couple girls' iced tea glasses, and wait for the fun to begin? In a crowded room like that, full of food smells, all you had to do was get a couple of people puking and let nature take its course. You got me, damn you."

"Natalie. I really need to win this pageant."

"Sure you do," I say sarcastically. "You totally need that million bucks. What've you got, a sick mother with medical bills spiraling out of control? Child support? A mad desire for a 'vette? Or something else?"

Suddenly it hits me. The aldactone.

"You're trans," I tell her.

She looks at the floor, then raises her head again and looks me right in the eyes.

I stare at the nude woman on the bed. Sure, she's somewhat wiry with small titties and her features are sharp and mannish to a certain extent, but she's got tits and a pussy. I see no scars anywhere.

"You must've had a great surgeon," I say.

"You're right. I realized that I was in the wrong body when I was in high school. Luckily, my parents were open-minded, so I was able to start my transition before puberty was well-advanced. I did hormone treatments until I graduated, then took a year off before college to have my surgery. I've been living as a woman ever since."

"But why did you enter a beauty pageant? Especially this pageant?" Again, the answer hits me before she speaks. "You've been trying to get A.T. to fuck you!"

"Adam Tymko is one of the most hateful transphobes in the world," she says. "Unfortunately, he's also a major influencer. You can't imagine the number of men and boys that he's poisoned against the trans community with that vile podcast of his. The express purpose of this pageant is to celebrate what he calls real women and stigmatize trans women. I've been a member of a group in San Francisco that supports transgenders for a number of years, and we decided it would be a great public relations coup if I could enter the pageant and win it. The fact that I've had sex repeatedly with A.T. and Taras is a bonus, too. How can those transphobes claim that we're not real women now?"

I can just imagine the media shitstorm if Miko were to win the pageant, then come out as trans. A.T.'s street cred would be in the toilet. Plus, his followers would probably desert him in droves if it they found out he had sex with a trans woman.

I've always been ambivalent about trans people, especially the women. Being bi myself and in a non-traditional relationship, I've experienced my share of the hate that LGBT people have to put up with. Eduardo was essentially not allowed to live in the same house with the rest of the fam for several years because of a bigoted child services agent. And one of the bravest persons I ever knew was a trans guy who hadn't transitioned yet, and died saving Danny's life from a crazy woman. But I can't help feeling

Shooters!

that there's something basically cringy about trans people. All of the hormones and surgery in the world will never turn a man into a woman, or a woman into a man. And I don't get how believing that you're something you're not can ever have a good outcome. I try my best not to let what I believe affect how I treat them, but I can't seem to help the way I feel.

But then there's what Miko has actually done.

"The fact remains that you poisoned people to give yourself a leg up in the pageant," I say.

She defends herself. "I didn't really hurt anybody."

"That's totally not your fault. You can't be sure what's going to happen when you slip somebody something like ipecac. People can have allergies, or medical conditions you don't know about."

She's looking at me with a pleading gaze. "So what are you going to do?"

"I don't see any way around telling A.T. about it. Maybe even the cops. The fact you're trans is a different story. It's none of my business— that's totally between you and A.T."

"There's no way I can talk you out of telling A.T. about the ipecac?"

"I don't think so."

"What if I dropped out of the pageant?"

I have to think about that. True, Miko committed a crime when she gave people the ipecac, essentially a poison. But is it my responsibility to go to the law about that?

"I guess that would be OK." I tell her. "But don't tell A.T. you're quitting. You know he'll try to talk you out of it. Just go, and don't come back."

Now tears are welling up and running down her cheeks. "It would be a really great thing if I won," she says. "I'd announce to the world that I'm trans just when A.T. gives me the mil. Imagine the effect of that. And imagine how much good I could do for the trans community if I had a million bucks to spend."

What I can imagine is A.T. strangling her on live TV, but I don't say it.

"None of that justifies giving people poison, Miko. You totally could have killed somebody."

"You're right." She raises an eyebrow. "You won't tell the cops?"

"Not if you're gone by tomorrow."

"You've got a deal."

It's getting near dinnertime, but I totally don't feel like eating. The pageant is suspended, until tomorrow morning, at least, which means no talent competition. That totally suits me—I couldn't imagine trying to pole dance, the way I feel right now. I'm also not thrilled with the idea of spending the night in this room with Miko. I think I've got her beat down, but I'm not sure what she might do at three in the morning with me asleep in the bed next to her.

Even though it's against the rules, I decide to go home and sleep in my own bed. I can get up early and be back here before the sun comes up. The only one who could tell on me is Miko, but she's got a secret I can tell, too.

Chapter 34

It's 6:00 a.m. when I get to the hotel Thursday morning. Miko is packing her shit when I come in. We don't say anything to each other.

I get a text from A.T. saying there's a meeting in the ballroom at 1:00. I still don't feel great, but after Miko leaves, I decide to chance a light breakfast and maybe catch a few more zzz's this morning after Miko's gone.

It's noon when I wake up. I dig a black Hellwitch t-shirt and a pair of cut-offs out of my suitcase and put them on. The shirt is a size too small and leaves part of my baby bump showing. That ought to get the brothers hot.

I walk over to the convention center. Murph waves me through the metal detector as I come in. Winking at me, he says, "It's my half-day. I'm just going off shift. I'll be havin' a drink at the Liberty later if you want to come and join me."

Dude must be eighty. I smile at him and pat my belly, saying "Thanks, but I'll pass. I'm off the booze for a while, you know."

"See ya in the mornin', then."

When I get to the ballroom, it looks like everybody but Miko and Gracie is there. The contestants are standing around in groups, talking quietly. The atmosphere is low key, like they're all waiting for the axe to fall. Danny and Kidd are standing unobtrusively in opposite corners near the stage.

A.T. and Taras come out from behind the curtains on stage. A.T. taps on the mic for attention. "Everybody grab a seat." When we've all done so, he continues, "I've got a few updates for you. First, the news about Grace Pratt is not good. She is in the ICU at University Hospital in critical condition. No visitors but immediate family. Her parents are flying in tonight." He allows a second or two for that to sink in, then taps the mic again. "Next thing. The pageant is back on. That means the big party starts tomorrow morning at ten. I want all of you here by nine. We've got top social media influencers, some A-list actors and a few forward-thinking politicians attending. We'll be broadcasting live to 180 countries and both local and national U.S media personnel will be in attendance, including Roderigo Hernandez from New York City, who has the biggest entertainment news show in the world. Even if you don't win, and just one of you will, this is your big chance to get your face and your name out there. So dress your sexiest and come prepared."

He pauses again while a buzz among the girls rises. A tingle grows in my belly as I consider the implications. M.B. insinuated that I ain't pulling my weight. Well here's a chance for me to meet important people that might help me do that. And Roderigo Hernandez is a friend of mine. Wait till the girls see me hanging with him!

A.T. continues, "So since we had an unfortunate break in our schedule, in order to revive interest in the pageant, I've decided to bring the million dollars in a day early. It will be up here, on stage, in cash, for all to see while the party is going on."

The buzz starts again, even louder this time. Danny immediately heads for the door, pulling his cell phone from his pocket as he goes.

***

"Is he nuts?" Amos Murdoch says after receiving Danny's call. "I shore hope the armored car people are going to provide security for that cash while it's on site, but I don't think we can count on it. You and Kidd need to be prepared to take that job on if the armored car guards won't. As a matter of fact, I'm comin' down there myself in the mornin'. I'll take charge of supervisin' everyone while you two are watchin' that money. And I'll find out from A.T. what his plans are for it later that night before he gives it away the next morning."

***

On the plaza in front of the convention center, Danny hangs up his call to Amos and prepares to go back inside. Scanning the area around him as a good Marine always does, he notices that the protestors and the cops are gone. The only people nearby are a couple of black guys— they look like gang bangers. One is on his cell phone. He'll have to mention to Nattie that she should go back to the hotel in a group with some of the other girls, or he'll have to accompany her himself.

Going upstairs and through the main doors, he nods to Ned, Murph's relief, at the metal detector, which squeals as Danny walks through. It's a free test of the equipment, Danny thinks. A 1911 better make it do that every time.

Coming to the top of the escalator, he sees a black girl in a skin-tight white dress with a slit in the chest revealing nearly all of her boobs but the nipples. Any man's eyes would be riveted to her chest, just waiting for a wardrobe malfunction. She's wearing a red sash—she's *Miss Fresno*. Danny's still madly in love with Nattie, even given her recent outrageous behavior, nevertheless he's been walking around with a hard on most of the time, surrounded by all of these hot babes. *Miss Fresno* slips a cell phone into a pouch around her waist, then looks up at Danny as he approaches. Her eyes widen in surprise, then she favors him with a ravishing smile.

The little man downstairs wakes up and salutes.

***

A couple of miles to the south, LeBrowne Ellis hangs up his phone, and looks around at the crowd of his boys surrounding him.

"It's on, homies," he says.

Chapter 35

It's 8:55 a.m. when Martin and Eduardo pull into the parking lot in front of Forrest Middle School.

"There it is, dude," says Martin. "Are you ready to go in there and get your revenge on those hos that dissed you?"

Eduardo is quivering like a setter on point. He felt like all the bedamned when Martin woke him a couple hours ago, with a headache and muscle aches. It was all he could do not to barf. Then, despite his protests, Martin fed him some strong black coffee. Fifteen minutes later, Eduardo felt like he could conquer the world. His vision was a little blurry, but the rest of his senses seemed sharper. His skin burned like he'd been in the sun too long and it was hard to sit still. Martin took care of that by bringing him to the car to ready the guns—they laid the ARs on the back seat with a mag in place, and each took a .45 and jammed it in their waistband. Martin gave Eduardo a vest that was too big, but it had ample pockets for AR mags. Spares for the pistol he could carry in his jeans.

"OK Ibáñez, here's the plan," Martin says. "The front door will be locked, so we'll have to shoot out the glass to get inside. Once we do, I'll take out the receptionist and anyone else behind the front desk while you shoot out the glass in the inner doors. When we go in, I'll go right and you go left. We'll end up in McCurdy's room, taking out anyone we meet in the halls. Then we'll go to the cafeteria. We'll have easy pickin's there. If we find Shultz or Davies, they're yours. If we don't, we'll just have to hunt them down." The older boy pauses, then, "You ready for this?"

Eduardo feels like he has to pee. He nods.

"Tell me, man! You ready for this? Say it!"

"Hell, yes," says Eduardo. "I'm ready for this!"

***

A white Chevy Silverado pick-up pulls into the parking lot behind the convention center. Parking here is restricted to essential personnel and the handicapped, so Amos Murdoch qualifies. He parks in the space marked with a stylized wheelchair next to A.T.'s cobalt blue Bentley. After killing the engine and setting the parking brake, he pushes a button on his wheelchair, and both doors on the driver's side swing upwards as a unit. A push on a second button causes the floor upon which the wheelchair rests to pivot 90 degrees and extend outside before lowering Amos and his chair to the ground. Once he's down, the old Marine releases the brake on his chair and works the joystick to drive away from the truck before raising the elevator again and tucking it inside, and lowering and locking the doors. He drives the chair around the building onto the ramp leading up to the front doors. He hits the button that opens the doors to the building and rolls inside to where Murph mans the metal detector. His chair won 't fit through, so he drives to the open area beside it to bypass it. He hikes his jacket back exposing the .45 on his hip for Murph to see.

"Wish they'd let me have one of those too," says Murph.

"Well, I wouldn't mind," Amos replies.

"Now you tell me," Murph responds with a grimace.

Amos rolls down the hall, past the cafeteria, the escalators and the elevator, turns the corner and goes down to the Media Center, where the red light is on. He squints through the narrow window and sees A.T. inside, wearing his headphones and mic, arms spread wide as he addresses his invisible audience. The old detective looks at the red light once more, back at A.T., then raps sharply on the glass. A.T. doesn't seem to notice.

"Screw this," Amos says under his breath. He opens the door and rolls inside.

"… tune in on your fave Tymkoverse channel at 10 a.m. EDT and check out the most epic party ever! All the sexy ladies will be there dressed their sexiest, and Roderigo, whom I'm going to ask to be my co-host, will also be there." He notices Amos, and motions for him to close the door and come in while he rattles off the list of A-list actors, major sports figures and social media influencers who have promised to attend.

"We've even got an American Idol winner to sing for us!' He consults the *Grande Complication.* "I've got to sign off now, guys, so I can get upstairs to meet my guests. See you soon!" He flips a switch, removes his headphones and glares at Amos. "Didn't you see the red light? It means…"

Amos cuts him off. "I know what it means. But it's time to get this show on the road. If you'll help me move some of these chairs to make a place for myself in front of the monitors…"

"Do it yourself, old man. I've got to get upstairs to my guests." A.T. storms out.

Amos sighs, then pulls out his cell to get in touch with Danny or Kidd.

***

Shooters!

A gray Cadillac Escalade pulls up behind Amos's pickup. LeBrowne and Irwin are in the back seat. LeBrowne hands a black duffle bag to Irwin.

"Here's yo' piece, m'man."

Irwin takes the bag and opens the zipper to reveal the ugly black rifle inside.

"Hey! There's no mag!"

"Watchoo think I'm stupid enough to give you a loaded gun you can use on me? You'll find a vest with eight mags in a sack in the litter basket around front. You know how to load it, right?"

"Just put the mag in with the bullets facing front."

"Dass right." LeBrowne takes Irwin's hand and puts it on the AR's charging handle. "Den just pull this back, let it go and you're ready to rock and roll. And one more thing." He turns the rifle so the receiver is facing up and points to the selector lever. "Dis baby is full auto. The lever has three settings—safe, fire and auto. Be careful with auto. You'll empty your mag in about two seconds."

If Irwin had balls he'd have a hard-on. Full auto! Oh, man!

"When the mag's empty, the bolt will stay back and leave the action open." LeBrowne fingers a little tab on the side of the rifle. "Pop in another mag, push this to close the action and you're ready to go again. Got it?"

Irwin nods. His hands are itching to get ahold of that gun.

LeBrowne gives Irwin the bag. "Now go do what you gotta do," he says.

***

At 9:00 a.m. on Friday, walking up to the convention center, I'm wearing a short jacket over a one-piece, backless body suit that has two pieces of fabric covering just my nipples, with straps descending to a thong below. My baby belly is on full display. As much as I hate 'em, I've got a pair of *faux* Tom Ford stilettos dangling from my right hand. I'll put those on, along with my red *Miss Capital City* sash, in the ladies' room on the second floor just before I go into the ballroom. I'll leave the jacket on the bench in the hall so I can make my entrance to the ballroom in style.

There are no protestors in front of the convention center this morning, but four cops are still here, standing in a group like they're waiting for something. Danny and Kidd are with them. Three people carrying TV

185

cameras are nearby, each one accompanied by a reporter holding a mic. One team is getting some shots of the convention center, and another of the police and Danny and Kidd. The third is simply waiting for the action to commence. A sparse crowd of about a dozen people is also there, probably fans looking to get a glimpse or pix of the celebs who'll be arriving for the party.

It looks like Danny spots me as I'm walking up, and he looks away. So we're back to that, are we? Fine. We'll do this any way he wants.

The last cameraman points his camera in my direction and brief frisson of nerves goes up my back. Then I realize they're likely not filming me. I look over my shoulder to see an armored car approaching.

***

A couple of blocks away, at police headquarters, a yellow light on a panel in the communications center winks on. The officer manning the panel flips a switch, touches her headphones, does a double take, then pics up a mic on the desk in front of her.

"All units in the vicinity of Forrest Middle School, respond code three to a possible emergency. Men with guns reported approaching the school."

She picks up a phone to inform the watch commander.

***

Eduardo winces when the receptionist's face dissolves into a red mist as Martin fires three quick rounds. A student at the copier freezes, and Martin takes him down next.

"Ibáñez! The door!"

Eduardo looks through the metal detector at the glass double doors that are blocking their entry to the school proper. He levels his rifle and touches off two rounds. The tempered glass shatters into thousands of fragments. Two students in the corridor inside freeze like jacklighted deer, and Martin mows one down. The other boy scampers down the hall and vanishes around a corner before Eduardo can fire.

Martin steps through the squealing metal detector and then the ruined doors, like an avenging god.

186

Shooters!

"C'mon Ibáñez! Go left!" He strides off down the corridor, turns right where the other student vanished, and a bolt of fire erupts from the muzzle of his rifle.

***

A police cruiser pulls up in front of the school and the two officers take in the shattered glass doors. A burst of rifle fire comes from inside the building.

"Holy shit!" Officer Boone ejaculates. Grabbing the mic from the dash, he presses the button and says. "We've got a code 2000 at Forrest Middle School! Send backup now!"

The comm officer at headquarters picks up her mic and makes an adjustment on her console. "Code 2000 at Forrest Middle School. All available units respond!"

The officers bail out of the car, draw their sidearms and take up positions of cover behind the vehicles.

***

In front of the convention center, Officer Lester touches her shoulder mic and speaks. Her bod abruptly straightens. She says something to the other officers, then steps over and briefly talks to Danny. Then all four officers trot toward me, passing me and continuing to the pedestrian mall.

The armored car and me arrive in front of the steps at the same time. Danny, forced to acknowledge me, holds out a hand like a traffic cop.

"Nattie! Stop there a minute."

The doors of the armored car are opening.

Fuck you, dude. I continue on up the stairs and into the building.

"Good morning, Natalie," Murph says from next to the metal detector.

I'm not carrying any metal, so I just walk on through, returning his greeting. I go down the corridor and ride the escalator to the second floor. When I get there, I turn and see Danny and Kidd coming in the front door. Danny is carrying a large briefcase.

I go straight to the ladies' to take off my jacket and put on my shoes.

Thomas A. Burns, Jr.

***

Students stand at their lockers as Eduardo enters the hall. He scans them, looking for the hated Schultz or Davies. They're not there. The kids stand bug-eyed and disbelieving—it's one thing to be told what to do when you see someone with a gun in school, but a very different thing to carry it out. Eduardo raises his rifle and fires. The ceiling lights wink out one by one and plastic and plaster rain down on the students' heads. They break and run like scared rabbits. A tingle starts in Eduardo's toes at the sight, running up his legs into his belly, then into his chest and face, feeling like liquid fire. He squeezes off a few more rounds just to hear the rifle roar.

He continues on, seeking the mofos who humiliated him.

***

Irwin comes around the building and sees no one in front of the convention center. He spots the litter basket and runs to it, finding a grocery bag inside, the handles knotted together. He leans his rifle against the trash receptacle, pulls out the bag and rips it open, and dons the vest he finds inside. It's heavy with mags and ammo and hangs on his shoulders like Marley's chains. Picking up his rifle, he secures the vest, removes a mag from a pocket and inserts it into the receiver, slaps it into place and pulls the charging handle. He checks the selector level and flips it to Auto, then looks around for somebody to shoot. He sees a group of women approaching, about thirty yards away and raises the rifle, then, thinking better of it, lowers it again, hiding it behind his leg. Better to let them go up the stairs and into the building then follow them inside. Fewer places to run and hide in there.

The girls pass him, chattering like squirrels without even noticing him.

Story of my life, he thinks bitterly. They go upstairs and through the glass doors.

Irwin licks his lips and follows.

***

I open the ballroom door. A cloud of food and booze smells wash over me, bringing tears to my eyes and making my stomach roil.

188

Shooters!

I will not puke, I will not puke…

I step inside, acutely aware of my high heels.

I will not fall on my ass!

There are about fifty people in the room. Heads turn as I come in, many pairs of eyes, male and female, fixing on me in my skimpy outfit. I get that familiar rush I used to experience on the stripper's pole, settling my stomach some. I look around spotting a familiar spaghetti western actor getting a drink at the bar, and have to work hard to prevent my jaw from dropping. Holy shit! I recognize another face I've seen on TV when Danny watches his Sunday football games. And there's the last winner of American Idol!

Danny must've come into the room while I was putting on my shoes. He's with A.T., handing him the briefcase. A.T. carries it up on stage, places it on an angled stand already in place, and opens the lid. It contains package after package of greenbacks.

The million dollars!

A slender guy with slicked-back black hair, a sharp goatee and a pencil mustache, who's wearing an electric blue suit, hollers from across the room.

"Natalie! Over here!"

It's Roderigo!

Trying to be nonchalant, I go to him and step into his open arms.

Jaws drop all throughout the room.

There's a giant TV screen above the stage, hanging in front of the curtains. It shows the scene in the ballroom, which is prolly being broadcast to the international audience. As I watch it over Roderigo's shoulder, it flickers, and suddenly transforms. Three people on a bed, two men with a woman between them. She's sucking off one while the other one rams into her from behind. It's A.T., Taras and Miko in our room yesterday! I'm not in the picture because my bed is out of view of the camera.

The camera. Where the fuck was the camera? I get it! Inside Frankie, the teddy bear! It had to be!

A woman steps out from behind the curtains. Tall and thin, she's got on a pair of bright red hotpants and a black vest above. She's not wearing a bra, so her small pointy tits flash the crowd. Her crimson sash reads *Miss San Francisco.*

It's Miko! I thought she gave in a little too easily when I told her to quit the pageant.

She's got a mic clipped to her collar. Her high voice floats out over the crowd, which hushes like someone turned down the volume knob.

"I thought all of you would like to see how a woman actually goes about competing in this pageant," she says. "All of the interviews and other pageant activities are only smoke and mirrors. This is how the million dollars will be won or lost."

A.T. and his brother are standing like statues, gazing at the screen. Then A.T. wheels around and addresses the crowd. "What you're seeing here happened last evening," he says. "It was all completely consensual, and had nothing whatsoever to do with winning or losing the pageant. However, because of this blatant violation of privacy, I am expelling Ms. Aiko from the pageant." He faces Miko and addresses her directly. "You can expect to hear from my lawyers."

Bright white letters appear at the bottom of the screen, beginning https://... It's a url! WTF?

"Members of the press here today, take down this url," Miko says. "If you go there, you will find my medical records, which I have made public today. They detail my transition from the man Masaharu Aiko to Mihara Aiko the woman. She smiles sweetly at A.T. "Want to explain to everyone how I'm not really a woman now, A.T.?"

A.T. stands stupefied for a couple seconds, then reaches for her with a roar of rage, clamping his hands around her throat.

The sound of automatic weapon fire drifts into the ballroom from downstairs.

***

Students scatter in front of Eduardo like leaves in a strong wind as he strides down the hall like the mighty Thor, fire spitting from the barrel of his rifle. He spots a familiar blonde girl disappearing into a side door.

Fuckin' Schultz!

Eduardo stops in front of the door, sees a blue circular sign with a figure in a dress and the word *Girls*.

Stupid bitch. She's trapped herself—there are no windows in the bathrooms.

He kicks the door open and enters, facing a counter of sinks across from a row of stalls. Two of the stall doors are partially open, while the third is fully closed.

Shooters!

Stupid bitch.

"If you come out, I might let you live. If you don't, I'll shoot you through the door."

He waits a minute, then the door opens inward and the terrified little girl steps out. She's wearing a white sweater with the head of a bear, the school logo, on the front, over a blue pleated skirt and knee socks. Her hands are held out in supplication as she stares at Eduardo wide-eyed.

"Please…" she whines.

Drug-fueled electricity surges through Eduardo's veins. He brings his rifle to eye level and points it at her face.

"Please what?" he asks.

"Please don't hurt me."

"Why not? You hurt me."

"I know. I'm sorry, I'm so sorry, so very sorry…" She's crying now.

"Whatchoo gonna do for me so I don't hurt you?"

"Anything! Anything you want!"

"Kneel down." He orders.

She does it. He approaches, places the muzzle of the rifle under her chin, exerting upward pressure so she has to look in his eyes.

He hears the sound of liquid running. A yellow pool is forming around his shoes. Her eyes glaze over, then close as she tumbles sideways.

He stands over her, his rifle pointed at her head.

***

Irwin comes through the glass doors just as the girls are passing through the metal detector under Murph's watchful eyes.

"Hey!" Irwin shouts and everyone turns to look at him. He knows they're not believing what they're seeing. His finger tightens on the trigger. He's totally unprepared for what happens next.

True to what LeBrowne told him, the rifle spits flame for about two seconds, bucking in his hands like a live boa on speed. He grips the gun tightly to avoid dropping it on the floor. The girls scream, one of them dropping like a lead weight and the others scurrying down the hall toward the escalators.

Murph stands stupidly with both hands on his belly. When he pulls them away, crimson drips from his fingers and his tripes spill out over the front of his uniform. He goes down.

Irwin fumbles for the mag release, then his fingers find it. He pushes it and the spent mag clatters to the floor. He scrabbles for another, extracts it from his vest, slams it into the receiver, and looks down the hall to see two of the girls running up the escalator. He brings the AR to his shoulder and pulls the trigger. Nothing happens. *Shit!* Then he remembers and pushes the bolt catch. Another girl is continuing down the hall, but she turns the corner across from the elevator before he can shoot. A fourth woman is frozen at the bottom of the escalator, holding on to it to remain standing. She half-turns to face him as he approaches. He notes in passing that she's beautiful, wearing a gold lamé party dress that barely covers her ample breasts and a white cowboy hat. Expanding red dots decorate the front of her dress, matching her red and gold sash. It reads *Miss Montana.*

Holding the rifle much tighter this time, he squeezes the trigger, sweeping it across her body waist high.

The stream of bullets basically cuts her in half.

This time he ejects the mag with confidence, smoothly withdrawing another and slamming it in place, then tripping the catch to close the action.

"Fucking Stacy."

He opens the cafeteria doors. The place is empty—everyone must be upstairs. He closes the door and goes to the escalator.

***

Amos recognizes the sounds in the hallway immediately. Looking at a monitor, he sees the shooter running down the hall, carrying an AR-15, full auto, 5.56 mm NATO, most likely. He grabs the arms of his chair and tries to stand, curses, then pulls the .45 from his holster and lays it in his lap. Another look at the monitors, he sees the girl in the cowboy hat collapse at the base of the escalator and the perp running up the stairs to commit more mayhem.

Nattie! She's up there!

He toggles the joystick, directing his chair out into the hall.

A half-naked girl runs by him, shouting, "He's got a gun!" She takes refuge in the media room.

Amos rides down the hall to the elevator.

Shooters!

***

A patrol car, siren blaring and red lights blazing, squeals to a stop in front of Forrest Middle School, where Officer Boone and his partner are still outside, crouched behind their vehicle. The doors of the newly arrived car burst open and the officers formerly on duty at the convention center bail out. Corporal Lester, the erstwhile driver, takes in the situation at a glance as a fresh rattle of gunfire sounds inside the school.

"Holy shit, Boone! What the fuck are you two doing still out here?"

"Didn't you hear that, Corp?" Boone says, referring to the gunfire. "We're doin' this by the book and waitin' for SWAT!"

"The book says you can make entry if you have exigent circumstances." Another crackle of gunfire comes from behind the shattered doors of the school. "What the fuck do you call that? Boone and Roy! Follow me in." she orders. "Davis and Harrison! Around back. Charles, you stay here and apprise SWAT of the situation when they arrive."

Lester draws her pistol and leads the other two officers inside.

***

Inside the school, the hallways have cleared—Eduardo assumes it's because everyone is sheltering in place like they've been trained to do during active shooter drills. He's heading for his homeroom where he hopes to find Davies and some of the others who humiliated him. If the door is locked he'll shoot his way in.

He hears sirens outside as he approaches Vice-principal Drayton's office. They tell him he hasn't got much time left. Drayton's door is open wide, and he looks inside. She's sitting in her desk chair, her mouth open wide, a red hole in her forehead and a couple more in her chest. Looks like Martin has already been here.

He hurries on to get to homeroom before the cops catch up with him.

***

Danny and Kidd haul ass for the ballroom doors after hearing the gunfire. Problem is, there are four sets of doors and only two of them, and they have to weave between all of the people in the room, who are starting to panic, to get there. Roderigo lets go of me and turns tail for the stage, fleeing the gunfire. On stage, A.T. lets go of Miko, who collapses to the floor. He dashes to the briefcase containing the million dollars, slams the lid shut, throws the latches, and disappears behind the curtains. Taras follows. Roderigo, now on stage, does the same.

Danny and Kidd have reached the doors and are checking them out, trying to figure out how to lock them, I think. Danny suddenly whirls, sticking his pistol in his belt, picks up a metal folding chair and collapses it, then he tries to shove it between the push bar and the body of the door.

Another pair of doors bursts open and someone enters. He's got a gun! A stream of fire erupts from the muzzle as he sprays a cascade of bullets around the room like they're coming out of a fire hose and the smell of gunpower fills the room. Screams echo, blood spurts, people fall. Danny and Kidd hit the deck even though no bullets have yet been directed their way. The AR abruptly stops shooting and the magazine falls to the floor a second later. As the shooter fumbles for another mag, he opens his mouth and shouts, "Natalie McMasters, I know you're here! Show yourself, you bitch, or I'll kill everybody in here!"

***

One floor below, Amos sits in front of the elevator. It seems as if it's been five minutes since he pushed the button, even though he knows it's only been seconds. The lighted button goes dark, a muted ding sounds and the elevator door slides open. Amos works the joystick and rolls inside, banging into walls as he rotates the control to turn his chair around so he can access the floor selection buttons. He has to use the barrel of his pistol to push 2. So much for the fucking Americans with Disabilities Act!

The doors slide shut and the elevator begins its leisurely ascent.

***

On the ballroom floor, Danny and Kidd both scramble for their pistols, but neither one has a clear shot because of the forest of tables, chairs and screaming people surrounding them. The experienced Marines both realize that the only way to draw a bead on the shooter is to stand up in the face of an automatic weapon. Not a great choice.

Shooters!

***

A.T. and Taras are hurrying to the rear door of the ballroom backstage. Footsteps echo behind them, lending wings to their feet. The back of a gray metal door with a red-lit exit sign above it comes into view. A.T. slams into the bar, thrusting it open.

A large black man points an impossibly huge chrome-plated revolver right between A.T.'s eyes. Holding out his other hand, he says, "I'll take that briefcase, y'all."

A.T. has no choice. He extends the briefcase to the banger. Behind him, Taras yells, "No!", and leaps forward.

Taras you fucking moron…

A.T. goes deaf as a tremendous BOOM sounds and his cheek is seared by the muzzle flash.

***

Holding his AR chest high, Eduardo looks into his homeroom. Martin is up front, straddling the body of Ms. McCurdy, who's lying in a pool of blood. The other students are sitting rigidly at their desks, like an audience at a macabre performance.

Martin's got his rifle trained at a dark-haired woman kneeling in front of him. It's *Máma* Lupe! She turns her head as Eduardo enters. Her eyes become as wide as saucers as she sees him standing there with his gun, and a tear rolls down her cheek.

Martin takes a step toward Lupe, extending his weapon so it nearly touches her nose.

Footsteps resound behind Eduardo and a voice shouts, "Capital City Police! Drop the weapons, now!"

Martin says to Lupe, "It's time to die, bitch."

BANG!

BANG!

Chapter 36

Hearing my name from the mouth of a crazed shooter is right up there as the fucking shock of my life. It takes about a nanosec for me to realize if I don't say something, a lot of people are going to die. And if I do speak up, there's a very good chance it might be me.

It's totally no choice at all.

"I'm Natalie. What do you want?"

"Shag your fucking ass over here, Stacy."

Stacy? Where have I heard that name before?

Hands raised, I check the shooter out as I weave my way toward him. I say him, but truly, I don't know WTF it is. Wearing long, dirty, curly, blonde hair full of dirt, a leopard-patterned sarong, knee sox and expensive-looking white women's sandals, a face covered with several layers of pancake and a thick coating of hideous, cherry red lipstick adorning the mouth, this creature looks like something conjured up by Stephen King.

Glaring at me malevolently, the thing says, "You don't know me, do you?"

"No, I don't. What do you want from me?"

It begins laughing like the Joker from Batman. The sound sends shivers down my spine. Pointing at my bulging belly, it says. "Did I do that? Of course not! I ass-fucked you."

Suddenly I'm back in that decrepit East Village flat. My ass is in the air, my face jammed into the fabric of a couch that stinks of sweat and old beer, sharp pain radiates into my belly and down my legs as he thrusts into me from behind. My legs are splayed open so I can't get any purchase from them, making my Tai-chi training worthless—I just have to lay there and take it. But when he finally lets me free, I throw him into the wall, then stand over him with my heel on his balls. I know I'll hurt him badly, maybe permanently, if I bear down with my full weight, but a red rage fills my brain and I do it anyway. His scream fills the cramped little room like the cry of a wounded bird. It makes me feel whole again, for a minute, anyway.

Now I'm standing face-to-face with him again. I remember the rheumy blue eyes, the crooked teeth, the curly blonde hair. Did I really kiss that nasty mouth, let him stick his tongue in mine? Yuck! I struggle to remember his name, which I've erased from my mind like a bad habit. I know if I don't remember it, he'll likely kill me where I stand.

"Do you know me, cunt? Say it. Say my name, and beg me not to kill you."

His name suddenly floods my mind, bringing waves of anguish along with it.

"Irwin! Irwin, please don't. I'm begging you…"

"Don't what, Stacy?"

The muzzle of the gun is as big as a sewer pipe. The foulness of his breath completes the image.

"Please don't kill me!"

A clatter to the right causes both of us to turn. Danny and Kidd are rising from the floor, bringing their pistols to bear. Irwin's finger tightens of the trigger and he waves his rifle like a magic wand, sending a short burst their way. Both men dive to the floor again, and I swear I see blood fly.

"Danny!"

Training his gun on my belly again, he grates, "Let's get out of here. And none of your kungfooey tricks! I can pull this trigger a lot faster than you can move."

I step toward the door and he encircles my neck with his arm, the rifle jammed in my spine at belly height. We step into the hall like a pair of Siamese twins.

A clattersqueak fills the air and my eyes open wide as I see a man in a wheelchair flying down the corridor, joystick in one hand, 1911 in the other, like some steampunk contraption. It's Uncle! His gun belches fire and I hear something snap next to my ear. I fall sideways as the pressure on my neck suddenly releases.

Irwin turns toward me again, reaching for my shoulder. I grab his wrist and twist my hips, bringing him round in a circle and releasing him in the direction of the balcony. Waving his machine gun around like a baton, his finger tightens on the trigger as he stumbles forward and fire belches from the muzzle of his rifle. Red spots blossom on Uncle's chest, and his wheelchair turns over, dumping him out on the floor. A crimson pool expands beneath him.

"Uncle! Noooo!"

I dive to the floor as Irwin's gun comes round to my direction. He hits the railing of the balcony and goes over, a stream of bullets stitching holes in the ceiling before it abruptly ceases. A passing scream is ripped from his

Shooters!

throat, then it is cut off short, and a muffled metallic thump reaches my ears.

Strong hands slide into my armpits, helping me upright. My eyes meet a round black face full of concern.

"Kidd! Where's Danny?"

"There was a medic in the crowd. She's with him now."

I'm briefly torn about who to go to, then I choose Uncle. There's nobody with him.

We hurry to him and Kidd tosses the wheelchair aside like a toy. He helps me turn Uncle on his back.

His face is stark white and he looks a million years old. His shirt front is nearly all red now. He opens his baby blue eyes, first seeing nothing, then a smile lights his face as they focus on me.

"Nattie," he says. "Did I get him?"

"He's dead as a dog, Amos," Kidd tells him.

Uncle smiles, then runs his eyes up and down my bod, taking in my near nudity. I'm suddenly ashamed.

"That's a helluva way to dress," he says.

His mouth flops wide and a couple of cups of blood gush out, running down his chin. His eyes cloud over, seeing nothing again.

Chapter 37

The two newscasters, sitting behind the news desk in the studio, stare at each other with grave faces under the hot lights.

"Well, Jill, we've made history today in Capital City."

"That's right, Tim, but it's not the kind of history we want to make. Two mass shootings in one day…"

"…and one of them a school shooting." Tim turns his head to the camera with a solemn expression. "It occurred about nine o'clock this morning at the Forrest Middle School. The school's receptionist, the vice-principal Anna Drayton and a teacher, Agnes McCurdy were killed, as well as six students, Tommy Fletcher, 11, LaShonda Curtis, also 11, Cecil Jamison, Buddy Harris, and Mary Jo Smathers, 12, and Erin Dodge 13. Over twenty more people, both teachers and students, were injured, some critically, and are currently at University Hospital. Their names are listed on our website. The alleged shooters were both students at the school. One of them was also killed, but police are not currently saying how he died. Their names are being withheld by law enforcement because they are minors."

Jill takes up the sad tale. "The other shooting occurred at Adam Tymko's downtown beauty pageant at approximately the same time as the Forrest Middle School shooting. A lone gunman, as yet unnamed, was involved, and apparently used a fully automatic assault rifle. Eight people were killed, including Angela Stratton, the winner of last year's *Miss Montana* pageant and a runner-up for Miss USA, actor Slim Jones, who had bit parts in over 50 Hollywood films, Lacey Spivak, a freelance journalist, Carl Johnson, who had simply purchased a ticket to attend the celebrity meet-and-greet and Augustus Murphy, a security guard employed by the 3M Detective Agency, which was in charge of security at the pageant. The CEO of the 3M Detective Agency, Amos Murdoch, was also killed by the shooter. Mr. Murdoch was confined to a wheelchair, but he reportedly made a valiant attempt to stop the shooter nonetheless. The shooter himself was apparently neutralized by Ms. Natalie McMasters, who was a contestant in the pageant as *Miss Capital City* and also Mr. Murdoch's niece. Ms. McMasters is unavailable for comment at this time. The shooter was critically injured and is currently in the ICU at University Hospital. And there's yet other news about the incident, isn't there, Tim?"

"Yes indeed, Jill. It has been alleged by an unnamed source that the pageant's first prize, one million dollars in cash, was stolen by a person or persons unknown during the shooting. Mr. Taras Tymko, the brother of Adam Tymko, the pageant organizer, was apparently killed during the purported theft. Police are not saying at this time whether the loss of the money was connected to the shooting. Adam Tymko has cancelled the pageant and is also unavailable for comment."

"Now, in other news…"

Chapter 38

It's Monday morning.

I'm at University Hospital. The news is not good.

Danny is here. He was shot three times in the shoulder and in his upper chest. One bullet came within inches of his heart. He's going to be OK, but he'll be in the hospital for a while.

Gracie Pratt's windpipe was crushed in the attack on her. She is presently a vegetable. The cops are pretty sure that it was Irwin who did it.

Eduardo is here, too. He was shot by CCPD officer Lester while shooting up his school. His wound is not fatal either, but he's under arrest and handcuffed to his bed.

Miko was here but was discharged. She had a bruised throat, but A.T. apparently didn't have hold of her long enough to do lasting damage. She walked right into a group of reporters outside, and expanded on her sexual encounters with A.T. and his brother.

Finally, Irwin is here as well. He survived the fall, but his back is broken, and it's likely he'll be a quadriplegic.

Uncle Amos's funeral is later this afternoon. He's going to be buried in his family's plot in the nearby town of Garton, where he grew up.

A.T. cancelled the pageant, because someone stole the million dollar prize and killed Taras in the process. Word is he's left town. It said on the 'net that the audience for *Tymko's Times* was cut in half after Miko's vid came out. I know I should feel sorry for him because of Taras, but whatever. If Uncle hadn't been working for those idiots, he'd still be alive.

I'm getting ready to visit Danny when my cell phone chirps.

"This is Nattie."

"Ms. McMasters, this is Shalyka at Capital OBGYN. Do you have time to talk? I have some news for you."

"I guess so. What is it?"

"We've got the paternity results back for your pregnancy. Unfortunately, they show that the father is a close relative of yours."

It was Ellis! I feel like I want to puke.

"Then I want to get rid of it."

"You haven't heard? That will be a problem. Congress has passed a new limit on pregnancy termination. It's now 12 weeks. You're at nearly 20 weeks."

"Isn't there an exception for rape and incest?"

"Yes, but it can take as much as four to six weeks to get it approved. That will put you at six to six and a half months."

OMG! Babies are born alive at that time.

"I'll have to talk to my family about this."

"Well, don't take too long. The longer you wait, the greater the chance of complications."

"I'll let you know in a few days."

Now I really need to talk to Danny!

I go to his room. He's sitting up in bed, watching a sports channel on TV. He looks up as I come in, but he doesn't smile. I move to the bed to give him a kiss, but he doesn't lean toward me to get it. So I stand back again.

"Hey," I say. "How you doing?"

"Fine." His eyes travel back to the TV.

"We need to talk."

Still he won't look at me. WTF? "So talk," he says.

I totally don't know how to say it, so I just come out with it. "My baby. It's not yours."

That gets him to turn his head, but his expression is angry, not concerned. Turning back to the TV, he says, "Then whose... never mind. It's none of my business. You said."

I can feel the tears welling up. I never told him that Ellis raped me. I was ashamed.

He continues. "Look, I've been thinking about this. It's obvious to me that you want to live your own life how you want to, and I'm just in your way. So I think the best thing for me is to leave. I'm not really your husband anyway, so there won't be any legal issues. And it might be better for you because you won't get tied up in 3M's mess. The guns Eddie and the other guy used to shoot up the school were 3Ms, you know. There's a good chance that me or Kidd or both of us might go to jail."

Jail! "I didn't hear anything about that!"

Shooters!

"Of course you didn't. You've been too concerned with your own mess." He looks at me again. "When you go to Amos's funeral later, please apologize to M.B. for me because I can't be there."

"I will." I don't know what else to say.

I'm fighting to hold back tears as I leave Danny's room. I know he's totally not serious, he's just hurt and sick. He'll come around when he gets better. He loves me. I know he does.

My next stop is Eduardo's room. There's a policeman in the hall outside his closed door. He stands up, stopping me as I approach. The nameplate on his uniform reads *Anderson*.

"This patient isn't allowed visitors," he says.

"He is my son," I reply.

Anderson looks at me with suspicion. "His mother is with him," he says.

"I know. She is my wife. I should have said he's my stepson." Now he looks totally confused.

"What's your name?" I tell him. He picks up a clipboard and looks at it. "Your name is not on the list," he says. "You can't go in."

"Just ask the woman inside. Her name is Maria Ibáñez. She'll tell you she's my wife."

"It doesn't matter," Anderson says. "If you're not on the list, you can't go in. You'll have to take it up with headquarters."

"I will."

I can't believe that Eduardo would do such a thing. I have to talk to him to find out what happened. The news said that the casualties at the school were worse than those at the pageant. The receptionist, vice-principal Drayton and Eduardo's teacher Ms. McCurdy were killed, as well as six students. Over twenty more people, teachers and students, were injured, some critically. The other boy involved, Martin Castro, was also killed, apparently by Eduardo.

I am totally afraid that Eduardo will go to jail for the rest of his life. And I'm not sure that he doesn't deserve to.

I pull out my phone to check the time. Yeet! I have to get moving to be on time for Uncle's funeral.

During the drive to Garton, I reflect on my time with Uncle Amos. He was Mom's brother. We saw him infrequently growing up, because he didn't like Daddy and the feeling was mutual. Daddy passed during my senior year in high school and when I came to State, Uncle offered me a job in his detective agency to help with my expenses. Mostly I just sat in a car watching people who made disability claims to their insurance companies, to verify they were really injured. But one day I got involved with a pervert who had kidnapped a young woman, and that began the chain of events that led to where I am today. Even with all of the arguments with Uncle over the years, I came to love him, and I'm sure he loved me too. I wipe away my tears. I can't get to bawling or I'll wreck the Jeep before I get there.

The service is at Garton Baptist Church. Like in a lot of small towns, the cemetery is out back. As I park the Jeep, I spot Mom, M.B., Shannie, and Reverend Makepeace out front, greeting mourners as they arrive. I'm not looking forward to the service—I'm an atheist and I don't believe that Uncle has gone anywhere. I'm just here out of respect for him and the family.

As I walk up, M.B. glances at me, then she and Shannie go into the church. Mom and the reverend wait for me. The reverend greets me and Mom gives me a big hug. "Oh, Nattie," she cries.

"We're going to start in five minutes," The reverend says, and goes inside. I start to follow, but Mom puts a hand on my shoulder.

"What?"

"I want to let you know. M.B. told me that she'll be leaving the house and the agency after the service. Apparently there are too many memories there, and she's not interested in running 3M with Amos gone. She's officially Shannie's adoptive mom, but she's going to leave her with me for a while, until school is done."

I'm puzzled. "I guess I get it, but why doesn't she tell me herself?"

"I think she's angry with you about what happened to Amos. It was a big shock with them still newlyweds."

"What happened to Uncle wasn't my fault, Mom." Or was it? If I hadn't hurt Irwin like that...

"I know that, Sweetiekins. I'm sure she'll come around with time."

"Well, Danny asked me to apologize to her because he can't be here."

"I'll take care of it."

The church service is what I expect from southern Baptists. A contingent of Marines shows up for the burial. Uncle's casket is draped with the flag and they fire three volleys over it. I totally lose it when they play Taps. They fold the flag and give it to M.B.

I'm surprised that Lupe isn't here. I thought she was fond of Uncle.

Shooters!

When we get back to Hyacinth House, Mom gives me another hug before she goes to her cottage. "Come down for dinner later. Bring Lupe, too."

"I will if she comes home."

Inside, a pall seems to hang over the house. I'm the only one here. I take the elevator to the second floor to go to my room to change, because I'm too damned tired to walk up the stairs.

Stepping into my room. I flip on the light. There's an envelope on my pillow.

Nattie –

I'm sorry for everything that has happened. I have always felt that two women being married to each other is wrong, and that God has been punishing me because of what I've done. We made it even worse when we called Danny our husband. I think it is finally time that I listened to the Lord.

I'm going to call Mr. McDougall for a divorce. I am going back to the church to confess my sins and pray to God to fix what is wrong with Eduardo. I do not blame you for any of this—it is all my fault. I should have known better.

I wish you would join a church also and bring Jesus into your life. I hate to think of you burning in hell for eternity.

This is very hard for me. Please do not look for me and make it harder.

Lupe.

Chapter 39

"Here's the head! Now push!"

My body is dead from the waist down because of the epidural, but I try to push as hard as I can, breathing in short puffs the way they showed me. There's a cloth barrier blocking my view of my lower body, so I can't see what Shalyka is doing.

"OK. The head is mostly out. Stop pushing. Let the contractions do the work."

Of course, I can't feel the contractions either, because of the anesthetic. I have to rely on Shalyka to keep me in the loop.

"Ah! Here's another one! Breathe. Breathe. Ok, now long deep breaths before the next one starts. We're almost done."

What do you mean, we? I'm doing all the work here!

"Ok, this should be the last one. Breathe!"

"It's a boy!"

In a moment, Shalyka lifts the baby above the barrier. He's tiny, and chalky white against her deep brown skin. His head is covered with cottony white peach fuzz. The umbilical cord hangs down between his legs. She wipes him with a towel. "Pull up your gown," she orders and I do, exposing my breasts. She puts him on my chest. My arms move automatically to embrace him. He looks up into my eyes with his sea blue ones. There's no question that I'm totally in love with him already!

I kiss him on top of the head and say, "Welcome to the world, little Amos Murdoch McMasters."

"I'm going to cut the cord, then take him to the ICU," Shalyka says.

Fear shoots through me. "Why? Is there something wrong?"

"I just think the doctor needs to look at him."

"Why?"

She hesitates, then she says it. "Because he looks like an albino to me."

"Albino! What does that even mean?"

"It just means that he might have a deficiency of pigmentation. Sometimes complications come along with it. We just want the doctor to examine him ASAP to check that he's OK."

I pull little Amos closer to me. "Can he stay just a little while longer?"

"Just a little," she says. In a very short time (it seems), "OK now, I'm gonna have to take him. You'll see him again soon."

She reaches down and puts her hands under his armpit and tugs. I resist a minute before letting him go. As our skin-to-skin contact is broken, aching emptiness floods into me, and I can feel the tears welling up.

"Goodbye, little Amos, goodbye."

They wheel me into recovery, where I'll stay for a while before going back to my room. They started me on magnesium sulfate before delivery to prevent something called postpartum preeclampsia. It's a muscle relaxant that makes you feel like a wet dishrag. A nurse sticks a needle into my IV line and pushes the plunger, and I go out like a light.

When I wake, I'm in my room. Mom is here. She's the only one who's stuck by me through the rest of my pregnancy and delivery. When I open my eyes, I hear her say, "Oh good! They've been waiting for you to wake so you can feed little Amos. I'll let them know you're back with us."

She goes out into the hall, likely to the nurses' station.

Time passes, and she doesn't come back. I start to freak out. Where is she? Has something happened to Amos?

A nurse enters with no Amos and triggers a blood pressure cuff that's already attached to my arm.

"What's going on? Where is my baby?"

"Shhh…" she says. The blood pressure cuff deflates, and she raises her eyebrows. She triggers the cuff again. It pinches my arm, deflates. She reaches to a tray near the bed and picks up a syringe, sticks the needle in the IV line again.

"No, wait…" Blackness descends again.

Chapter 40

All I can remember about my drugdreams is that they are troubled and anxious. My eyes pop open. The medstench hits my nose and I remember where I am.

"Amos! Where is my baby!"

A hand clasps mine. I turn my head, expecting to see Mom. But it's Danny!

His expression is concerned. I've seen that look before and it's never good.

"What?" I say. "Where is Amos? Where is my son?"

Now tears are running down his cheeks.

"OMG! What's happened? Where is my boy?" I holler those last four words.

Danny adds another hand to his grasp and squeezes harder.

Mom speaks from across the room.

"He's gone, Nattie. I'm so sorry."

"What do you mean, gone? Is he dead? Is my baby dead?"

"Not dead," Danny says. My heart moves from my throat back into my chest. "Taken."

"Taken? What the fuck do you mean, taken? Who took him?"

Another voice. Female. "It appears to have been your sister," M.B. says.

"My sister? You mean Bella? She's dead!"

"Apparently not," M.B. says. "There is a video. A nurse took him from the nursery, supposedly to bring him to you for feeding. Obviously, he never got here." A beat. "The nurse looked just like you."

I can't breathe! I dissolve into tears. "I want my baby!" I wail.

Danny bends down to take me into his arms, hugging me for all he's worth. "I'm sorry, Nattie. I'm so sorry," he says over and over.

Later that afternoon, the mag sulfate has mostly worn off and I can move again. The docs have agreed to release me in the morning.

"I'm coming back, if you'll have me," says Danny. "I can't leave you now. We can't let this stand."

"Don't come back if you just feel sorry for me," I tell him. "I'll find Amos somehow. I'll never quit looking for him."

"I know," Danny says. "But I'm coming back because I love you. I always have."

The tears come back and I hug him, never wanting to let go.

"I'm coming back, too," M.B. says. "Amos's will says that he wanted me to take his place and keep 3M going. I can't not comply with his last request. And someone has to look out for poor Eduardo."

***

Later, back at Hyacinth House, Danny, Mom, M.B. and me are all in Uncle's office. A vid is running on her monitor. A woman in a nurse's uni who looks just like me is wheeling a basket from the nursery down the hall. Cameras follow her until she disappears into a storage closet. In a few minutes, she comes out again, this time wearing civilian clothes. She's in a wheelchair, holding the baby, who's dressed to go outside. A woman I've seen before, dressed as an orderly, wheels them to an elevator. The scene cuts to the lobby, where they're discharged. The woman's name is Geraldine McCauley. She is the consort of a man called Jerome Ellis.

All these people are supposed to be dead. I saw all of them get into a helicopter, which blew up into a million pieces just a few minutes later.

Apparently they were never on it.

"So 3M's first order of business will be to find your son, Nattie. We'll do whatever it takes. Danny, Kidd and I are all on board."

I can't answer. I just hug her.

As we're adjourning downstairs for a late lunch, the doorbell rings.

Chapter 41

I open the door and stare wide-eyed at the woman standing on the porch. Half-a-head shorter than me, round-bodied with café-au-lait skin, chocolate eyes puffy and red from crying and long, straight black hair that hangs to her waist.

Lupe, my soon-to-be ex-wife.

"Why did you ring the bell?" I ask her. "This is your home."

"Not anymore," she says, and my heart misses a beat. "I said I was leaving you."

Then what are you doing here?"

"I want to come back," she says. "I cannot desert you when you have lost your baby.

I don't even think about it. I just take a step forward, sweep her up into my arms and cover her face with kisses. I end with a long one on her mouth, which seems that it will never end.

We're both breathless when the kiss breaks.

"You must help our son," she says. "Eduardo. We must not lose both of our boys."

'Lupe, I don't know. They say he killed people."

"He says that the only one he killed was that other boy. That Martin Castro, who was going to kill me. I believe him."

"Then I do too," I tell her. "I will try to help him. But I must find Amos, too. I know who has him."

"Who?"

"Jerome Ellis. And my sister."

"Where are they?"

"I don't know. But I will find them."

If it's the last thing I do!

——— The End ———

213

Did you enjoy Shooters!? Have you read the other Natalie McMasters Mysteries? If not, get your copy of the first book, Stripper! from Amazon now at the link below:

https://www.amazon.com/gp/product/B07C87Y2FH?notRedirectToSDP=1&ref_=dbs_mng_calw_0&storeType=ebooks

And be sure to sign up for my newsletter at:

https://www.3mdetectiveagency.com/contact/

Follow me on:

Facebook:
https://www.facebook.com/groups/541595279667727

Twitter: @3Mdetective

Blog:
https://www.3mdetectiveagency.com/blog/

Instagram: 3mdetective

Goodreads:
https://www.goodreads.com/author/show/17956517.Thomas_A_Burns_Jr_

Bookbub
https://www.bookbub.com/profile/thomas-a-burns-jr

Tumblr
https://www.tumblr.com/blog/nataliemcmasters

Praise for the Natalie McMasters Mysteries

Stripper! A Natalie McMasters Novel (2018)

***** - Extremely well written. The plot was very entertaining and the characters were well developed and likeable. Told from the first-person perspective of Natalie McMasters – the book is a real page turner. Great read! – Amazon review

***** - Excellent crime/mystery story, kept me turning the pages. Burns has created a fascinating lead character--Nattie McMasters. She's young, sexy, and courageous. – Amazon review

Revenge! A Natalie McMasters Mystery (2018)

***** - A fast-paced story, Intriguing true-to-life characters with an explosive ending. Looking forward to the next book! – Amazon review

***** - This was an unexpected gem. I was fully gripped from page one to the last word as the pace was fast without much down time. Natalie was the type of character I appreciate, with dimension. While hard, and often crass, there is also a vulnerability to her that makes her more than the average cardboard sassy heroine. – Amazon review

Trafficked! A Natalie McMasters Mystery (2019)

***** - Bluntly put, this ain't your average mystery book. It's gritty, raw, and "human" in the worst way possible. And I enjoyed it every dark minute of it! – Amazon review

**** - There was blood, whipping, love making, sewer stench, a tour of Manhattan and Kosher food, honor, despair, and a healthy dollop of deceit and mystery solving. Burns is a good writer and is on to something good with his Natalie McMasters Mysteries. Amazon review

Venom! A Natalie McMasters Mystery (2020)

***** - Venom is a twisty page-turner with non-stop action and an ending you won't soon forget. Thomas Burns is adept with character and setting description. Natalie McMasters will steal your heart! .Amazon Review

***** - I have loved this exciting series from the start and this installment did not disappoint! Full of suspense and emotion Venom showed even more character development and showed a vulnerable side to them all. I was immersed in the story and invested in the outcome. Amazon Review

Sniper! A Natalie McMasters Mystery (2020)

***** - Thomas A. Burns, Jr. has written another page turner. It seems there is never a good place to put the book aside to pick it up later. SNIPER! is an emotionally charged adrenaline rush right up to the last page. .Amazon Review

***** - This was a fabulous read! I have rarely read a book this edgy and cutting, best have some Jack Daniels to chase it. With themes ripped from today's headlines, SNIPER is a tour de force ride with a troubled young woman and her unusual family and social circle. Nattie is forceful, opinionated, and quick to give in to impulses - whether to take down a bad guy, bolster a loved one or have sex. SNIPER's plot is a fast-paced collision of gun control, 2nd amendment (plus 1st and 4th amendment) rights, political correctness, mob violence, PTSD, addiction (of all kinds) and parental rights. Yet these themes move the plot, which speaks to the author's skill. Amazon Review

Killers! A Natalie McMasters Mystery (2021) - Winner of the Silver Falchion Award for Best Action Adventure of 2021 from the Killer Nashville! International Writer's Conference

A wild romp to find a murderer has a little bit of everything: gore, fun, and humor. The narration and action have tension throughout as the characters are on an intense mission. The author and characters have a strong passion for the plan that is laid out. This sixth installment in this series with these characters stands alone even though the characters continue to change and evolve throughout the series. Publisher's Weekly Booklife Review

***** - In the new Natalie McMasters mystery, KILLERS!, that petite powerhouse heading Thomas Burns's series is back with a powerful opener that never lets go. This time she's determined to find the killer of her therapist friend and surrogate mom. Natalie has a complicated history, and is currently one third of a throuple. That leads to interesting complications and subplots while the twists escalate in several directions. Chasing clues and serial killers, stumbling across more dead bodies, there will be gunfights and a look into the world of BDSM before it's all finished. And how does the murder of an aged Chinaman from Alabama fit in? Burns explores it all, as Tai Chi and southern culture collide with a maniacal killer, a sexual sadist known as The Marquis. But he's not the only sicko Natalie and her team will encounter. Graphic and all too real, Killers! explores a vastly different world with non-stop action. Amazon Review from Anthony and multiple Award-winning author M.K. Graff

***** - Ripping good read! Thomas Burns returns with another Natalie McMasters winner. Action explodes off the first page, when Natalie attends her friend's funeral, only to see her friend's murderer watching from the edge of the crowd. In that instant, Natalie knows she's next on this serial killer's list. Accompanied by an unlikely series of friends, she sets out to find and destroy this man known as The Marquis, before he can complete his destruction of those she loves. Burns builds the atmosphere and suspense through a variety of well-depicted, isolated settings. The headlong pace is relentless, rarely stopping for so much as a breather. Strong character development and a plot that doesn't disappoint grab the reader from the first page and won't let go. Let's hope this isn't the last Natalie McMasters mystery. This reader couldn't put the book down. Amazon review from Betsy Ashton, author of the Mad Max Mysteries

***** - Wham Bam! Killers! takes off like a rocket and never slows its pace. The story begins with Nattie McMasters at the funeral of her friend. While at the graveside, she sees the serial killer who murdered her friend. He's watching her and Nattie knows she's next on his list. She does her best not only to protect her family and friends, but to hunt down the evil villain known as The Marquis. Author Thomas Burns takes the reader on a wild ride, complete with non-stop action and intensity. Amazon Review from Brenda Donelan, author of the University Mystery series.

***** - Natalie McMasters is back. In all her glory! Watch out! Natalie McMaster is back, hellbent on hunting down a crazed killer before she becomes his next victim. She assembles a motley cast of characters to help and they embark on a course of non-stop action, a series of twists and turns, and unforgettable characters on both sides of the law. Kudos to Thomas A. Burns for giving us the kick-ass Natalie McMasters. Amazon Review from Maggie King, author of the Hazel Rose Book Group Mysteries.

***** - Best Natalie McMasters crime novel yet! 5 Stars! Crime novelist Tom Burns hits another one out of the ballpark with this (very) fast-paced detective story. Once more, his irrepressible Nattie McMasters gets caught in a web of murder & mayhem. This time she comes face to face with nothing short of pure evil and the evil reaches out to touch her and her circle of lovers, family, and friends. Sultry tidewater Georgia provides an interesting locale for this tale. You can almost smell the brackish water and feel the heavy air. Burns's pacing and delivery surpass his previous novels, drawing the reader into the world of a psychotic mastermind who is unstoppable and whose deviant passions are unquenchable. Amazon review – Scott W. O'Connell, author of the Yankee Doodle Spy series

Sister! A Natalie McMasters Mystery (2022)

***** - Sister! is a tightly paced thrill ride from author Thomas A. Burns, Jr. The plot jumps between Natalie searching for a mysterious woman who may (or may not) be her sister, and Eduardo, Natalie's adopted son, running away from home after a fight with his birth mother, Lupe. Burns deftly keeps the action moving as the two plots come together in a page turning ending. This is a book that sucks you in and can easily be read in one sitting. Burns' characters are well written, and even if this is the first book you read in the series (as it was for me), Burns does a nice job of letting you get to know them all inside and out while the story progresses. While I highly recommend the book, it deals with some adult material. There are scenes of child abuse which, while not graphic and certainly appropriate for the story, were definitely hard to read, and the book is not for the squeamish. I wholeheartedly give Sister! a five star rating, and I look forward to reading the other books in the Natalie McMasters series. – Derrick Belanger, Publisher, Belanger Books

***** - Thomas Burns brings Natalie McMasters back in a hair-raising tale of mistaken identity. Natalie is waiting for her name to be called at her college graduation ceremony when police sweep in and arrest her. Some who could be her twin was captured on security cameras robbing a convenience store and killing one person. Only through the assistance of a friend, who is in the FBI, vouchers for her alibi. But, Natalie being Natalie, can't leave the investigation alone. She wants to know who this woman is and why she could be Natalie's twin sister. A quick visit to her mother only clouds the issue. The woman could indeed by her twin. Natalie and her extended family are up against power and money as the clues unravel. The tension is absolute, and the ending stunning. You might want to sleep with the lights on for a night or two. – Betsy Ashton, Author of the Mad Max Mysteries, Betrayal, and Eyes Without a Face

***** - Sister!, the latest installment by Thomas A. Burns packs a punch in the first chapter and the tension only increases from there. Natalie McMasters finds herself accused of a crime she didn't commit. While working to prove her innocence, she learns of family secrets which will impact the rest of her life. The tone of this book was eerie and unsettling, dealing with uncomfortable issues that are all too prevalent in our daily news cycle. But no matter how disturbing the subject matter, I could not stop reading. Burns paints a vivid picture of his characters and the dilemmas they face. One twist leads to another which culminates in an ending you won't expect. I'm already waiting for the next book in the series! . – Brenda Donelan, Author of the University Mystery Series

About the Author

Thomas A. Burns Jr. writes the Natalie McMasters Mysteries from the small town of Wendell, North Carolina, where he lives with his wife and son, four cats and a Cardigan Welsh Corgi. He was born and grew up in New Jersey, attended Xavier High School in Manhattan, earned B.S degrees in Zoology and Microbiology at Michigan State University and a M.S. in Microbiology at North Carolina State University. As a kid, Tom started reading mysteries with the Hardy Boys, Ken Holt, and Rick Brant, then graduated to the classic stories by authors such as A. Conan Doyle, Dorothy Sayers, John Dickson Carr, Erle Stanley Gardner and Rex Stout, to name a few. Tom has written fiction as a hobby all of his life, starting with Man from U.N.C.L.E. stories in marble-backed copybooks in grade school. He built a career as technical, science and medical writer and editor for nearly thirty years in industry and government. Now that he's a full time novelist, he's excited to publish his own mystery series, as well as to write stories about his second most favorite detective, Sherlock Holmes. His Holmes story, *The Camberwell Poisoner,* recently appeared in the March – June 2021 issue of *The Strand Magazine.* Tom has also written a Lovecraftian horror novel, The Legacy of the Unborn, under the pen name of Silas K. Henderson—a sequel to H.P. Lovecraft's masterpiece At the Mountains of Madness.